The Courage of Others

James Hitt

Published by Open Books

Copyright © 2015 by James Hitt

Cover image "Folded Clouds" Copyright ©OakleyOriginals

Learn more about the artist at
flickr.com/photos/oakleyoriginals

PART I
A HERO'S WELCOME

1

The War Department sent the telegram dated October 25, 1919. Mister Egbert Jenkins, the local telegrapher, breathing heavily because of his heart condition, shuffled two blocks to our store to deliver the news the moment he received it. Coming along the walk, he saw me standing behind the store window holding a couple of hats that I was about to place on dummies. He held up the paper and waved it expecting me to understand its importance. "Is your aunt here, Davy?" he said, his voice muffled by the glass.

Before I could reply, he came through the front door and spotted Aunt Esther at the counter half hidden behind a stack of bib overalls.

He crossed the floor and handed her the telegram. She took it, her eyes pinched in worry, which said she expected the worst, but as she began to read, her face lit with hope, and she began to cry, not the kind of hysterical sobbing I've seen from other women, but rather a few silent tears followed by a sniffle or two. Reaching into her apron pocket, she pulled out a handkerchief and dabbed her eyes, now rimmed in red. I had never seen her cry, not once in the ten years I'd lived with her and Uncle Marsh, not even at the funeral of my mother, her older sister, whose death had brought me to their home in the first place.

Mr. Jenkins reached across the counter and patted her hand. "Now, now Esther, everything's going to be fine. He's coming home."

Embarrassed, I looked away and placed the hats on the dummies, pretending to position each just so and wondering what had made Aunt Esther cry. The telegram obviously brought good news, so why would a person cry over good news? I felt much the same as my aunt—I was glad Uncle Marsh was coming home—yet no one would see me cry. Of course there was another explanation. A part of me felt a little intimidated. After all, Aunt Esther and I had run the business as well as our own lives for the past year and a half, and things ran smoothly. Now I wondered how our lives were going to change.

Don't get me wrong. I was proud of Uncle Marsh, and any doubts were the doubts of a sixteen-year-old kid who didn't like change. From the first day I entered their house, he treated me like I was his own son, praising me for my achievements, chastising me for my sins with a stern, cold look that proved far worse than any whipping. He never laid a hand on me, never once, not even when Ben Cooperson and I stole a pack of smokes from Wiggins' General Store, although on that occasion he hauled my butt to the sheriff's office where fat Harvey Ralston locked me up for a couple of hours. I was eleven at the time, and that scared the bejesus out of me.

Uncle Marsh enlisted in May 1917. Five years previously, he distinguished himself fighting against Poncho Villa, earning sergeant's stripes in the process. So the town sent their hero off on the local express with a cheering crowd and twin trumpets playing "Onward Christian Soldiers." Most figured the war would be over in three months. American troops would put a quick end to the Kaiser's plan of world domination.

Yet for me, and for most people of Twin Forks, the

European conflict remained a distant, almost meaningless event. Only the newsreels that the Tower Theater showed each week brought the war home. When I saw men fighting and dying on the battlefield, I shook my head and said how terrible it was. But in reality the bodies flopped down and died like rag dolls, not at all like the actors who died far more romantically in motion pictures like D. W. Griffith's *Hearts of the World*, which was, for me, far more real. If the Higgins boy and the Pasley boy and Uncle Marsh hadn't gone off to fight, the people of Twin Forks might have ignored it altogether.

The Higgins boy came home with a stump for a left leg. The Pasley boy was blown to pieces at Chateau-Thierry, and the army shipped his remains home in a sealed coffin. Uncle Marsh, the first to go, *was* the last to return. Three months before, word reached us that he'd suffered some kind of injury on the battlefield and had spent the rest of that year convalescing in a hospital in Paris. The War Department's letter proved vague on the exact circumstances, and the few letters from Uncle Marsh failed to elaborate, which only added to our fears. What was he not telling us and why?

That first Saturday after we received the news, Aunt Esther and I rose early and dressed. I slicked down my hair, put on a clean pair of overalls and shirt, and slipped my feet into a pair of freshly shined boots. I was ready a good twenty minutes before Aunt Esther, who continued to preen herself long after I wandered down to the store to wait for her. I snitched one of the smaller jawbreakers from the glass jar under the counter, and it was almost all gone by the time Aunt Esther came down.

She was dressed in a dark gray, winter dress, the hem almost touching the ground. At the time, my aunt must have been in her early thirties, but in those days, once a woman married, she seemed to become old immediately. Perhaps it was the way women rolled their hair in tight buns that gave their faces a pinched, hard look, or perhaps it was their dresses that hid their bodies under layers of cotton and wool. In my aunt's case, the past year wrought additional changes beyond her makeup and dress. Her hair, once coal black, now sported strands of gray, and as we stepped out the door, the bright sunlight exposed every new wrinkle around her eyes and mouth brought on by her anxiety over Uncle Marsh.

This morning, for the first time since Uncle Marsh left, she painted her lips with rouge, only a touch to give them a bit of color, and the same with her cheeks. She loosened her hair so that it dropped over her shoulders, and that alone took five years off her appearance. She was smiling, which I hadn't seen much of since my uncle's departure and which softened her features even more. I never thought my aunt physically beautiful, but this morning I saw evidence why men might call her a handsome woman.

"Let's go meet Marsh." She slipped on a wide brim hat, the kind ladies wore to keep the sun off their faces rather than those they wore for vanity, yet that simple piece of apparel added a touch of the regal, and she walked with her head a little higher, her shoulders a little more squared.

I closed the front door without locking it. In those days when we stepped out, we never bothered to lock our doors. We trusted our neighbors. We didn't fear them.

We'd walked barely a dozen paces toward the train station when, passing an alley between Wiggins General Store and the Tower Theater, we heard the grunts and screams of boys scuffling. There, Tommy Barron, the mayor's son, sat on a colored boy half his size, the kid's arms pinned under his knees. Tommy dangled a worm in his right hand, intending, I believe, to force it into the boy's mouth, but the boy spun his head right, then left, his lips pressed tightly together.

Tommy was a big kid, as tall as me although a year younger. His chest and belly rolled outward before narrowing to his hips and spindly legs. At school the kids called him Tommikins behind his back. Tommikins was a silly cartoon character in the *Dallas Morning News*, drawn by the same artist who did Mutt and Jeff, and his body shape looked exactly like Tommy Barron's. In addition to his rather oddly shaped body, his face showed the ravages of acne, permanent scars having already formed on his forehead and cheeks where he picked at pustules until they bled and scabbed over.

Off to one side, four other kids watched, their eyes alight with perverted pleasure, and one of them screamed for Tommikins to 'stuff the goddamn worm down the nigger's throat.' Tommikins played to his audience. He jiggled the worm and laughed. The boy under him bucked and kicked trying to dislodge the bully, but the mayor's son forced all his weight into his knees, and with his left hand, seized the hair of the smaller boy, forcing his head back.

The sight of this injustice brought my aunt to a sharp halt. "Tommy Barron, you stop that this instant!"

Her shrill command startled the boys, who looked at her in wide-eyed astonishment, and that gave the colored kid leverage to squirm out from under Tommy's grasp. He was even smaller than I first thought, no older than ten or eleven. Tears streaked his dusty cheeks. Off balance, Tommikins slammed his open palm against the kid's cheek, splattering the darker skin with yellow juice. As the boy made it to his feet, Tommikins threw a wild punch at his backside. The boy fled down the alley and disappeared around the rear of Wiggins' store.

My aunt pointed a thin finger at Tommikins. "I'm going to tell your father about this, Tommy Barron."

Tommikins drew his lips into a sneer and climbed to his feet, his pants covered in dust. "You think my daddy will care I beat up a nigger? Nobody cares, not my daddy, not nobody, except for the nigger himself—and a nigger-loving old lady."

I started to go for him, but Aunt Esther caught my arm. For a moment, Tommikins' eyes widened in surprise, but when he saw I wasn't going to make a scene, he stuck his thumbs in his belt and strode off down the alley, his feet kicking up small clouds of dust. The other kids followed.

My aunt watched a moment longer, the rigid set of her jaw and the flush in her cheeks telling me she was about as angry as I had ever seen her. "A boy like that isn't worth a gob of spit," she said.

"Are you going to tell his daddy?" I asked. We were to meet Mayor Lon Barron at the train station, and she would have her chance then.

Not many kids liked Tommikins. He was a bully, especially toward those younger and smaller. Although he and I had never butted heads, I didn't like him, and if his daddy gave him a whipping, I wouldn't feel sorry for him.

Aunt Esther didn't speak again until we were almost at the train platform. "Tommy Barron was right. His father won't care. More the pity for that." She lifted her fingers and tapped her lips as she always did before she made a point. "I won't risk spoiling Marsh's homecoming."

We found Mayor Lon Barron waiting with Deputy Sheriff Jim Kennison on the station platform. Lon, his hands behind his back, stood gazing up the tracks. As befitting his position as President of First Bank and Trust, he wore a dark vest suit, a watch fob hanging from one pocket, a small diamond stickpin attached to his tie. The shoulders of his coat held a fine layer of dandruff, and white flakes dotted his coal black hair, which was plastered to his head with such insistency that I would have sworn he'd used axle grease to mold its shape. Twice he'd run successful campaigns for mayor, and as his success grew, so had his girth. People joked that his belly was so big that, once he put on his shoes, he needed a full-length mirror to see them. A cigar as thick as Lon's thumb hung from his lips at an oblique angle, and he puffed great clouds of smoke that swirled around his head.

"I think I hear the train," he said, but I heard nothing. That was Lon, always a little impatient, wanting things to happen before they did.

Jim tipped his hat. "An important day, ma'am; I'm mighty happy for you."

Aunt Esther clasped her handbag to her breast. "It's just that...well, his letters never sounded encouraging. I don't know what to expect."

In August of the previous year, Jim had arrived in Twin Forks as a deputy sheriff, taking over from Harvey Ralston who'd passed on from a failed heart. Although he'd never met Uncle Marsh, Jim stood with us because Lon insisted that the town's two proper officials should be on hand to greet a true American hero. Jim, nearsighted and with an astigmatism, wore spectacles, which kept him out of the Great War, but most people, especially women, thought him handsome. A good six feet in height and sporting a mop of curly blond hair, he carried himself erect and appeared fit for about any physical duty. His shirt issued by the sheriff's department hugged his chest and thin waist. Often I witnessed women, some as old as thirty and married, eye him with a particular interest, which I thought disgusting since he was only twenty-two, a scant six years older than I.

"Yes, ma'am; not knowing is the hardest thing there is." Jim removed his Stetson and ran his fingers through his thick, golden hair. Despite the time of the year, the day had warmed, and the fall sun bounced off the white pebbles that lined the track bed, making us squint against the glare. "I'm sure the army wouldn't send him home him if he wasn't fine."

Jim slapped the Stetson on his head and looked at me with a half-formed smile. Even though he was a deputy sheriff and sparking Susanna Barron, the mayor's daughter, Jim was nothing more than a big kid himself. Around Lon and people like Lon he always appeared out of place, a big country boy a little overwhelmed by his success.

Whatever Jim's shortcomings, I envied him. Susanna Barron was the best looking girl in Twin Forks, and I had a crush on her, so bad that whenever I thought of her, my chest felt like it was weighted down with a hundred pounds of rocks. But she was two years older than me, and I was nobody, kept from the orphanage because relatives had taken me in. Jim had the backing of her father and was going somewhere in county politics.

Around the far curve, black smoke showed above the trees, and we heard the rumble of the Sunshine Special, which ran between St. Louis and El Paso. In its seven years of existence, I must have seen it pass through Twin Forks a hundred times, but it had made only one previous stop to deposit the Higgins boy minus his leg. People in our part of the county rode their wagons into town or strode on their own two feet, and those who traveled to the big city used a local that ran once daily between Fort Worth and Dallas. As I said, we were an insular community, concerned more with the price of cotton than stock markets or foreign wars.

As the train began to slow a mile out, Aunt Esther, Jim and I stood beside Lon, and I felt my usual excitement when a train rumbled through. To me, a train symbolized those far romantic places that I only read about in books and magazines. I was haunted by the romance of the rails, I was in love with long distances. From the first day I arrived in Twin Forks, I knew I didn't belong in this backwater burg where it took a once-in-a-lifetime occasion for the Sunshine Special to stop. There was a larger world waiting for me, and one day I would go off to college and find it. One day.

The train rolled to a stop, the cars rattling together, the brakes squealing, steam pouring from the engine. Black smoke rolled over us and cleared when a gust of wind drove it away. A short, bow-legged conductor jumped from one of the cars and placed a wooden step before the exit. We waited almost a full minute before one man, leaning on the arm of the conductor, lowered himself to the platform. He carried a faded green valise, and the sleeves of his plaid shirt hung below his wrists so only his fingers showed. His slacks, two sizes too large, were tied around the waist with rope to keep them up, and this gave him the appearance of one of those baggy pants comics in a Mack Sennett comedy. Only his face kept me from laughing. His eyes were so deeply embedded in his skull that they appeared as black holes, and gray splotches covered his skin like a dog with mange. He walked with a shuffle, as if putting one foot in front of the other was the greatest of efforts. When I saw him, I thought: Who is this old man and where is Uncle Marsh?

Before he had left us, Uncle Marsh was the most striking figure in Twin Forks, six feet in height, broad in the shoulders with muscles that rippled all the way up his arms. Once a local farmer came to town to pick up a load of lumber, and when a wagon wheel collapsed, the wagon and load dropped on the man, pinning him. If the load had shifted a foot, maybe less, the weight would have crushed his chest. Uncle Marsh, witnessing the accident from his store, rushed out to help, and using only his back and legs, lifted the wagon and its load high enough for others to drag that farmer from underneath the wagon. Sometimes in small towns like Twin Forks, tales like this get blown out of proportion, but I heard it from at least half a dozen people who were there, and they all told it pretty much the same way, so I figured it must be true.

The conductor snatched up the wooden step, blew his whistle, and the Sunshine Special jerked twice, the cars slamming together before it gained momentum to roll on. The old man glanced at the departing train and then back at us, and I saw into the eyes—I couldn't help it. He looked straight at me. "You've sprouted some since I left, Davy," he said.

At that moment Jim, Lon Barron and Aunt Esther must have understood, as I did, why the army had sent Uncle Marsh home. They sent him home to die.

Aunt Esther enfolded Uncle Marsh in her arms. She

was still holding him when his body began to shake like an earthquake that rumbles unexpectedly to the surface from deep within the earth, slow at first then gaining strength until the whole world is shaking. He covered his mouth, and coughed so long and hard he appeared to be suffering a seizure. Slowly the coughing subsided.

Lon had his hand extended, but when Uncle Marsh began to cough, he stepped back, his expression one of concern if not outright fear.

Uncle Marsh ran an arm over his mouth, smearing a spot of blood across his sleeve. Sweat beaded his forehead, and his thin face drooped with fatigue. "Nothing you can catch, Lon." Uncle Marsh sounded like his throat was full of sand and rock.

Jim stepped forward, offering his hand, and for that I admired him. "I'm Jim Kennison, deputy sheriff. It's a pleasure to meet you, sir."

Uncle Marsh's grip was limp, his hand held in place by Jim.

"Let's get you home, Marsh," Lon said.

Lon owned one of the dozen or so automobiles in our part of the county—a brand new four-cylinder McLauglin Buick, a symbol of his status that he showed off whenever he got the chance. Aunt Esther and I could have ushered Uncle Marsh home, but Lon insisted that he deliver us, so we climbed into the back seat. I hugged one window, Uncle Marsh the other, Aunt Esther in the middle. Pressed together as we were, I could smell Uncle Marsh even over Lon's cigar. He smelled like stale sweat and mildewed leather, compliments of the long train ride.

Lon drove right down the middle of the street, bouncing along the ruts, kicking up a storm of dust, and frightening a team owned by Zeb Cain that shied away as we passed. We'd traveled all of a hundred yards before Lon halted the automobile in front of our dry goods store, above which we lived. Here Aunt Esther twice brought stillborn babies into the world, and after the second, the doctor informed her that her childbearing days were over. The miscarriages had messed up her insides. Here they had brought me ten years before when I came to them at the age of six, and here I had grown into the person I was. I called them Uncle Marsh and Aunt Esther, but I knew them far better than my real mother and father who, each year, receded further and further into the dark recesses of memory.

A fine coat of dust clung to the windows of our dry goods store. Where once roses adorned the sides of the building, weeds and crabgrass had now assumed control. I helped Aunt Esther around the store as much as she let me, but right from the first day I moved in, both she and Uncle Marsh had insisted that school came first. I performed my chores, few that they were, but my first responsibility was my studies. As a result, the appearance of the store had deteriorated, and now I felt ashamed that I had not insisted on doing more.

As soon as the car rolled to a stop, I was out and running around the other side to open the door for Uncle Marsh. He slid out, but even before his feet touched the ground, he began to fall. I caught him, my arms encircling a chest that was all bone. He weighed so little that I could have held him up with one hand. His valise tumbled onto the dirt, spilling out an army issued uniform and medals that clinked like tin soldiers.

Aunt Esther came from the other side, and with one arm around his shoulders, led my uncle toward the back stairs. Kneeling, I stuffed the clothes back into the valise and picked up the medals, more than half a dozen, among which I discovered a Metal of Honor and a Purple Heart. None weighed more than a few ounces, and I thought them wholly inadequate as compensation for what he had endured. Yet I could not help but feel a sense of pride in my uncle, who not only survived where so many had fallen but who his country had recognized for his bravery and duty.

I had dropped below the sight of Lon Barron and Jim, and they must have forgotten I was there. Lon waited until Uncle Marsh and Aunt Esther were out of earshot before he said, "You remember I mentioned a town get-together to celebrate Marsh's homecoming? Well, forget it. It ain't happening."

"He sure is tight-lipped, ain't he, Mayor?" Jim said

"That was just Marsh being Marsh. As long as I've known him, I never heard him speak more than twenty words at any one time." Lon plucked the cigar from his mouth and studied the stub before tossing it onto the street. "I don't doubt Marsh is a hero, but who wants to see a hero that looks like that?"

"Those sores on his face—" Jim removed the wire-rimmed spectacles and rubbed his nose. "How do you suppose he got them?"

"Maybe it's some disease he picked up over there. Maybe from a French woman, for all I know." Lon stomped the clutch and shoved the car into gear. "Hell, we did our civic duty, and more power to us. Let's go get a beer."

That crack about a French woman made me good and angry. Uncle Marsh wasn't the kind of man to play around with women, not that kind of man at all.

Standing, I held the valise in one hand, the medals in the other. With my knee, I slammed the car door as the Buick moved forward. Jim glanced over his shoulder and saw me, his eyes drifting to the medals. Like a little kid whose mother overhears him talking dirty, his face reddened with embarrassment.

I caught up to Uncle Marsh and Aunt Esther on the landing. While she opened the back door, he leaned most of his weight upon the banister, breathing hard, like he had run a mile without stopping. Aunt Esther took his arm, leaning him into her, and together they stepped into the kitchen. In an effort to stop time, she had kept everything in its place as he would have remembered: the chairs, the tables, the lamps, the pictures on the walls, even the knick-knacks on shelves. His face lit with instant and grateful recognition. His familiar world had not changed, and in that, he felt some sense of comfort.

Laying the valise on the kitchen table, I came up beside him, and he gripped my shoulder, his thin fingers digging in. Fearing he was about to collapse, I slipped an arm around his waist, and taking his weight from Aunt Esther, guided him into the living room where I deposited him onto his big easy chair, the soft cushions enfolding him like an old friend. Stepping back, I studied his scarred face, the splotches close to bright red from his exertions, his skin drawn so tightly over his facial bones it appeared almost translucent. In addition, his sockets were so deeply embedded in his skull that the pupils reflected little light. Twice I had seen people in the last stages of cancer, and they had looked healthier than Uncle Marsh.

Reaching up, he fingered one of the spots on his cheek, exploring the area as if trying to judge its size. "I must look a'fright, Davy."

I started to protest, but what could I say that wouldn't sound insincere? Instead I said, "Do they hurt?"

He coughed, covering his mouth with the back of his hand. When he spoke again, his voice was raspy. "Hurts a little in here." He tapped his chest over his heart. "Fine otherwise. As for these—" He touched a pink spot. "—the doctors told me plenty of sun would help rid them."

I held out the medals. "These fell out of your valise. They got dust on them."

"They got more than dust on them, son." He waved his hand as if dismissing their importance. "Put 'em away in a drawer, far back, where I don't have to see them."

It was an odd remark that I didn't understand, and I started to ask him to explain, but his tortured expression told me to keep quiet.

Aunt Esther came back from the kitchen carrying a glass of water. With a shaking hand, Uncle Marsh lifted the glass to his lips, and water spilled off his chin and spotted his shirt.

Aunt Esther kneeled before her husband and laid a hand on his knee. "What happened, Marsh? Your letters didn't say much. I thought—well, Davy and me didn't know what to think. Was it as bad as we heard?"

"Worse," he said.

He drank the rest of the water, and Aunt Esther took the glass and placed it on the end table. "You're all worn out."

"Two days on the train," he said. "Hard days sitting there wondering. That's all there was to do."

She leaned forward and ran her fingers through his hair, now thinner than it used to be, and like hers, speckled with gray. "Maybe you should lie down for a while."

I helped him stand, and arm in arm, we made our way to the bedroom. There I sat him on the side of their bed, and Aunt Esther removed his shoes and socks, his shirt and trousers. The sight of his concave chest and thin legs must have embarrassed him, and he lay back, snatching at the sheet. He lacked the strength for even that small job, and Aunt Esther pulled the cover up around his neck. Leaning over, she took his face in her hands and kissed his forehead, his eyes, and his lips. "I ain't never letting you go to war again," she said.

"Don't suppose anybody will ever ask."

"Then I've got you for good now," my aunt said.

2

*T*he next morning I awoke to a piano playing "Shall We Gather at the River," which drifted all the way from Twin Forks Baptist Church. During the night I had kicked off the covers, and I was clammy with sweat, all due to the unseasonably warm weather. Whenever the Sunday morning weather was good, the Baptists opened the front doors around seven, and Mae Brennan, who had to be close to ninety and a little tone deaf, played hymns to remind the parishioners that Sunday school began at ten, church services at eleven. I got a little annoyed when that happened because Sunday was the one day of the week I got to sleep late, but Mrs. Brennan's stone fingers invariably denied me that pleasure.

I rolled out of bed, dressed and went to the kitchen. I found it deserted, which surprised me. Even on Sunday mornings, Aunt Esther was up and about long before seven. I would find her at the kitchen table reading the *Dallas Morning News*, a full breakfast ready and waiting. I heard Uncle Marsh snoring loudly, and I figured Aunt Esther didn't want to disturb his sleep.

I went down the back stairs and around to the front for the newspaper. Rounding the building I almost collided

15

with Mr. Jenkins, the telegrapher, out for his morning constitutional, although as far as I could see, the exercise did little good other than cause him to sputter and gasp more than usual. But Doc Gibbs prescribed exercise, and Mr. Jenkins would follow the doctor's orders even if it killed him.

He drew up short and nodded, too out of breath to speak at first. I bid him good morning, and that gave him time to find his voice. "How's Marsh?" he asked.

What could I say to such a question except to deflect it by a half-truth. "As well as can be expected," I said.

"You tell your uncle—you tell him—as soon as he's up to it—" He paused a moment until he recovered. "As soon as he's up to it, I'll be around to see him."

With that, he struck my shoulder with a beefy hand and staggered past, heading for his office to sit before the telegraph and wait for messages to come clicking across the wires. For him, his job was seven days a week, twelve hours a day. His wife had passed away during the influenza epidemic, and he was a lost, lonely man whose sole purpose in life was to tap out wires with greater speed and accuracy than men much younger than he. Under the circumstances, I thought it gracious of him to ask after Uncle Marsh.

I picked the morning newspaper from its delivery box. Mr. Wiggins who owned the general store two doors down raised a thin arm in greeting. Like most old people I knew, he had trouble sleeping, and most mornings, the weather permitting, he pulled his rocking chair out onto the sidewalk and rocked away the day. Three years before, he had given the store to his son and daughter-in-law. Since then, he made no secret of the fact that they, along with their three kids, drove him crazy, and this was his only escape. "Give my regards to your uncle," he said. Despite his age, Mr. Wiggins wasn't feeble, and his voice easily carried the distance between us. "Tell him that when he feels up to it, we can play checkers, like we use to. I've been looking forward to it since I heard he was coming home."

The following day, a Monday, people began to drop by the moment that Aunt Esther opened the store, and before I got home from school, nearly everybody in Twin Forks had made an appearance. Mayor Lon Barron and Jim Kennison must have spread the word, so people knew the extent of Uncle Marsh's illness. No one expected to see him, no one really wanted to see him, but they felt the need to extend their good wishes. During the week others came, too, those who lived on and worked the farms but who only came to town for supplies.

For all their felicitations, I doubted, as each of them must have doubted, that Uncle March would ever be well enough to visit with Mr. Jenkins or play checkers with Mr. Wiggins or socialize with any of them ever again. Most days he climbed out of bed only to use the chamber pot, and even that little bit of exercise tired him so that afterward he fell back into a restless sleep. He grew even thinner, if that were possible, his coughing more violent, and often after one of his fits, he spit blood. Doctor Gibbs came twice a week, climbing our creaking back stairs, although he was so fraught with rheumatism that it may have been his knees that creaked. With his stethoscope, he listened to my uncle's heart, and with his knuckles tapped my uncle's back and listened there, too. He would peer deeply into Uncle March's eyes as if he might discern some cause for the malady, but when no answer presented itself, he would pull a few colorless pills from his bag and stuff them in Aunt Esther's hand. "I've got no experience with anything like this," he told us more than once. "You ought to get Marsh over to that new veterans' hospital in Dallas. Until then, add a couple of beers to his meals. Beer has plenty of vitamins and will give him strength."

The first time Doc Gibbs broached the subject of the hospital, Aunt Esther waited until she heard the door close and Doc Gibbs' feet on the stairs before she faced Uncle

March with the question, although I suspect she knew his answer even before he uttered it. "I'd rather die in my own bed," he said.

My aunt passed her hand across her mouth and pointed a finger at my uncle in that particular gesture she had when she meant to emphasize her point. "You ain't dying anytime soon, Marsh Langston. I won't allow it."

Aunt Esther cooked and cleaned and saw to the store as she had for the past year and a half, but to these tasks she now added caring for Uncle Marsh. I helped as best I could, but every time I tried to assume a chore beyond my usual load, she shooed me back to my books. One afternoon when she had to see to shopping, she allowed me to spell her an hour or so by sitting with Uncle Marsh while he slept. At one point, he began to toss and turn, and finally kicked off his covers. Without warning, he bolted upright, his eyes wide as if he were startled by a loud noise, except the house was as quiet as an empty church. He saw me, and his expression changed from what I can only describe as fear to one of irritation. He growled like an angry bear. "Get back to your studies, Davy. I don't need a nursemaid."

I patted the book on my lap, an old tattered copy of *Silas Marner.* "I've got my work right here. I've been reading while you've been resting."

"Go on, get out of here, boy." He spoke with a fierce harshness I had seldom heard from him. I jumped to my feet, almost knocking over the straight-back chair. He must have seen the consternation on my face, and in a softer tone, he said, "I don't mean to be abrupt, Davy. I appreciate all you're doing, but I'm not ready to take off for the Promised Land. When I do, I'll give you a call. Until then, go about your business."

So I left him alone, although I went no further than the kitchen table where I sat and read until Aunt Esther came up the rear stairs and through door, her arms full of groceries. "Why aren't you with Marsh?" she asked, and when I told her, she twisted her lips in an attitude of mock annoyance. "That man is as stubborn as a constipated mule."

I began to worry about Aunt Esther. When she worked in the dry goods store, she wore her hair in a bun, stacked and pinned, and her dress, if a little drab, was always clean and presentable. Now wild strands of hair flew in all directions, her dresses needed ironing, and on more than one occasion, I noticed a stocking hanging around an ankle.

Late one March evening, as I sat at the kitchen table still working my way through *Silas Marner*, Aunt Esther came in to say goodnight. Her hollow cheeks held dark shadows, swollen bags hung under her eyes, and the eyes themselves were half hidden by drooping lids. When she bent over to kiss me on the forehead, she swayed and had to catch my shoulder to remain upright. I sprang to my feet and sat her on the chair. She leaned both elbows on the table and placed her head in her hands. I poured her a glass of water. Her hands shook, and some of the water spilled over the edge. Setting the glass aside, she said, "I haven't ate much today. I've made myself a little dizzy."

"You're getting yourself sick," I said. "This is the season for ague fever, and that can lay a person low for weeks. You can't let that happen."

She regarded me with a long, silent stare, then asked, "What are you saying, Davy?"

"You're taking on too much."

She thought on that a good minute before she nodded. "Maybe it is time to get some help."

"I'm not doing my share," I said. "I should take on extra work around here."

She reached out, took my hand in hers and patted it. "I promised your mama that you'd get an education, that you'd be the first member of this family to go to college. You're a sweet boy, but sometimes a little shortsighted. Neglecting your studies isn't the answer. Maybe Sunday morning, you and me will take a little stroll over to Boonesville. I think I know somebody there who might help."

At least half a dozen times in the company of Uncle Marsh, I visited that colored shantytown above Piker's Bluff, which overlooked the Trinity River. Before Uncle Marsh left for the war, he hired a couple of men from there to help Aunt Esther at the beginning of each month to unload supplies. They proved to be good workers, the Bowen brothers, both young with new wives, and each with a child on the way. Aunt Esther paid them good wages too, as much as she would have paid a white person, which caused problems with Lon Barron.

One Monday morning, the mayor came barreling into our store on his spindly legs, his belly preceding him, the buttons on his vest straining to hold. He slammed an open palm on the counter and screwed his face into a paroxysm of outraged dignity. "Darn it, Esther, I hear you're paying top wages to those colored boys."

I stood off to one side, ready to say goodbye to Aunt Esther as I was on my way to school, and Lon threw a glance my way as if he expected me to back him up. He had narrow little eyes—some might call them beady—which made him appear as if he were always figuring a way to weedle you out of your pocket change.

"Marsh told me to pay top wages." Aunt Esther wiped her mouth and pointed a thin finger at the Mayor. "I'm doing what Marsh wants."

"When you pay a colored boy the same as a white man, you're saying his work is equal to a white man's. Now you know that ain't so."

"Don't know no such thing, Lon Barron," my aunt said.

"All that extra money you give them—why they don't even spend it here in town. Young Mr. Wiggins told me so. They go over to Augustus or Hollister, and we never see a penny of that money."

"They shop here—with us—and with others, too, but they won't have nothing to do with young Mr. Wiggins." Aunt Esther crossed her arms over her chest, and her face became hard, what Uncle Marsh called brittle. "When they buy his meat, he uses his thumb to drive up the weight on the scale. He adds sand to their salt. He sells them vegetables that are just this side of rotten. It's no wonder they stopped coming to him. His father never cheated them, but he does. They'd rather walk five miles to Augustus where at least they get fair treatment."

"Those colored people saying they was cheated?"

"No, Lon, I'm saying it. I've stood right in Wiggins' store and watched him doing it."

"If Marsh was here—" Lon began.

"—he'd tell you the same as me," she said.

He removed his bowler and ran his fingers around the inside hatband. That small action gave him time to consider his next point, and when he spoke, he adopted a more reasonable and conciliatory tone. "Look, Esther, this ain't about me hating those people. Fact is, I pity them. No ma'am, this is about social order." He put his hands on the counter and leaned forward, his belly pressing against the edge. "Look what's happened in Russia, where the Bolsheviks have turned the social order upside down. That whole country is in chaos. Now I'm the mayor here, and it's my job to make sure that don't happen here, too."

My aunt flashed a sardonic smile. "You get up every morning feeling that way, Lon? If so, you must be plumb tuckered out by noon. Any man would be if he carried around that much weight on his shoulders. It's a miracle you ain't bent double."

At that point, Lon must have realized that he could get nowhere with Aunt Esther, and red-faced, he stomped out of the store. Grinning, I tucked my schoolbooks underneath my arm and kissed Aunt Esther goodbye. I stepped onto the boardwalk where I discovered Lon Barron unwrapping a cigar. He tossed the paper wrapper into the wind, which whisked it down the street. He shifted his eyes to me, and my smile must have miffed him. A scowl darkened his face. "What's so funny, kid?" he asked.

"Nothing's funny, Mayor," I said. "It's a nice day, that's all."

He pointed the unlit cigar at me as if it were a pistol. "You sassing me? You better watch it, kid. You better watch it before somebody knocks that sassiness right out of you." He spoke the last words through his teeth. His nostrils flared, and he balled one hand into a fist as he struggled to gain control. To some extent, he succeeded because he took a deep breath, and his next words sounded more deliberate, more calculating. "You don't know nothing about social order, kid, but you'll learn. Your aunt is making a big mistake that'll cause misery to those she's trying to help. You'll see."

I was proud of Aunt Esther for standing up to the mayor, but my feelings had nothing to do with the fact that she stood up for colored people. I admired that she wouldn't let Lon bully her. Of course that was Aunt Esther for you. She never let anyone bully her. Now, however, she was talking about going to Boonesville to find help.

"Boonesville?" I said. "Why would we go there?"

"You have some objection to those people?" my aunt asked.

"Well...they're colored. I mean—"

"You've got to look beyond a person's skin, Davy," Aunt Esther said. "You read books all the time. I would've thought you'd learned that by now."

When colored people came to our store and I waited on them, I treated them the same as I treated white people. Many I knew by first names. Sure they called me 'Mr. Davy' instead of 'Davy', but I figured that was their way. It didn't mean anything. I said, "I never once treated a colored person bad. Never once! I never called one a bad name, I never talked down to one."

"You're a good boy, Davy, and you'd never set out to hurt a person on purpose. But the fact that you're questioning me about those poor folk up on the hill—well, that gives me pause."

"The whole town—" I began.

"—sees only this." With her thumb and forefinger, she pinched loose skin on her arm. "I expect you to see more."

"This whole town thinks one way, and you and Uncle Marsh another. Is everybody in town wrong but you two?"

A look came into her eyes that said she was disappointed in me, and that made me feel a lot worse than if she had been angry. "You need to talk to your uncle when he's better." Even her voice held a note of disappointment. "He can explain it better than me."

For a long time I sat at the table mulling over my aunt's words, disturbed that I looked small in her eyes. Finally, I directed my attention back to *Silas Marner*, trying to concentrate on the words as best I could, but after fifteen or twenty minutes, when I realized I remembered nothing of what I'd read, I gave up and went to bed.

3

At half past six Saturday morning, Aunt Esther and I set out for Boonesville. She pinned a wide brimmed hat to her hair and wore her walking boots. Because of the cool weather, she threw a thin jacket over her shoulders. Other than my boots, I wore my overalls and a plaid shirt. A light wind blew in from the Gulf, but it brought no clouds and no smell of rain, and with each step we kicked up a cloud of dust. Soon my lips began to chap, which made me wish I had dabbed them with a little petroleum jelly as Aunt Esther had suggested, but I was sixteen, and smearing my lips with petroleum jelly was for girls.

After three quarters of an hour, we came to the hill on which Boonesville rested. Aunt Esther paused to look up, but from our vantage point we could see only brush and trees. She stepped off, keeping to the trail with me a few steps behind. The weeds grew high on either side, and in the undergrowth, cicadas buzzed. An occasional yellow jacket floated by, intent on keeping out of our way, and once a horned toad scurried across our path, raising a trail of dust. Funny thing about horned toads: they're so flat and low to the ground, yet fast and sleek. They don't do any harm, not to humans. Maybe to insects, but that's a good thing. Yet most people, if you asked them, would say they were ugly and useless.

Boonesville looked down upon the Trinity River, which flowed a winding route over two hundred miles to the Gulf of Mexico. Below the bluff sat a patch of fallow ground, probably no more than half an acre, where the residents planted corn and other vegetables, often bringing in small cash crops. The white people of the area harbored little resentment. While fertile, the tiny piece of farmland flooded every few years, washing away the crops.

The dirt path wound its way up the gentle slope and through groves of elms, their gnarled and knotty limbs green with new growth as well as occasional clumps of mistletoe. The morning sun cascaded through the branches, bathing the ground in dappled light. From ahead, where the path curved left, came the voices of young children squealing and chattering. We rounded the curve and entered Boonesville.

Perhaps the town had changed since Uncle Marsh had brought me here, but if so, I couldn't see it. Three dozen shacks filled the bluff on my last visit, and the same three dozen were still there. Most appeared in various stages of decay, and if a strong wind came up, the whole damned town would wind up in the Trinity. In building their community, the coloreds scrounged wood from deserted houses, and so each structure was one of a kind, yet they shared a dilapidated decadence that made one indistinguishable from another. They also shared a common feature: the windows didn't have screens, but pieces of cardboard nailed to the sills and punched with holes that would let in the light but keep out insects.

Off to our left, three small children played, and the moment they saw us, their eyes widened, and they ceased their chatter. Even a couple of mangy dogs quit yapping and slunk away, their tails between their legs. The responses of the kids and the dogs were understandable. They seldom saw white people in their shantytown, and when they did, it usually meant trouble. Granted, my aunt and I didn't present a particularly threatening appearance, but we were white, and in the eyes of the children and the dogs, that was enough.

A colored man, thin and bleary-eyed, sat by the side of the nearest shanty, and the moment he spotted us, he pushed himself to his feet and stayed erect by shoving his back against the wall. Sweeping a battered hat from his head, he held it over his belly. "Mornin' Miss Esther." Even though five feet or more separated us, I smelled his whiskey breath. "I hear Mr. Marsh is back. I sure hope he doin' fine."

"That's kind of you, LeeRoy," my aunt said. "Can you tell me where Sister Rose lives?"

With his hat, he pointed to a shack on the far edge of the bluff. It stood straighter than the others, and wood shingles rather than tarpaper covered the roof. The frame even displayed a coat of whitewash. No trash littered the front, which in itself separated it from the other dwellings. On each side of the front door stood rose bushes, their naked stems trimmed and brown.

If I had given much thought to why Aunt Esther brought us to Boonesville, I would have figured out the answer. Years before on one of our infrequent visits here, Uncle Marsh introduced me to Sister Rose, yet I suppose I had not spoken half a dozen words to her since. Still, I knew her reputation. Many townspeople called her a witch because she dabbled in all sorts of potions and herbs. Some even claimed she used those powers to cast evil spells on white people. As a result of such slanderous rumors, she seldom came to town because, I am sure, she preferred to avoid encounters with the stupid and ignorant.

Aunt Esther knocked on the door, the solid wood hard against her small knuckles. When no one answered, she knocked again. This time the door flew open, and we faced a young man, seventeen or eighteen, broad shouldered, his skin dark like the night. He looked down upon us with a detached anger, as if our presence offended him, and his chiseled face reminded me of an ebony mask I had once seen in a history textbook,

"Whose come calling, Daniel?" a voice said from inside. Although I could not see Sister Rose, I recognized her voice, soft and melodic, and in its own way, cultured. Every other colored woman and man I knew talked in that particular Southern colloquial dialect so prevalent among their race, but not Sister Rose. She sounded more white than most white people, although I would never have said it to her face. And it didn't sound as if she was putting on airs. Her words and voice were unforced and natural.

When the young man failed to respond right away, Sister Rose said, "Where are your manners? Invite our guests inside."

The young man stepped aside, and we entered

The smell of boiled collard greens permeated the one room house. In a far corner a wash basin full of soapy water and plates rested on the kitchen table, and the young man's sleeves were rolled up past his elbows. Beads of water and soap suds clung to his forearms.

Sister Rose sat with her back to a window, and in her lap she clutched an open book so old and weathered that the pages had yellowed and curled. A brown water stain discolored the top, and the cardboard jacket hung loose from the binding. When she saw us, she laid the book on the floor next to her rocker, allowing me to see the title: *Pride and Prejudice* by Jane Austen. To her right were two shelves—nothing more than wood planks supported by old bricks—which held an additional fifteen or twenty books, more than I had seen in any one place except the schoolhouse. As far as I knew, nobody in town except Miss Pilgrim owned so many books, and I couldn't remember seeing another adult reading anything other than the Bible. My uncle was unusual in the fact that every day he read the newspaper from cover to cover. Yet here was a colored woman reading a novel, and who possessed her own private library. A few townspeople owned copies of *Ben Hur*, but I never heard one person say he or she had actually read it, although Lon Barron bragged that the past spring he'd attended a stage performance over in Dallas. He admitted he slept through a good portion of it, but he woke for the chariot race. "Damndest thing you ever did see," he said once. "It was like they were actually racing those two-wheel wagons right there on the stage."

Sister Rose stood, a tall woman who held herself erect, proud. "Why, if it isn't Miss Esther." She didn't offer her hand or approach Aunt Esther; that would have been too forward. She was the aristocrat of Boonesville, if such a thing were possible, but in the white world, she was only one more colored woman, nothing more.

Aunt Esther crossed the room and extended her hand. "I expect you know my boy, Davy," Aunt Esther said.

Sister Rose took my aunt's hand as she appraised me with her dark eyes. "I hear tell your boy is a scholar."

I didn't know how to respond, feeling that if I agreed, I would be bragging; if I denied it, I would be lying. As a result, I kept my mouth shut.

Sister Rose said, "My boy studies some himself, don't you, Daniel?"

"Some," Daniel said, his voice the deepest bass I'd ever heard, a voice made for singing or poetry. Many times I had seen him around Twin Forks, a book sticking from his overalls, although I figured it was a way of shoving it in our faces and saying: "I got a book and can read better than you." He had a book in his pocket now, the spine showing the first word of the title: *Pudd'nhead*.

"What can I do for you, Miss Esther?" Sister Rose asked.

"As I'm sure you've heard, my man has come home. He's doing poorly—real poorly. I need someone to look after him while I run the store. I hear you're good at helping those that are suffering."

Sister Rose stiffened. "I know what people in town say. They say I'm a witch, that I have magic cures. I'm no witch, Miss Esther. I know a few herbs, a few roots that can help those in pain, but I'm no witch."

"Never meant no such thing," Aunt Esther said. "I need you to sit with him, look after his needs. Davy does what he can—and he would like to do more—but I won't have his studies suffering. So I need help. I can pay fifty cents a week. I know it ain't much—"

"That's a real generous offer," Sister Rose said.

"You'll do it then?"

"I'll bring my boy around, too. You wouldn't mind, would you, Daniel?"

"Whatever you need, Mama," the young man said.

"Would you like us to come with you today?" asked Sister Rose. "We could walk back with you right now."

We were unprepared for such kindness, and Aunt Esther was taken aback. Tears gathered in the corners of her eyes, but she pushed her lips together and willed herself not to shed them. She took a moment to find her voice. "Maybe you could bring along some of those potions, if you think they might help Marsh," she said.

Sister Rose kneeled before a cabinet, opening the bottom draw where a number of bottles of all sizes and shapes sat in perfectly aligned rows. She took three of them, studying each first, before she placed them in in a brown cloth bag. She stood and passed the bag to her son who tied the top into a knot and wound it around his wrist. "We can go now, Miss Esther, if you're ready," she said.

We walked the two miles back to town, Aunt Esther and Sister Rose leading, Daniel and I following ten or twelve paces back so we didn't catch their dust. The boy kept a hostile silence, and I wondered if he were mad because his mother had asked him to accompany us. He was a head taller than I, and I had to look up to see his sculptured expression, the kind that would cause the people of Twin Forks to call him 'uppity.' Whatever his attitude, it made me uncomfortable. In an effort to break the tension, I pointed to the book in his back pocket. "I've read *Pudd'nhead Wilson.*"

"So?"

My teacher, Miss Pilgrim, had loaned me the book, and I recalled the fierce rush with which I devoured the novel in two consecutive nights. Because I loved it so, I wanted to talk about it with someone other than Miss Pilgrim, and all I got for my trouble was, 'So?' Right then I figured he had never read the novel, that as I suspected, he wore the book for show.

"Good book," I said. "That's all."

I was tempted to say more, to tell him to go to hell, but instead I fumed all the way into town. 'Uppity' was a good word for him, I thought.

4

*W*e climbed the back stairs to our store where Aunt Esther discovered the door ajar. Her face darkened as she marched straight to the bedroom, not bothering to take off her hat, the wide brim flapping in cadence with each step. She halted at the bedroom door, her hands on her hips, the back of her neck burning red.

Uncle Marsh sat up in bed, his face pale, one fist to his mouth trying to suppress a cough. His jowls were more pronounced, his eyes pinched, his pupils like glass. At his bedside sat Wilfred Joyner, the Baptist preacher who led the largest congregation in Twin Forks. I counted Uncle Marsh and Aunt Esther as religious people—they believed in God and Jesus Christ and they read their Bible—but we seldom attended church, and never once Preacher Joyner's congregation. Accepting Sunday as a day for rest, my adopted parents believed listening to a preacher, especially Brother Joyner, was only one more form of work.

Joyner stood over six feet, a thin rail of a man with a prominent Adam's Apple that reminded me of Irving's character Ichabod Crane, but he owned a booming voice that, if the church doors remained opened, carried all the way up the street. He was the Jonathan Edwards of Twin Forks whose sermons never varied in their hell-fire and damnation, but I suspect he was a secret drinker. His bulbous nose, discolored with busted blood vessels certainly suggested it. He also loved his cigars, and one afternoon he came by our store smoking when an ash flew off and landed on the tip of his nose. For the next ten minutes, he tried to persuade Aunt Esther and me to attend his services, all that time that black ash rocking up and down like a teeter totter. After that, I could never take anything he said seriously.

But I wasn't laughing now. Neither was Aunt Esther.

When he saw my aunt in the doorway, he stood and offered a condescending smile. In his left hand he clutched a Bible, the leather cover so worn that the gold letting was unreadable.

"Preacher, ain't you got no sense at all?" Aunt Esther said. "Can't you see my man is exhausted? Can't you see he doesn't need to waste his strength palavering?"

The preacher looked beyond Aunt Esther to Sister Rose, and he raised a disapproving eyebrow. "Marsh and I were discussing his immortal soul."

"His immortal soul will keep until he's feeling better." Aunt Esther reached up and unpinned her hat, holding it in one hand while in the other she thrust forward the long pin like a sword as if she were ready to impale the preacher.

"Well—" Brother Joyner drew out the word as if speaking to a child who couldn't quite understand his meaning. He focused again on Uncle Marsh. "—I thought that perhaps now, after your experiences over there, you would join the fold—join our fellowship in Christ. I know that there were no atheists in the trenches, Marsh. I know that, in your hour of need, you called out for your savior. It's time now you joined us."

Uncle Marsh pressed his lips together as if trying to hold his tongue.

Preacher Joyner said, "Perhaps if we pray, Marsh?"

"Had enough praying for one lifetime, Preacher." Uncle Marsh focused his feverish gaze on Joyner, and had he the strength, I believe he would have risen from that bed and tossed the preacher out by the seat of his pants. He was that angry. "As for the trenches, you weren't there. Let me say this, and then we're done. When we was shooting at them and they was shooting at us, we didn't think much about God and praying. We thought only about staying alive. Those that prayed died as quick as those that didn't. Sometimes quicker 'cause they weren't paying attention to what mattered."

Joyner stood very still, and all the while, I suspect, he was trying to find words to deflect Uncle Marsh's attack. Instead, he directed his attack at Aunt Esther. With the Bible, he pointed at Sister Rose. "You do know who this woman is, Esther? I have no prejudices against coloreds. They are what they are, the cursed descendants of Ham, but this woman with all her secret cures and potions walks with Satan. By bringing her into your home, you're jeopardizing your whole family, including the soul of this innocent boy." He gave me a cursory glance, but I doubted he cared much for my soul. I was only leverage for his argument.

"Sister Rose is here to help with Marsh," Aunt Esther said. "That's all I care about. It's time to be on your way, Preacher, so I can see to my man."

"Beware this *Sister* Rose..." He emphasized the word 'Sister' so that it sounded derogatory, ugly. "...and remember *Ecclesiastes* 13:1: 'He that toucheth pitch shall be defiled therewith.'"

I guess I could have kept still, stayed my place, but the devil got into me, and I said, "'As a man thinks in his heart, so is he.' *Proverbs,* 23:7." Having at the insistence of Uncle Marsh and Aunt Esther read the Bible from cover to cover, I had memorized a few passages, and whenever I found it useful, pulled one out of my head.

Preacher Joyner regarded me with open hostility. "You're blaspheming, boy. You're using the Lord's words in vain."

"No sir, only quoting the Bible, like you." I spoke in a rational, conversational tone, but Preacher Joyner saw through my words. I suppose everybody in the room did.

In that deep tone that always silenced me, Uncle Marsh said, "Davy."

Although the preacher struggled to control his temper, his face flushed and his cheeks quivered. "I've warned you, Esther. That's all I can do. I'm sure if you ask God, He will lead you down the right path."

He gathered up his hat from the end table, and Aunt Esther and I stepped aside to allow him to pass. As he did so, I smelled tobacco so ingrained in his clothes that I wondered if it ever came out. But I also caught another odor, faintly hidden by the cigar smoke, and which confirmed my earlier suspicion. He breathed heavily, a smoker's breath, but I caught the faintest whiff of whiskey, the homemade hooch that Ernie sold at his saloon. Ever since the doctor had ordered beer as a supplement to my uncle's diet, the responsibility for picking up a pint and bringing it home had fallen to me. During the past few weeks, I made daily trips to Ernie's, and I was all too familiar with that smell. He sold his hooch for a nickel a glass, whereas he charged more than twice as much for a shot of Jack Daniel's or Canadian Rye.

Once we heard the door slam, Uncle Marsh shifted his attention to me. "Davy—"

"Yes sir," I said.

"—sometimes you're too smart for your own good."

I think he wanted to say more—remind me that I was still a boy and should respect my elders—but he would chastise me no further in front of guests.

"Sister Rose, it's good to see you again, though I must apologize for our departed company." My uncle extended a hand, and Sister Rose crossed to the bed to take it.

"No need to apologize for those you can't control," she said.

Daniel took his mother's place at the foot of the bed, and Uncle Marsh said, "You've filled out, Daniel—just like Davy. You've grown into a man."

"Sorry you're doing poorly, Mr. Marsh." Daniel stood stiffly, reflecting, I suppose, his discomfort at being in the home of a white person, yet his words sounded sincere and his expression held no hint of perfidy. I marveled at his courteous response, so opposite the manner in which he treated me.

Uncle Marsh dropped his hand from Sister Rose as if he didn't have the strength to hold it up any longer. His breathing grew more labored, his sides heaving like an old horse that had run too far and too fast, and he began to cough, sending his whole body into a paroxysm of shaking.

Aunt Esther said, "Davy, go to the kitchen and fetch the beer pail. Hurry now; get it filled."

I ran from the room, and behind me Sister Rose said, "Daniel, you go along with Davy."

I scooped the empty beer pail from the kitchen counter, and as I headed for the door, I found Daniel waiting. I started to tell him not to bother, that I didn't need him tagging along, but I thought: Let him come if he wants. What do I care?

Ernie's Bar was a little more than a block from our store, and we covered the distance in less than a minute. I pushed through the swinging doors, Daniel right behind me. At any other time, more attuned to the social conventions, I might have asked him to wait outside, or he might have done it on his own, but at that moment the urgency of our task clouded our better judgment.

We pushed through the swinging doors. Off to our left sat Mayor Lon Barron and Deputy Sheriff Jim Kennison, a beer in front of each, and the moment we entered, they stopped talking and focused their attention on us. Four other patrons sat in a far corner, old Mr. Wiggins and three of his cronies playing forty-two, the dominoes lined before each like toy soldiers. They stopped playing and stared, too.

The mayor had hung his coat on the back of his chair, and sweat darkened his shirt. Jim's shirt was in the same condition, and mud covered both men's boots. On more than one occasion I heard the mayor say that public officials must look their best at all times, that even one spot on their clothes was unacceptable. Now they both wore sweat and mud like badges of honor.

Ernie, the owner of the bar, stood behind the counter, and I handed him the beer pail. "My uncle needs this right away."

With a nod, Ernie took the pail and tilted it under the tap.

Lon Barron emitted a sigh of exasperation and said, "Boy, what the hell you doing in here?"

At first I thought he was speaking to me, but when I faced them, I saw both he and Jim had their attentions directed at Daniel.

Daniel waved a thumb. "I'm with him."

Lon sat with one leg crossed over the other, his face screwed up like he smelled rotten eggs. "That don't give you the right to come in the front along with white folk."

Daniel shrugged, his stoic expression failing to mask his insolent eyes. "Never been in here before, Mr. Mayor." Despite his use of the term 'Mister', his tone held no respect, no humility.

Lon dropped a heavy foot to the floor. "That's no excuse, boy."

Ernie said, "The mayor's right. Next time, you go around to the back, regardless who you come with."

Daniel glanced at the bartender: "Yes, sir. Next time..."

"Ain't it a little early for a pint, boy?" Jim said, but his attempt at humor landed flat. No one laughed, no one even smiled.

"You two gentlemen are having yours, so I guess it's

not too early," Daniel said.

Jim narrowed his eyes, his jaw tightening. "Mayor Lon and me spent the whole morning pulling Ollie McPherson out of his well, so I don't need any sass from you. Understand?"

"I came with this boy because my mama told me to," Daniel said.

Calling me "this boy" annoyed me, but I said nothing. Ernie laid the pail on the counter, and foam rolled over the sides. He jerked a towel from his belt and wiped the wood with a fierce intensity as if he were angry at the beer for spilling itself. His hand slammed against the pail, and a third of the contents sloshed over the lip. In angry frustration, the little bartender glowered at Daniel. "Five cent fine for coming in the front door and for making me spill this beer. You hear me? Five cent fine. Put your nickel here on the bar, boy." With his index finger Ernie tapped the bar.

"Mr. Ernie, I came here with—" He paused as if trying to recall my name. "—him. I came because Mama asked me. Now I don't have a nickel. But I promise I won't ever come in the front again."

Daniel started for the door, but before he reached it, Jim pushed back his chair, came to his feet and stepped in front of him. Jim was tall and used to looking down on people, but Daniel was as tall as Jim and carried more weight and muscle. I doubt Daniel's stature worried Jim. Jim wore a badge, and I think he believed it protected him like armor. He tried to screw an expression that appeared hard and determined, but his spectacles along with that mop of curly blonde hair made him seem more studious than threatening. He rested the heel of his hand on the butt of his double-action .45. I don't believe he intended anything by it—I had seen Jim take that stance in the middle of a casual conversation—but Daniel caught the move and forced a crooked smiled. "Are you going to shoot me over a nickel, Mr. Deputy? That's a cheap price, even for a colored boy's life."

Daniel's speech, so proper, so precise, sounded more white than black, and that irritated Jim. He wanted his coloreds to sound like coloreds.

"Like I told you, next time I'll come in the back. I'll keep my word." Daniel stepped around him. "You have a nice day, Mr. Deputy. You, too, Mr. Mayor."

Daniel strolled through the swinging doors, their hinges squealing at his departure, and Jim made no further move to stop him.

Lon slammed an open palm on the table, and his extra chin jiggled with the impact. "That smart aleck son-bitch needs to be taught a lesson!"

Jim squinted at the mayor through his thick lens. "You think I should have shot him, Mayor? Over a nickel?"

"It's not about money. It's the principle of the thing. If it'd been me—if I was the deputy sheriff—he wouldn't have got away with a thing like that." Lon swept up his mug and drained the contents. Finished, he banged the empty glass on the table, and with the back of his hand, wiped foam from his lips. "You don't know who that boy is, do you? That's Sister Rose's boy. You know who she is, don't you?"

"Heard of her," said Jim.

"Rumors say the old witch wants to set up a school to teach little pickaninnys to read and write. If it's true, it's a goddamn waste of time. Book learning confuses them, takes their mind off work, and upsets the proper balance of things."

"I saw he had a book stuck in his overalls," Jim said.

"I've seen him all the time off by himself, reading. Something unnatural in that. And he talks all so fine and proper. I tell you, Jim, I'm beginning to think he's a Bolshevik."

"Maybe that boy ought to be taken down a peg or two, but shooting him over a nickel?" Jim shook his head. "I couldn't do that, Mayor."

"Yeah, I've noticed that about you, Jim." Lon's voice held a note of disappointment. "You got a big streak of kindness in you. Not a bad thing ordinarily, but a man in your position, especially if he wants to move up in the world—like becoming county sheriff—that man has to act when the time demands it." Lon stood, and reaching into his vest pocket, pulled out a dime and tossed it on the table. "Maybe you're right. Maybe this wasn't the time and place to deal with that boy. But I'm keeping my eye on him."

Ernie handed me the beer pail, now refilled. "I'll put it on your uncle's tab, Davy," he said.

With the mention of my name, Lon Barron glared at me. "What the hell are you doing with that boy, Davy Stoneman? I have a good mind to have a talk with your aunt. Explain to her the kind of company you're keeping."

Holding the beer pail with both hands so not to spill any, I started for the exit.

"You hear what I'm saying, boy?" Lon said.

I didn't want to argue, but Lon insisted on making an issue out of Daniel. I stopped and faced him. "Sister Rose has come to help us. She sent Daniel with me, and I guess it was my fault he came through the front door." To Ernie I said, "Sorry, Ernie. It's my fault, not his."

Ernie twitched his nose like a frightened rabbit and looked to the mayor for guidance.

"Sister Rose is at your place?" Lon Barron gave Jim an incredulous look, as if I had told the biggest lie in the whole wide world. "I'll definitely see Esther about this. She needs to send that woman packing."

"The preacher tried that already, Mayor," I said. "He didn't have any more luck than I suspect you'll have."

The mayor's eyes burned the back of my neck as I pushed through the swinging doors.

I found Daniel waiting for me by the corner of the saloon, and side by side and without a word we walked back to the store. In the kitchen I poured a beer for Uncle

41

Marsh. I found him sitting in bed, his back propped by three or four pillows. Sister Rose stood at his side, holding out a glass that contained a light brown liquid.

"What's this?" Uncle Marsh sounded weak and tired.

Sister Rose said, "Sassafras tea with a pinch of mallows to take the edge off the coughing, and butterfly weed to give you strength. Nothing to cause harm."

He drank with his face screwed up, as if he expected it to taste bitter, but when he lowered the glass, he said, "Not half bad." He motioned me forward, and I handed him the beer. He took two swallows and passed the glass to Aunt Esther. "Now this tastes like dog piss."

"My mixture makes some food and drink taste off kilter," Sister Rose said. "Give it half an hour. Everything will taste fine then." She reached into her dress pocket and drew out a book, the corners worn so thin that the cardboard showed through the cloth cover. "You don't mind if I sit a while, do you? That way your wife can see to your store and do whatever chores she needs to do."

"Don't mind at all," said Uncle Marsh.

"I thought I might read to you, if you'd like."

"You gonna read me the Bible?" he asked. "That's the only book I ever had read to me."

"Not the Bible." She opened the book, and licking her index finger, flipped the pages until she came to the first chapter. "Miss Esther, you go do your work. If you need my boy for anything, you tell him." Once again, my aunt, faced with Sister Rose's generosity, appeared stricken, as if she had a case of the gripes. With a nod, she left the room. I stood in the doorway to listen as Sister Rose began in her deep sing-song voice. "*It was the best of times; it was the worst of times.*"

I found Aunt Esther in the kitchen pouring the beer from the glass back into the pail. She lifted the pail by the handle, but Daniel took it from her, and with his free hand opened the icebox and placed the pail on a nearly-empty shelf. He nudged the door shut with his knee. "My mama knows what she's doing," he said. "No need to fret."

"Not fretting, not one bit," Aunt Esther said. "Fact is, your mama gave me a little perk up, too. Evening Primrose, she said. To help my rheumatism." Smiling, she patted Daniel on the shoulder. "Now I'm going downstairs to open the store. If I need you boys, I'll call."

The moment Aunt Esther stepped out of the kitchen, Daniel said, "My throat's parched. That was a long walk from our place."

I pulled two glasses from the cabinet and filled them from the kitchen pump. I chugged that water, some of it running down my chin and spotting my collar. I refilled our glasses, and this time we drank more slowly. Finished, Daniel laid his empty glass on the kitchen counter. "You got a mouth on you, boy." His tone held neither malice nor rancor. "First with that preacher, then with the Mayor; you got grit, I'll say that for you."

"What about you?" I said. "You sassed Jim Kennison. Mayor Lon said that if he was deputy sheriff, he wouldn't let you get away with it."

"That's the difference between me and you. You sass a man, the worse you get is a licking from your folks. I sass the same man, I'm liable to get lynched." He shrugged, his mind drifting back to the bar and what might have happened. "Naw, I didn't sass that deputy sheriff. Not really. If I had—" With a shrug, he put the incident out of his mind. "So, you've read *Pudd'nhead Wilson*." He pulled the book from his overalls. "I still got forty pages to go, so I don't know how it ends—don't you tell me now—but maybe when I finish—"

The lower right corner of the cover was half-chewed away. Shocked, I said, "I read that book."

"Yeah, you said that."

"No—" I pointed an accusing finger at the book, "—I mean I read *that* book, *that* very copy. Miss Pilgrim, my teacher, loaned it to me. She told me her dog ate that missing corner."

"You think I stole it." Casting a cold stare on me, he spun away and stomped out of the kitchen, slamming the door so hard the floor shook.

For a full minute I stood in the middle of the kitchen, a part of me believing he had stolen it. How else would he have gotten it? Yet, if a white boy had shown me the same book, I would have accepted without question that Miss Pilgrim had loaned it to him, too.

At that moment, I saw myself as no better than Lon Barron. Maybe I was worse. At least Lon flaunted his prejudice openly. Mine was like a hickey you'd try to cover with calamine lotion.

When I summoned the courage, I followed Daniel outside and found him seated on the stairs, the book open, his fingers running over a page. At first he pretended he didn't know I was there. I seated myself a couple of steps below. "You didn't steal the book. Miss Pilgrim loaned it you, like she did to me."

He looked up at me then. "You thought I stole it. I know you did."

"For a second I did, and that was stupid of me."

His eyes bore into me. "Is this how a white boy apologizes to a poor colored boy?"

"It's my apology," I said.

"You're not very good at it, are you?" He closed the book, no longer pretending to read.

"What else do you want me to do? Get a horsehair rope and walk down the middle of the street whipping myself?"

That brought the first smile I had seen from him, the corners of his mouth curling up like he had tasted sweet potato pie. "I'd pay a nickel to see that."

"You don't have a nickel," I said.

He reached into his overalls and pulled out a buffalo head nickel and a few pennies. "You want to earn yourself a nickel?"

Shocked, I said, "You could've paid Ernie."

"I wasn't going to give that peckerwood a nickel because he said so. Anyway, it wasn't the money. It was the principle of the thing."

"Jim Kennison might have shot you. And what if he had? What would your principles be worth then?"

"Other than having seen him around town, I don't know this deputy sheriff, but he don't have the look of a man who would shoot a person—even me—over a nickel. Some in this town would, but not him." He ran his fingers over the cover of the book, studying it. "There's not much in this world that I have beside principles. This book I'm reading—even it's not mine. Would I die for a principle? I don't know. I'd die for my mama, if I had to. So I guess I'd die for love. As for principle—I don't have much else, so I guess I might, if it came to that." He glanced around the alley as if to make sure no one could hear, and he lowered his voice. "Look, you were right about Miss Pilgrim. She loaned me the book, and if you tell anyone, you can get her in a whole peck of trouble. The school board—the mayor runs it, and if he finds out, he'll fire her."

"I'll guarantee you two things," I said. "First, I won't walk down the street beating myself with a horsehair rope. Second, I won't say a word about Miss Pilgrim loaning you the book."

"And what do you want?" he asked.

"Just stop calling me 'boy'," I said.

He laughed, showing both rows of white teeth that contrasted with his dark skin. "Sounds like a deal...Davy."

5

$\mathcal{A}$fter Daniel and his mother left, I sat by the window with the last rays of sunlight filtering through the glass, and considered my stupidity. What on God's earth had possessed me in my silence to accuse Daniel of stealing the book? The answer was easy to see. I lived in a world that imprisoned Daniel and Sister Rose and others like them with unjust laws and strict social codes. Plenty of times I heard men like Lon Barron rationalize this arbitrary caste system. Each time the argument followed much the same path: We brought colored people to this country as slaves, and once freed, they possessed little knowledge or ability to survive. They were inferior in intellect and a burden on the white man. But we needed to keep them in their place, we needed restrictive laws, we needed to prevent them from learning too much, otherwise social chaos would result. Such reasoning had infected me in the most subtle and insidious way, and I hated myself for it.

Just before nine on Sunday morning, a knock came at our back door, and I followed Aunt Esther to see who it was. When she opened it, we discovered Sister Rose, although we didn't expect her, not on the Sabbath. "I brought around some more of my tonic," she said.

"Thought it might help Mr. Marsh."

The air was cool, despite the presence of the mid-November sun and the absence of clouds, but north central Texas, and for that matter, most of the Midwest, was in the midst of a drought. Dust clung to her long skirt and lace-up boots, and a fine layer coated her dark face.

"Marsh isn't up yet," Aunt Esther said. "He slept a full night for the first time since he came home. Even his dreams didn't wake him." She opened the door wider and motioned for Sister Rose to enter. "Let's have a cup of coffee before he's up and about."

This time Sister Rose acted surprised. I doubt many white people, if any, had invited her into their house for coffee, and she hung back. "Please," said my aunt, and with that, Sister Rose entered. She took a seat at the kitchen table while Aunt Esther pulled two of her fine China cups from the cabinet, the ones she only brought out on special occasions.

I closed the back door, but not before taking a look outside to see if Daniel was there.

Aunt Esther was tilting the pot over Sister Rose's cup. "Daniel didn't come," I said.

"He promised to help Solomon and his daughter Rachel with a little repair work on their house. My boy is always helping somebody."

I guess about everybody around Twin Forks knew of Solomon and his daughter Rachel who lived on and worked the land that was owned by Miss Pilgrim. A couple of years before Miss Pilgrim had come into possession of the old Hartwell farm. Almost immediately she had installed Solomon and his daughter as tenants, which had created a storm of trouble. Some people demanded that she resign her teaching position, which she refused to do, and the school board had no cause for action. The property belonged to her, and in Texas, property was sacrosanct. A person could do with it pretty much as he or she wanted as long as it didn't include gambling or serving hard liquor.

"Daniel said he'd come round tomorrow after your school is out," Sister Rose said.

The mention of school reminded me of a remark Lon Barron had made in the bar. "Is it true you're planning to open a school of your own?" I asked.

Aunt Esther said, "Davy, that's none of your business."

Even before I could apologize, Sister Rose said, "I'm not taking offense, Miss Esther, and I don't mind answering the boy's question." She smiled, her face becoming softer, less angular. "There are boys and girls up in Boonesville and nearby who need to learn to read and write. Some are almost as old as you, and all they can do is make their mark. Now and then I teach a few individually, but they need something more formal. We have a building, the old Squire place; it's been deserted more than ten years. It needs plenty of work. Daniel and I do what we can when we can. I think we'll be ready come this spring."

After that, I wandered off to my room to struggle with *Silas Marner*, but as I passed Uncle Marsh's room, I heard him moving around, and I looked inside. He was buttoning his pajama bottoms, having finished with the chamber pot. We had an outhouse, like most other folks, but it was downstairs and out back, too far for him to go in his condition.

He buttoned his pajama bottoms and sat on the bed, his cheeks flushed. Not that he looked well or anything close, but he had a bit more color than the day before.

When I told him that Sister Rose was with Aunt Esther, he pointed to the chamber pot. "Empty that, Davy. And tell the ladies I'll see them as soon as I wash up."

"Need help?" I asked.

"Not this morning," he said.

I stood there a moment while he sat on the bed trying to catch his breath. When I didn't leave right away, he said, "You got something on your mind?"

"I'd like to ask you a question, if you feel up to it."

"Ask away," he said.

"I was talking to Aunt Esther the other day about colored folk."

Before I could finish, he held up his hand, stopping me. "Esther already told me. I know her concerns, and they're my concerns, too. When you look at a person, you got to know that the color of his skin don't tell you what's inside."

"The whole town says one thing, but you and Aunt Esther say another. I'm not saying you're wrong. I just want to know why."

"I know how people here feel about colored people, and sure, Esther and I go against the grain." He rubbed his chin, eying me. "I could give you all sorts of reasons, but reasons carry little weight. Best if I tell you a story. Understand, I take no pride in what I'm about to tell you, but I'm telling you because you asked and because you're old enough to hear the truth, even though it shames me."

He was breathing hard, and I felt guilty that I'd broached the subject. I started to tell him to forget I asked, that we could discuss it later, but from the set of his jaw and the fire in his eyes, I could see he was too determined to quit now.

"I was about your age when my papa passed on, and I came into possession of this store. Soon after, some fellows dropped by and suggested that I attend a meeting that night at the Mitchell farm. 'Course I knew what it was about even before I went. My papa warned me that in this town, to be successful in business, a man had to be a member of the Klan."

"You went to a Klan meeting?" I said, astonished.

"I joined," he said. "That's why I take no pride in this story. I joined because I believed that if I didn't, nobody would buy from me. I'd go broke, lose everything. It was a stupid reason, and my only excuse was that I was young and didn't know any better, not until I went on a night raid."

"In a white sheet and all?" I asked.

"Still got it, if you want to see. I packed it away in the back of the closet. I keep it there to remind me what a fool I was." He looked at me but past me, as he recalled a night so long ago. "I watched and did nothing while they dragged a colored man from his home and beat him in front of his family. I can still see the man's little daughter with her face buried in her mother's skirts. We beat him with rawhide whips 'til his back was nothing but bleeding flesh. I tell you, Davy, it makes me sick to this day, what we did to that poor man. And you know what his crime was?" He focused those deep-set eyes on me. "He didn't step off the sidewalk and tip his hat when he passed a white woman on the street. All that pain and suffering over that."

"You said *we* beat him..."

"You're asking if I wielded one of the whips." He shook his head ever so slightly. "I stood and watched, too much the coward to do anything else. I had no idea of his 'crime' before we got there. I told myself I had no idea what was going to happen either. That was a lie. In my heart I knew, and I hate myself for what I failed to do."

"How many were with you?" I asked.

"Sixteen or seventeen." He held up his hand again before I could make my point. "You're going to say there were too many, that it wouldn't have done any good if I'd tried to stop it. For years I used that reason to excuse my actions. Maybe I couldn't have changed things, but the fact is that I didn't try. Right then and there, I began to see that everything I'd been taught about people of color was lies. Most white people wanted to keep coloreds in their place. They called them shiftless and lazy, but the first time I hired a couple of men from Boonesville, they worked better and harder than any white boys I'd ever hired. I got to know them after that, not only those two, but others who came and worked for me or shopped here."

"You made friends with them?"

"I won't say any of those people became friends. That would've been too dangerous, not for me, but for them. But when you get to know a fella and you do him a favor and he does you one, well, you see him different, and the color of his skin ain't important."

He reached across to the table, picked up the glass, and took a sip of water. He cleared his throat, and I could tell that he had talked too much. His voice had grown hoarse. But he wasn't finished. "Colored people have a hard row to hoe, and most make do without complaining. They take a lot more guff than I would, and I don't say that as a criticism. If I'd been born colored, I wouldn't have lived this long, not with my temper." He paused to catch his breath, then he said, "Davy, I want you to remember one thing."

"Yes sir?"

"You're real smart, and you're going to amount to something someday, but there are others as smart as you who don't have the same advantages. That means you have a responsibility. You see what I'm getting at?"

"I believe I do," I said.

I emptied the chamber pot in the outhouse and returned to the kitchen, all set to head back to my own room when another knock sounded at our back door. I went to answer and discovered Lon Barron, his belly pressing against his Sunday-go-to-meeting vest. Right behind him, poised on her toes and looking over his shoulder, was his daughter Susanna, a black and white parasol shading her light, delicate features.

"Fetch your aunt, boy." Lon spoke in a brusque, commanding voice.

Aunt Esther, her eyes alight with irritation, stormed into the kitchen. "And what's so important that you have to use that tone, Lon Barron?"

"That woman's here, Sister Rose." He stepped past me and moved in close to Aunt Esther, trying to intimidate her with his bulk. "There's no use lying. Susanna and I were on our way to church. We saw her come up these very stairs."

"Why would I lie?" Aunt Esther crossed her arms and struck a pugnacious pose, leading with her chin like an over-eager fighter.

Easing myself onto the porch, I set the empty chamber pot down and closed the door so that Susanna and I would not have to endure the dramatics. She pushed her lips together in a pout. "I want to hear."

Without a doubt, she was the best-looking girl I had ever seen. Her dress curved outward over her breasts, narrowed to her waist and curved once more over her hips. The dress itself was the latest fashion, although perhaps a little daring for Twin Forks, the hem rising all the way above her ankles. With her blond hair in ringlets and piled on top of her head, she looked as if she had stepped off a cover of *American Beauty* painted by Charles Dana Gibson himself, and I possessed little ability to deny her. I opened the door so that we could hear and see.

Her father stood with his back to us, his hands on his wide hips. "So when I heard it from Preacher Joyner, too, I couldn't believe it. That woman is not welcome in this town."

"This is my town, too," my aunt said. "And she's welcome in this house as long as Marsh and me say so."

"I'm trying to be reasonable here. The fact that she's a colored woman has nothing to do with it—I told you that before—but this woman practices witchcraft. Preacher Joyner, and Mrs. Manning, and the Farleys have all told me the stories of her magic cure-alls."

Aunt Esther was growing tired of the mayor. "Why don't you get out of here, Lon, before I get riled?"

The mayor puffed out his cheeks and expelled a loud grunt. "If Marsh was here right this minute, and if he was a well man—"

"I'm right here, Lon. Talk to me."

The voice drew our attention to the kitchen doorway,

and there stood Uncle Marsh, his thin body wrapped in a robe, his bare feet planted against the hardwood floor.

To my left I heard Susanna gasp.

Uncle Marsh presented quite a picture. His tussled hair shot off in all directions, his thin face appeared skeletal, and the splotches on his face pulsated with heat. At that moment he was about the most frightening figure I had ever seen, a character straight out of a Bram Stoker novel.

"I was telling your wife—" the mayor began.

"I heard what you was telling her," my uncle said, "but you didn't hear what she was telling you."

"People in this town...there's talk, Marsh. There's talk." The veins of the mayor's neck stood rigid, and his face had grown red. "That woman and what she stands for—she's trouble, and we don't need her kind stirring up trouble." The mayor stared at Uncle Marsh while he searched for some point, some evidence that would cement his argument. "And that boy of hers—he's a bad one."

Uncle Marsh grinned, and I swear, he appeared almost sinister. "That's pathetic, Lon, trying to blame the boy in order to get rid of the mother." Uncle Marsh laughed aloud, and Lon Barron's face darkened with suppressed rage. The one thing the mayor couldn't abide was being the object of ridicule.

He fumed a few seconds longer before whirling on his heels and fleeing our house in much the same fashion as the preacher had fled before him. As he passed me, I noticed a vein on his temple beating against the skin as if it wanted out. He grabbed Susanna by the elbow so hard that she winced, and together they descended the stairs.

By the time I closed the door and stepped back inside, Sister Rose had come into the kitchen. "Maybe it's best I leave," she said.

Aunt Esther ran an open palm across her mouth like she was wiping away a bad taste. "Sister Rose, you pay no mind to Lon Barron or that preacher. They've got no say who we invite into our home."

"I've lived with his kind all my life," Sister Rose said. "When a person like me or Daniel do things they don't like—well, they're like gila monsters, Miss Esther. They sink their teeth in and don't let go."

"Do you fear what he'll do?" Uncle Marsh asked.

"I don't want to cause you folks any trouble," she said.

"Then that's settled." Uncle Marsh said. "If Lon Barron gives you any trouble, you come to me. I'll see that it stops."

Even though he was a bit perkier than the day before, Uncle Marsh still looked as if he would have trouble walking a dozen paces. He leaned against the door jamb and clutched the robe to his chest. He was so frail and sickly that his promise to take care of the mayor seemed a hollow gesture at best, yet I thought I detected a light in his eyes—or maybe behind his eyes—that hinted at better days to come. Or perhaps I only imagined it. Or perhaps it was nothing more than the fact that he had bested Lon Barron, and that small victory had given him a sense of hope.

That light faded though, and he said in a weak voice, "Right now, Sister Rose, I think I might enjoy a little more of that tonic." And he shuffled off to the bedroom.

6

The next morning I awoke before six and readied myself for school. By seven-thirty I was helping Miss Pilgrim set up for the day. I was her oldest student, and part of my day included passing out the M'Guffey readers and afterward helping some of the first and second graders with their alphabet and numbers. Around ten, Miss Pilgrim sent me off to the back room—a storeroom with a window—to do my own lessons and composition, which she would discuss with me in the afternoon.

I finished the last few pages of *Silas Marner*, glad to be rid of it, and then wrote an essay on the effects of greed in the novel. I finished the last sentence as Miss Pilgrim rang the bell for lunch. I came out of the room as the rest of the class scrambled through the front door. Rather than rush outside, I went to Miss Pilgrim, who sat behind her desk. She peered at me through those thick lenses that magnified her eyes. She was a thin woman, much thinner than Sister Rose or Aunt Esther, but despite her diminutive size, she had a way of looking at you that could zero you to the bone. Most kids I knew either hated her or thought her too strict. With me, she had proven to be a taskmaster but a fair one.

"I know you loaned Daniel a book," I said.

Miss Pilgrim looked beyond me to the door and lowered her voice so only I could hear. "And how does that make you feel?"

I discovered it difficult to answer her question in simple terms. Without a doubt, a part of me felt a sense of jealousy that she loaned the same books to another person—whether that person was colored or white made no difference—and another part of me rejoiced that she had loaned it to Daniel. In that respect, I believed that the color of his skin did matter. Miss Pilgrim's act was one of defiance, and like most boys my age I harbored a rebel inside. Occasionally, like when I quoted scripture to the preacher, I freed my rebel, but most of the time, as an act of self-preservation, I kept it chained and hidden. Still, I admired such courage in others.

"I like Daniel," I said.

"He's a good young man, a bright young man, like you, Davy," Miss Pilgrim said. "It would be unconscionable of me to ignore a student who wanted to learn. You understand what I'm saying, don't you?"

After that, Miss Pilgrim sent me out to be with the other boys and girls. On the grounds, I found my usual spot on the shaded east side and, hunkering down, opened my lunch pail. Before I could remove the contents, Tommy Barron, the mayor's son, marched up to me followed by the entire student body. On their faces, I saw anticipation and expectation.

He kicked the bottom of my shoe. "My father says you got that crazy old nigger woman working for you. What have you got to say about that?"

"Don't kick my shoe," I said.

"I asked you a question." He kicked the bottom of my shoe again.

He stood over me, his hands balled into fists. He kicked my shoe a third time and I lashed out, the heel of my boot slamming his shin and driving him back with a howl. I sprang to my feet to face him. I could tell right away that he didn't like that. He backed off a step and fixed a hostile stare on me. He must have seen me as an easy target—I never roughhoused or wrestled with the other boys. I didn't play football, and I seldom cursed, and I doubt that he expected me to put up much of a fight.

A little first grader, Emily McCabe said, "Davy never fights."

Her comment seemed to spur Tommikins' courage, and he slammed a palm against my shoulder. "I asked you a question, Davy Stoneman!"

I might not have fought even then. Not only was I slow to rile, but I think I feared violence, feared getting hurt, feared hurting someone. In all my time in Twin Forks, I had fought only one other boy, Bernie Kellermann, over an incident involving a little girl. He had bitten me, and I blackened his eye.

"Go away, Tommikins," I said.

His face swelled in anger when I used his nickname. He thrust his beet-red face forward until we were separated by only inches, and when he spoke, he spewed spittle. "That nigger woman your wet nurse?"

What I did next came from no conscious effort, no planned response. Rising on the balls of my feet, I threw my whole weight behind a punch, and my fist connected with Tommikin's nose, so solidly that I heard the crunch of bone and cartilage. The blow sent him reeling backward, blood spraying the kids to his right. A couple of the girls screamed. Tommikins covered his nose with both hands, blood streaming between his fingers and tears welling in his eyes.

Drawn by the commotion, Miss Pilgrim rounded the corner of the building, her thin, gray hair caught by the wind, her tight bun unraveling. She had a rule about fighting: if you fought at school, you got sent home for the day. No excuses, no exceptions.

Tommikins spied Miss Pilgrim, and holding out his

bloody hands, showed her his damaged nose. "He hit me! The nigger lover hit me!"

With that, I stepped in and delivered a roundhouse left that caught Tommikins flush in the mouth. He fell backwards, with his arms spread wide, and hit the ground with a convincing thud. Dust swirled around his body in a kind of shroud, and he began bawling as if I'd broken every bone in his body.

I looked at Miss Pilgrim who stood open-mouthed. "That first one is for today; the second for tomorrow. I'll see you Wednesday, Miss Pilgrim."

I closed my lunch pail and stepped off toward home. Miss Pilgrim caught me at the swings, tugging on my sleeve.

"Can't talk right now, Miss Pilgrim," I said without looking at her. How could I? I knew my actions disappointed her, but it didn't matter. My insides boiled, and I wanted to pound some more on Tommikins.

When I got home, I marched right into Uncle Marsh's room and found him alone, sitting up in bed, the *Dallas Morning News* laid across his lap, the headline in bold relief: WILSON STUMPS FOR LEAGUE OF NATIONS: TRAIN PASSES THROUGH DALLAS.

Uncle Marsh looked up from the paper, his brow coming together in a question as he spotted my left hand, the knuckles raw and bleeding.

I said, "I'm home early because I punched Tommy Barron in the nose. I'm home tomorrow because I punched him in the mouth, too." The other time I had gotten into a fight, Uncle Marsh made me apologize, and I said, "I won't say I'm sorry, not to Tommikins or his father. You or Aunt Esther can take a belt to me if you feel the need, but I'll not say I'm sorry."

Uncle Marsh folded the paper, and with it, pointed me to the chair. "Maybe you better tell me what happened."

As I gave the details, his face darkened. "I can't say you did right hitting the boy, but I can't fault you either." He regarded me with those blue eyes that appeared so deep that you could never see to the bottom. "Still, you did get into a fight. I don't suppose I can let that go unpunished."

"No, sir, I guess not," I said.

My uncle raised his voice and said, "Sister Rose, would you come in here, please?"

Sister Rose appeared in the doorway. "Davy here won't be attending school tomorrow or the next day. What's Daniel doing?" my uncle asked.

She smiled as if she understood the direction of his thoughts. "Why, he'll be working on the old Squires' house, the one we're making into a school."

"Then that's your punishment," Uncle Marsh said. "You'll spend the next two days helping Daniel."

7

I arose at my usual time, dressed and hurried to the kitchen, drawn there by the smell of coffee. My aunt ladled out eggs mixed with bacon grease, piled on potatoes, and rounded it off with biscuits and gravy. "When a man does work like you'll be doing, he needs a hearty breakfast," she said.

While I ate, she stood behind me cleaning dishes in the washtub. A couple of times the heavy skillet slammed against the tin, making a racket, but otherwise I ate in silence until Aunt Esther wiped her hands with a dishtowel and seated herself across from me. "How do you feel this morning, Davy?"

"I feel fine."

"I mean about the fight with Tommy Barron. That's not like you, to get into a fight."

"I guess if Tommy Barron said it to me again, I'd swat him again. Otherwise, I'll leave him alone."

"You don't hold a grudge then?" she asked.

"I'm not sorry—no ma'am—but as far as I'm concerned, that's the end of it."

I was a bit miffed, and the tone of my voice reflected my irritation. Did Aunt Esther really think I'd go looking for another fight? After all, this was only my second fight since I had come to live with them, and I doubt that any boy in the school could have boasted a better record.

Reaching across the table she patted my hand. "You're a good boy, and I'm proud of you. You know that. But I guess I'm wondering the reason you hit Tommy Barron. Was it because he insulted you, or insulted Sister Rose?"

Her question confused me, and seeing this, she said, "Did you hit him because Sister Rose is a colored woman, and this boy accused you of having something to do with her? In that case, it's you who felt insulted. Or did you hit him because he said something bad about Sister Rose? There is a difference, Davy. You see that don't you?"

I laid my fork aside. My aunt had seen straight to a point that I had failed to consider. Why had I hit Tommikins? Part of the answer was easy enough to see. He forced the issue by kicking my shoe and shoving me around. Still, had he not made that crack about me and Sister Rose, I might not have hit him even then.

Up to this point, I saw my fight with Tommikins as justified and even a bit noble, but now Aunt Esther made me see the act in a darker light. "I guess I don't rightly know why I hit him," I said. "Maybe it was more than one reason."

"You're an upstanding boy, Davy, but that old saying 'nobody's perfect' has truth to it." She patted my hand again. "The trick to living is a simple one: you learn to spot your flaws, and you work to get rid of them. You'll never reach perfection. No human ever does. Even Jesus had a temper. It's in the striving where we find ourselves, where we find the people we're destined to be."

After finishing breakfast I went to Uncle Marsh and found Sister Rose at his bedside. She held *A Tale of Two Cities* in one hand, but she had not yet begun to read.

"You got everything you need for today?" my uncle asked.

"I packed all the tools last night like you told me," I

said. "Maybe Sister Rose can tell me how to get there. I'm not exactly sure."

Sister Rose gave me directions to the house, an old structure a quarter of a mile from Boonesville. Once she described it, I remembered having seen it when Uncle Marsh took me hunting. Over ten years before, a white family by the name of Squires owned the place, but one day they packed their few belongings and headed north. Since then, brush and trees had reclaimed the land.

"We had a time getting rid of the vines and creepers," Sister Rose said. "Why, every branch we cut away seemed to grow back the very next day. It covered half the roof and most of the walls. We hacked and hacked until our fingers bled. It took us more than six months to get rid of it."

"If the house was in such bad shape, why did you choose it?" I asked.

"Because it was all we could find. And the little children need something."

"But why you?" I asked.

"I had a calling."

"From God?"

"That's a little personal, Davy," Uncle Marsh said.

"I don't mind, Mr. Marsh. Davy's full of good questions, and he deserves answers." Sister Rose shifted her weight to face me squarely. "I figure that if God's out there, he's not too interested in my affairs. No, my calling is more personal. I was lucky that someone once took an interest in me, enough to teach me to read. It's a gift received, a gift offered."

"Do you believe in God, Sister Rose?"

My uncle gritted his teeth and was on the verge of protesting once more, but Sister Rose said, "Let me answer the boy, if that's all right with you, Mr. Marsh." My uncle nodded, although he appeared irritated at my forwardness. She said, "I believe in God, and I believe in Jesus Christ, Our Lord and Savior."

"The same ones that Preacher Joyner believes in?"

"We both believe in the Bible, that it's divinely inspired, but I suspect we differ on some points. You see, I believe that if we look deep, we can find God in our hearts, that to some extent He's in all of us. I doubt the preacher sees it that way."

"And Daniel?" I asked.

"I think he's still looking for answers."

Uncle Marsh waved his hand, shooing me from the room. "You're tiring me with all your questions."

As I left the house, I faced the first northern of the season, the kind where the wind comes storming down from Canada without one mountain ridge in its path to soften the blow or sheer the front in another direction. In that kind of weather, temperatures can drop twenty or thirty degrees in an hour. I wore my wool jacket, fur-lined gloves, and heavy boots, and still the wind cut right through me. My every breath sent a frosty cloud swirling away.

I let the wind carry me along as I hurried up the river trail, the dark Trinity flowing beside me. A couple of miles from town I reached the path that led to Boonesville. I passed this, entering the woods that spread out for miles, all elm and oak littered with scrub brush. Thin limbs reached over the trail like skeletal fingers and clawed at my overalls and coat. The wind howled above the trees.

Quite unexpectedly I came upon the house. One minute the forest surrounded me, so thick that I could see less than ten feet ahead, and in the next I stepped into a clearing much as Sister Rose described. A half a dozen tree stumps dotted the open ground that pointed the way to a dilapidated frame house whose paint had long ago weathered. The roof displayed a patchwork of tar tiles, some green, some red, three or four so black they appeared as holes. Window frames contained no glass. Instead, potato sacks hung behind each to protect the interior from the wind. The front door stood open, and inside I saw Daniel already at work, hammering away at a floorboard. The porch was yet to be built, and I climbed over the stoop to enter.

Daniel brought the hammer down one last time. "What kept you? It's the shank of the morning?"

"I had some chores to do first." I dropped the knapsack, the tools clanging together like discordant music. "You better put me to work before I freeze right where I'm standing."

As if to make my point, the wind surged, and the tops of the trees swayed and dipped. The potato sacks covering the windows flapped, and the house shuddered. "From the outside, this place looks as if it's ready to fall down," I said.

"It's not much to look at, but it would take a twister landing smack on top of us to bring it down."

"This isn't twister weather," I said.

"Around colored folk, it's always twister weather."

He told me to begin tearing out the floorboards he had yet to replace, all of which showed rot. I jerked the crowbar from my pack and began to rip away, slamming the curved end into the floor, splitting it open so that I could get underneath, and then using my weight as leverage until the board popped up or splintered. The work provided a certain satisfaction in that I never thought about my actions, I slammed and pulled, slammed and pulled, and after half an hour, I took off my coat and laid it aside. Sweat dampened my shirt. I stayed warm until noon when I shredded the last board and Daniel called a halt for lunch.

I slipped on my coat, not wanting to catch a chill, and we huddled in a corner. Opening my lunch pail, I pulled out two sandwiches, offering one to Daniel. "I don't take handouts," he said.

"Your mama fixed these."

He took it, and I reached into the pack again, pulled out two tin cups and a mug of coffee. "Your mama fixed this, too, but it's my family's cup. You don't mind drinking out of it, do you?"

"I guess not," he said.

After that, I told him about Mayor Lon Barron's visit Sunday morning to protest his mother's presence. Then I asked: "Why does Preacher Joyner hate your mama so?"

He continued to chew his bread and meat before washing it down with a swallow of lukewarm coffee. He laid his cup aside, and cupping his hands together, blew on them. "Early last summer, Preacher Joyner came to Boonesville to spread the gospel. No one invited him. He just showed up. Pretty soon he was thumping his Bible and telling us that we were spiders held over a pit of fire, and it was only God's grace that kept Him from dropping us in that fiery pit. But if we came to the Lord right then, if we let the preacher baptize us in the river, then maybe our souls could be saved.

"My mama and I stood listening like everyone else. When he finally ran out of words, my mama said: 'I don't care much for your god. He doesn't sound very nice.' With that, she walked away. So did every other person there. We left that preacher standing all by himself. He must have stood there for over ten minutes. I watched him from the window of our house. Finally, he marched off back to town. Now, because my mama uses a few potions and herbs to help people, the preacher calls her a witch and has all of Twin Forks believing it, but it's a lie, and he knows it."

"I don't like him, Daniel, not one bit, but he sounded like he believed what he was saying about your mama," I said.

Daniel shrugged. "Maybe he's talked himself into believing such foolishness. Maybe he's good at persuading people. Isn't that a preacher's job, persuading people?"

From outside, a booming voice called, "Daniel, you in there?"

A man with skin as dark as Daniel's appeared in the doorway. He wore a heavy coat and a battered fedora pulled low over his face that hid all but his short beard speckled with gray. He gripped the insides of the door jamb and hauled himself up, the boards groaning under his weight. He raised his head, and I recognized him, Solomon, who showed up at our store three or four times a year, and before Uncle Marsh left, the two men would spend a couple of hours playing checkers and talking. Maybe he would buy a shirt or a pair of pants or maybe he wouldn't buy a thing. Either way was fine with Uncle Marsh.

Based on his grizzled hair and beard, I judged him to be in his early fifties, maybe older, although his unlined face belied that. If there were one thing about him that was old, it was his eyes that seemed older than the rivers themselves.

He saw me kneeling, a nail between my lips, a hammer in my hand, and he raised one eyebrow. "We thought we'd come and give you a hand."

Solomon hauled up a girl, her dress rising to her knees. She lifted her head, and it was like a fist slammed in my stomach. It pained me to look at her. She was the best looking colored girl I had ever seen, her skin all satiny, her eyes nighttime dark, her lashes long and feathery, her figure the equal of Susanna Barron's.

Then I realized my stupidity. She wasn't the best looking colored girl I had ever seen, she was the best looking girl I had ever seen, better looking than any moving picture star including Mabel Normand or the Gish sisters. Most white girls I knew used lip rouge and face powder, but this girl wore only what nature provided, and she outshone them all. One flaw marred her face, a small scar that curved around the bottom of her chin, so old that I figured it a childhood injury.

A sense of shame overwhelmed me, and I tore my gaze from her. How could I have such a reaction to a dusky girl whose appearance was so alien to all I believed defined beauty? My face burned with shame, but I managed to get to my feet, hoping our visitors hadn't seen my discomfort.

"This is Solomon," Daniel said.

I spit out the nail and held out my hand. "Yessir, it's good to see you again."

Because of rheumatism, two of his fingers bent inward at an odd angle, and years of backbreaking work had transformed his palm into ridges of sandpaper callouses, but his grip was solid and strong, the kind that Uncle Marsh used to give before he went off to fight the Hun. "You Mr. Marsh's boy. You've growed some." He nodded and released my hand. "This is my granddaughter Rachel."

I suspected she was around my age, but when I looked into those dark eyes, she appeared, like her grandfather, to be older, wiser, or perhaps only wary. After all, I was a white boy that she didn't know and to whom she had never spoken a word.

"I hear Mr. Marsh is ailing," said Solomon. His deep voice resonated in the confines of that one room house. "You tell him we all hopes he gets better real soon."

"Yes sir, I'll do that."

From the moment Solomon spotted me, his brow reflected consternation. Even when he spoke of Uncle Marsh, he continued to appear worried and out-of-sorts. To Daniel he said, "You think it's right to have this boy here working with you?"

"Mr. Marsh told him to come," Daniel said. Then, as if he felt the need to defend me, he said, "He's a good worker. Look what he's done this morning." He pointed to the part of the floor that I had ripped apart and begun to repair.

"I don't doubt he's a good worker. I don't doubt he's good boy." Solomon faced me, his expression full of regret. "What I'm about to say—you don't take it personal, Mr. Davy. You being here—well, it could mean trouble for Daniel."

"No one knows I'm here except my folks and Sister Rose," I said.

"Now me and Rachel know—and if someone else happens along, they'll know, too. Now, Mr. Davy, this ain't about you. From all I've heard, you is a good person. You is Mr. Marsh's boy—you couldn't be anything else. But that don't always count for much. We is colored, you is white. People don't like the two mixin'. You understand, don't you, Mr. Davy?"

"I guess," I said

For the first time Rachel spoke, and her voice held a lyrical quality. "Some white folks in town don't like Sister Rose. If people knew you were here, they might take it out on her and Daniel."

Another gust of wind surged against the makeshift curtains, sending a chill through the room. "Maybe I should go," I said.

"I want you here, Davy, if you want to stay. I don't care what anybody says or does." Daniel showed no hint of indecision or doubt.

I thought his attitude might have angered Solomon, but the old man laid a hand on Daniel's shoulder. "You be careful, you hear." He looked at me with those big, ancient eyes. "You both be careful." With that he removed his coat and began to roll up his sleeves. "No more palavering. Let's get to work."

By then the sun already cast shadows to the east. Less than four hours remained until dusk. We set about laying the new floor, and with the four of us, the work went quickly and smoothly. Daniel and Solomon sawed boards to the right lengths while Rachel and I laid them in place and nailed them down. The pounding resounded even above the wind.

I kept sneaking peaks at Rachel, hoping she might throw a smile my way, but she remained all business, her face stony as she concentrated on the work. Perhaps she sensed me looking and made an effort not to respond.

After the first hour or so, Solomon began to hum a tune: "Amazing Grace". I loved that old tune. I joined in for the last verse. When we finished, Daniel said, "You may not hit all the notes, Davy, but at least you put your heart into it."

"I hit every note," I said. "They're just not always the right ones."

We laughed together, and that simple act of sharing seemed to free us. After that we talked as we worked, nothing important that I can remember, little things, unimportant things, comforting things that people share as a way to make time pass. As twilight grew near, I packed my knapsack and told Daniel I would come again the next day.

I jumped from the floor to the ground and threw my tool bag over my shoulder. Daniel and Solomon had their backs to me as they packed up their own tools, but Rachel was looking at me. The faintest hint of a smile touched her lips, A Mona Lisa smile, if that, and my chest felt weighted with stones so heavy that I wasn't sure I could move one foot in front of the other. Solomon glanced over his shoulder, and perhaps he saw what transpired between us. He said, "Hand me that screwdriver, Darlin'."

That broke the spell. Rachel bent her knees, picked the tool from the floor and handed it to her grandfather. I headed off toward home.

Ten minutes later I walked the path beside the Trinity River singing to myself, starting with "Take me Out to the Old Ball Game" before moving on to "Cowboy's Lament." I finished with a couple of verses of "Amazing Grace."

Passing the Barron house, so bright with electrical lights that it looked like a lit-up Halloween pumpkin, I heard a voice call out: "Davy! Davy Stoneman!"

Susanna Barron charged out her front door wrapped in a heavy coat that dropped to her knees and a long, flowery scarf that encircled her neck. She held her arms around her thin waist as if to ward off the cold, and her breath sent white clouds into the night. "Davy Stoneman, I have a bone to pick with you and your family."

She must have spotted me coming up the road and saw this as her chance to give me a tongue-lashing. The evening shadows played over her high, aristocratic cheekbones.

"You're angry because I thumped your brother," I said.

She waved a hand in dismissal. "That old pollywog! If he gets a thumping, he deserves it. Give him another, if you like." She shook her head. "No, it's your uncle. He was wrong—all wrong—what he said to my father. You know it, too. That woman working for your family—there ought to be a law against her kind. My father was only saying what was right, and your uncle..."

She droned on, and I stopped listening. My thoughts drifted to Rachel. I knew little of her, but what I knew, I liked. At that moment, I liked her a lot better than Susanna Barron.

"And you! You stuck up for those people!" Susanna hurled the words as an insult.

I hefted the bag so that my tools rattled together. "Goodnight, Susanna."

As I walked away I heard her stamp her foot in exasperation. "Davy Stoneman!" she shouted.

I doubt that many men or boys ever walked away from Susanna Barron.

"Davy Stoneman!" she called again.

Without looking back, I said, "Sleep tight, Susanna."

PART II
WINTER STORMS

8

I went again the following day to help renovate the dilapidated building, and many days thereafter. Even when I was back at school, as soon as Miss Pilgrim dismissed us, I took off for the old Squires place, having left my tools there so that I didn't have to drag them back and forth.

The sky remained leaden for most of November and well into December, the clouds hanging around the top of the trees, and a biting wind blew in from the north. On one particular Saturday morning, a week or so before Christmas, I arrived before nine, and Daniel and I worked less than an hour when Daniel, blowing on his hands, called it quits. No wonder. His coat, as thin as newspaper, showed bare thread at the cuffs and collar, and the cold must have cut right to the bone.

We walked back through the woods until we came to the path that led to Boonesville where Daniel, his head lowered against the wind, muttered a 'goodbye' and trudged up the slope. Less than half way to town, I felt little taps on my coat and hat as sleet slanted in from behind. Soon patches of ice began to line ruts in the road.

That December remains in my memory as the harshest winter I ever spent in North Central Texas. For three straight weeks, we got snow or sleet or a combination of both. As one storm moved out, another arrived, so the earth remained white and frozen. Icicles six and seven inches long hung from the rain gutters and eaves of every house and building, snow piled up along the streets, and the trees bowed under the extra weight. During the day the sun might come out for an hour or two and melt the top layer of snow, but during the night, it froze all over again. On a couple of nights the temperature dropped so low that ice formed along the edges of the Trinity River, an unheard of occurrence in the history of Twin Forks. Because of the weather, few people came to town, and a couple of days we didn't see a single customer.

One Sunday morning, Preacher Joyner gave a sermon entitled 'The Wrath of the Lord' in which he claimed God, angry at heathen beliefs tolerated within our community, sent these storms as a punishment. If we expected forgiveness, we must cast out evil.

I heard of this later, of course. Mrs. Manning came around to buy her little daughter a new coat and told Aunt Esther and me the whole sermon in detail. When her daughter at last discovered the right coat, a heavy mackinaw with a high collar, my Aunt said stiffly, "Seven dollars."

Mrs. Manning opened her purse and counted out seven one dollar bills. "I hope to see you and your boy at church. You will come, won't you?"

"I don't think that's likely with Marsh ailing," Aunt Esther said.

"All the more reason to come and hear the Lord's word," Mrs. Manning said. "Prayer is the only answer, my dear. You know that."

After Mrs. Manning and her daughter left, Aunt Esther opened the cash register and slammed the bills into the tray.

Ten or fifteen minutes later, as I worked in the storeroom unpacking a box of BVDs, Aunt Esther found me. "Maybe Cora Manning was right. Maybe Marsh and me have been neglectful of your spiritual needs."

"I've got better things to do than listen to Preacher Joyner." I tossed the empty box under the sorting table and kicked it against the wall.

"Do you hate religion, boy? I don't think I could stand it if we've caused that."

"No ma'am, I don't hate religion," I said, "but I do hate people who say they believe in one thing and then do the exact opposite."

Aunt Esther patted me on the arm. "Then we'll say no more about it. But if you change your mind, you let us know. I figure we can find a decent church, even if we have to go all the way to Hollister."

Right through the worst of the storms, Sister Rose came every morning, showing up at our door at eight, Daniel escorting her, both shivering from the cold. They stood before the iron stove that hissed and spit in the corner, holding their hands before them as if in supplication. Both their coats showed wear, the hems so ragged that loose threads hung like the icicles outside.

A week after the storms began, as the long shadows of night descended and Daniel and Sister Rose prepared to leave, Aunt Esther caught them at the door, two wool coats thrown over her arm. "These are for you."

I could see Sister Rose all ready to refuse the gift, and the expression on Daniel's face suggested outrage that my aunt had offered charity. Aunt Esther said, "You come all this way in this weather and you take care of Marsh. All I can pay is fifty cents a week. You're a charitable person, and what you are doing for us is charity. So these coats are payment for all you've done."

Sister Rose reached out to touch the thick wool. "These are too expensive, Mrs. Esther. We can't take these."

"These are last year's coats," Aunt Esther said. "You'd be doing us a favor to take them off our hands."

It was a lie, of course. I had seen my aunt remove the

coats from the racks where a new shipment had arrived the week before, but she gave them the excuse they needed. Removing their old coats they donned the new ones, thick and heavy, and their faces lit with smiles. They left, and from the front window, I watched as they struggled against the wind, their old coats thrown over their shoulders and destined for people worse off than themselves.

If my aunt had told a lie in one respect, in another she hadn't. The coats might not have been last year's models, but we certainly owed Sister Rose and Daniel more than fifty cents a week. Each day she showed up despite the weather, and each day she gave Uncle Marsh more of her tonic, and each day she read him more of *A Tale of Two Cities*. Because of her, Uncle Marsh had grown stronger. We saw it in the flush of his cheeks and in the extra weight on his arms and chest that filled out depressions and cavities. As December came to its end, and we moved closer to the new decade, Uncle Marsh climbed out of bed, dressed and came down to sit with Aunt Esther behind the counter. When I arrived home from school, I found him there, beaming like a kid whose mother had promised him a piece of sugar candy. He sat with her over an hour before climbing back to his room, exhausted, although that night he slept so soundly that he swore he never once rolled over in bed. Each day that followed, he stayed downstairs a little longer until, by mid-January, he extended his time to over two hours.

I came home one afternoon to find him and Sister Rose in the front of our store, Aunt Esther in the back unpacking a box of overalls. Sister Rose was reading aloud—the last chapter of *A Tale of Two Cities*, where Sidney Carlton consoles the girl before they go to their deaths. I sat on a bench and unbuttoned my jacket, but otherwise made no effort to interrupt. I listened to the end with the same rapt attention as my uncle while Sister Rose, in her deep, almost masculine voice, read the concluding lines.

Sister Rose closed the book, and for a while, none of us spoke. At last Uncle Marsh said, "Save for the Bible, I never read a book in my life. I don't say that with pride. But I tell you, Sister Rose, I never thought a book could make me feel...I never thought—" Embarrassed, he cleared his throat. "You got another book for tomorrow?"

9

During these weeks I saw little of Daniel. On the worse days, when ice and snow covered the ground, he escorted his mother to town and came again to walk her home. When he arrived, I was already gone. In the evening, I retreated to my books and studies. In late spring, comprehensive exams would come around, those that determined which colleges might accept me, and I needed to be ready. Miss Pilgrim passed along information on money given by Southern Methodist University that appeared made for me. It gave two hundred and fifty dollars a year to a *lucky* orphan whose grades showed a wide range of knowledge and skills. If I attended college at all, it would have to be with a scholarship or a grant, because Uncle Marsh and Aunt Esther, regardless of what they had promised my mother, didn't have that kind of money.

Often during those long, cold days and nights, I thought of Rachel, wondering where she was and what she was doing. I made no conscious effort to think of her, but I couldn't help myself. I half hoped she and her father might come to town, and that I would see her, but they never did. Even if they had, I wouldn't have known how to act or what to say.

Even though the winter storms had slowed the town to a standstill, many people, hearing that Uncle Marsh was up and about, came to see him. Old Mr. Wiggins and my uncle played checkers for hours on end. Mister Jenkins, the telegrapher, came by twice a week to discuss politics. They damned the Republicans and praised the Democrats, although neither favored the policies of President Wilson. Hank Sears, who looked like Abraham Lincoln without the beard, brought his wife and their seven kids one Saturday to pay their respects. Johnny Earl, in from Dallas where he drove a streetcar, stopped by and left a few tokens so that we could ride for free if we ever got to the big city. Mr. Misener, who owned the livery, dropped by one afternoon to share a plug of Moore's Red Leaf. They passed the afternoon discussing business, mostly Mr. Misener complaining that now, because people wanted automobiles, fewer and fewer had use for his services. Forced by circumstances, he'd bought a Liberty automobile to rent to customers. As I stacked boxes in the storeroom, I heard Mr. Misener say, "I declare, Marsh, the world's changing so fast it makes a fellow's head spin like a top."

I figured Mr. Misener was crazy. As far as I could see, nothing ever changed in Twin Forks.

Lon Barron poked his head in a couple of times pretending interest in Uncle Marsh's health, although he never stayed more than a minute or two. However, Jim Kennison came by almost every day and sat awhile, his long legs thrust out before him blocking the aisle so that if anyone entered the store, he had to stand to get out of their way. Jim kept Uncle Marsh abreast of all the mundane happenings in and around town—whose mare produced a foal, who was getting married, who was having kids, who was angry with whom. I swear, they gossiped more than two old ladies.

Jim admired Uncle Marsh. I found this out one Saturday morning when he came by and found me behind the counter. "Where's your uncle?" he asked.

"Doc Gibbs is with him upstairs," I said.

Worry creased his brow. "He's not taken a turn for the worse?"

"Just his weekly checkup," I said.

Jim smiled, his frown disappearing. "Your uncle's a good man—a real good man."

"The best man I know," I said.

Jim removed his spectacles, and with his handkerchief, wiped one lens, then the other. "Does he ever talk about the war, Davy?"

"I don't press him," I said. "I figure he'd just as soon forget it, if he could."

"I couldn't go myself, you know." He tapped the frames of the spectacles as he placed them back over his nose. "Too nearsighted. I wanted to go. I wanted to go real bad, but the pain your uncle's seen—well, maybe I got lucky. Maybe being a hero ain't all it's cracked up to be." He flashed a sudden ingratiating smile. "He's looking better these days, don't you think?"

"Sister Rose has really helped him," I said.

"The colored lady, huh?" He thought on it a moment and said, "Then I guess we owe her a lot. Yes, sir, I guess we do."

Whenever a townsperson made an appearance, Sister Rose took refuge upstairs. When I told her that she shouldn't let those people drive her away, she said, "People come to see your uncle. I'd be a distraction."

"A distraction?"

"If they saw me, then soon it would be all about me. No use putting your uncle in such a position."

Then, at the beginning of March, the sun came from behind the ever-present gray skies, the snow melted, and one Saturday I walked to the old Squires place to find Daniel hard at work repairing the damage caused by the storms. A small section of the east roof had collapsed, letting in the snow and sleet. Floor boards bulged and dipped like waves in a pond, which meant we would have to re-do much of our previous work. One of the cross beams, full of wood rot, showed wide cracks, and debris littered the buckled floor. We spent most of the morning cleaning up the mess.

After lunch, we cut away the rotten wood and replaced it with a partial section from another abandoned house. Daniel stood on the ladder while I hefted the beam. Once he slipped it in place, he began to hammer home nails, the blows echoing through the one room house. I held the ladder, rickety at best, which shook with each blow. The position of the beam forced Daniel to arch his back and neck in awkward positions. His arms soon grew tired, and I took over his job while he steadied the ladder.

I held a couple of nails in my teeth, and with one hand gripping the hammer, I stood with my head in the shadows trying to see where to begin. I slipped a nail from my lips, placed it over a joint, but before I could deliver the first blow, a voice said, "What the hell you niggers doing in there?"

Startled, I whipped my head around so fast that I almost lost my balance. The ladder shook, and only Daniel's grip saved me from a bad fall.

Two men stood in the doorway and peered inside. Zeb Cain, his yellow and crooked teeth bared like an angry dog, cradled a shotgun, and a long hunting knife hung from his belt. He was a big solid man, a good head taller and probably seventy pounds heavier than me. He got in one scrap after another, usually because he drank too much and talked too loudly, which often ended in a brawl. Seldom did a month pass that he hadn't spent a night in the city jail, and twice he spent time in the county lockup in Dallas, one incarceration lasting over a month because he and another guy went at each other with knives.

Behind him stood Pap Caldwell, hugging a shotgun to

his corpulent chest. Years before, when I first arrived in Twin Forks, the man weighed probably a hundred and sixty and sported a full head of coal black hair, but since then he'd added at least seventy pounds and his hair had receded until only small tuffs spouted around his ears. He wore a battered and faded fedora, which even indoors he kept glued to his bald pate. Standing on tiptoes, he peered over the shoulder of Zeb Cain.

Both men owned small farms, although neither could claim much success. Like other men I knew, they spent too much time at Ernie's bar playing forty-two and drinking Lone Star while their fields produced less and less each year as the soil played out.

Cain spit, and a brown wad splattered on the warped boards. "I asked you niggers a question. What the hell you doing?" He motioned with the shotgun. "You come down, boy. I want to see who's making this racket and disturbing our hunting."

I took the nails from my mouth and came down from the shadows. Pap squinted as he studied my face. "Why, it's Marsh Langdon's kid."

"What the hell you doing here?" Cain asked.

The impertinence of his question, as well as his insolent tone, angered me. "That's none of your damn business," I said.

"Davy." Daniel whispered my name as a warning.

Cain said, "You be civil or I'll slap some manners into you, boy."

My grip tightened on the hammer, and I glared at the man, ready to hurl another insult, but Daniel stepped in front of me. "I'm real sorry we disturbed your hunting. If you want, we'll stop right now."

Daniel's servile attitude appeared to mollify Cain, although he continued to glare at me with annoyance. Leaning forward, he examined the interior. "Whose place is this, anyway?"

"Nobody's place, Mr. Cain," Daniel said.

"Then why the hell you fixin' it up?" he asked.

Daniel fell silent. If people knew that Daniel and his mother were in the process of building a school, they would put an end to it.

"We're building a church!" Daniel's voice boomed with such evangelical zeal that I flinched as if he had taken a swing at me. "Hallelujah! That's what we're building here. Praise the Lord!" He jumped up and down clapping his hands. "Hallelujah! I know you gentlemen would like to join us in a little prayer, so why don't you step into our place of worship. Together we can kneel and pray in Christian fellowship."

Cain said, "What the hell you trying to pull, nigger?"

"John 3:16 says, God gave his only begotten son so that we all might have everlasting life. Because of Jesus' sacrifice, God offers us an eternal life. Come, pray with us. Lift your voices to the Lord! Let Him hear you sing His praises."

Cain spit, sending another brown wad spewing over the floor. "Let me tell you boy—" He leveled a thin finger at me, his nail so dirty it appeared as if he'd painted it black. "—Marsh is going to hear about this. You can bet your bottom dollar on that."

I warned myself to keep my mouth shut. Zeb Cain was nothing more than a bigoted failure, but my mouth seemed to operate all on its own. "Yessir, you do that. I'm sure my uncle will have a thing or two to say to you, too. He might even tell you to go straight—"

"Hallelujah! Hallelujah!" screamed Daniel. "Praise the Lord! Glory to God!"

"He's a proselyting nigger." Pap Caldwell laughed aloud. "I ain't never seen no proselyting nigger."

Cain whirled and stomped off, waving his hand in a dismissive gesture. Pap shook his head as if he couldn't quite believe his eyes, and then followed his friend. Without looking back, Cain shouted, "Your uncle is going to hear about you and that crazy nigger, Davy Stoneman!"

When at last the trees and brush swallowed the two men, Daniel roared 'Hallelujah!' His voice bounced off the thin walls. "We are saved, Brother Davy! We are saved!"

I stared at Daniel, who continued to smile broadly, his white teeth flashing in the mid-day light. "Daniel, I would've told that son-of-a—" I began.

"Remember I once told you that deputy sheriff wasn't the kind of man to shoot me over a nickel. But this Zeb Cain—he's different. He'd shoot me for the fun of it."

10

*W*hen I got home that afternoon, I discovered Uncle Marsh sitting alone at a workbench, a dismantled rifle laid out before him. In one hand he held a can of gun oil, in the other an old rag. Our store carried a rifle and a couple of shotguns on display behind the cash register. No other business in town, including Wiggins' General Store, carried guns, and if people didn't buy from us, they had to travel all the way to Hollister or Dallas. Whenever a new gun arrived, Uncle Marsh tore it down, cleaned it, and reassembled it before putting it out for sale. While he was off fighting the Hun, the job had fallen to me, but this was the first new rifle we had acquired in well over a year.

Uncle Marsh grinned broadly. "Never seen anything quite like this, have you, Davy?" He tapped the wooden stock. "Bill Misener offered it in trade. A Winchester 1895 .405 caliber. A real gem in perfect working order. Needed a good cleaning is all. Bill threw in half a dozen boxes of shells. Maybe when I feel a little better, you and me might go hunting again."

I took a seat across from him, but at that moment, hunting held little importance. "I need to tell you about what happened."

I described the encounter with Zeb Cain and Pap Caldwell. As he listened, his brow furrowed and his initial joy at seeing me was replaced by a more somber expression. When I finished, he said, "That was smart thinking on Daniel's part. As long Cain and his friend believe the two of you are working on a church, I don't see any harm done. Still—" He paused, his fingers tapping a pattern on the stock of the Winchester. "—if word gets out, somebody might guess the truth. Then there could be trouble. Might be best if you stay away until we see how the wind's blowing."

"Daniel's my friend," I said.

Uncle Marsh picked out the breech bolt and began to polish it. He continued for almost a full minute. That was Uncle Marsh for you. He liked to think things through, consider all the possibilities, before he made a decision. Working with his hands aided him, as if a direct connection existed between his fingers and his brain. At last he said, "You're old enough to make up your own mind, Davy, so I'll not forbid you to go. Still, it worries me, and it's bound to worry Esther. When trouble develops between whites and coloreds, it has a way of getting out of hand real quick."

"What makes a man like Zeb Cain?" I asked. "Why is he so mean and hateful?"

Uncle Marsh leaned back in his chair and studied my face with those intense blue eyes. "A question I can't rightly answer. People aren't born that way. Something happens, I guess, that sours them and makes them what they are."

"Daniel and Sister Rose don't deserve the treatment that's been dished out," I said.

"No, they don't." My uncle picked out the magazine firing spring, held it to the light, and with careful precision, wiped away a speck of dust. "Just keep alert." He nodded to a package on the counter. "That's for Bill Misener. Take it to him."

After I put away my tools, I grabbed the package and headed for the livery. Already past six, the street was encased in shadows. Halfway to the stable, a voice called, "Where you headed, Davy?" Jim Kennison crossed the street. He wore a heavy coat open at the neck.

"Delivering these dry goods to Mr. Misener," I said, hefting the package.

"Mind if I walk with you a spell?"

We passed the Tower Theater, the marquee announcing the arrival of *The Country Cousin*, a new film starring Elaine Hammerstein and based on a Booth Tarkington play. "Are you going to see that?" Jim asked.

"Doesn't look like anything I'd like," I said.

"I go every time a new moving picture comes to town." His voice held a note of pride. "Never miss one. You know why? It's not the main feature. It's the cliffhanger. Right now it's a Ruth Roland. Last week she was in this tunnel looking for her sweetheart, but the villain set a trap so that the mine would blow up with her in it."

Pretending to be shocked, I said, "She got killed?"

"No, no, it's a cliffhanger." He chuckled at my feigned ignorance. "See, a cliffhanger has chapters, and at the end of each chapter, it looks like the hero's going to be killed. Then the next chapter opens with the hero escaping. Ain't you never seen a cliffhanger, Davy? Gee, they're a lot of fun." We walked a few more steps before he said, "But I didn't come over here to talk about moving pictures."

"Didn't think so."

He touched my arm and together we halted a dozen paces from the livery. Shadows blanketed us so deeply that I could see only his spectacles reflecting the light from the theater. His face was a dark mask. "This is kind of serious."

"I'm gathering that," I said.

"Zeb Cain and Pap Caldwell are at Ernie's having a beer and jawing." Jim removed his Stetson and ran his fingers through his hair. "They said they ran into you and

Sister Rose's boy out at the old Squires place. They said the two of you were working on the house. Building a church, they said."

"So?"

"Cain said Sister Rose's boy is crazy as a hoot owl. He kept saying they ought to go back out there and burn the place to the ground. I told them best to let things be." He slapped the Stetson back on his head. "The other boys said the same thing. No good could come in burning a church they said. That *is* what you're building, ain't it, Davy? A church?"

"What else would we be building?"

"I don't think any of the boys liked it that you was helping out." Jim paused as if waiting for a reply, but when I offered none, he said, "You ought to try that Ruth Roland cliffhanger. You'd really like it." He waved goodbye and crossed the street heading for Ernie's.

I found Mr. Misener in the rear of the livery, a lamp lighting the interior as he polished the leather seats of the carriage that he rented for marriages and funerals. He was nearly my uncle's age, although he looked every bit the hayseed. He wore bib overalls, a plaid shirt and a broad-brim straw hat, and as he worked, he smoked his pipe, tilted at an angle so the smoke drifted away from his face. He told me to drop the package on his desk in his office. When I came out, I found him standing in the middle of the livery holding his pipe in one hand. "I got a lot more than I expected for that old rifle," he said. "Pass along a 'Thank you kindly' to your uncle."

"My uncle is cleaning the Winchester right now."

"Might've kept it if I liked to hunt, but I never used it once in my whole life. It was sitting around collecting dust. Still, it was Granddaddy's." With that, he went back to the carriage, but even at a distance of ten paces, I saw that while his eyes appeared to study the leather, they were focused on a time far removed from my own.

Back at the store I discovered Uncle Marsh absent,

Aunt Esther behind the counter. She held out the beer pail and told me to go to Ernie's to get it filled. "Marsh needs his vitamins," she said.

So I headed up the street and pushed through the swinging doors. As usual on a Saturday night, men crowded the place, a half dozen standing at the bar drinking Lone Star, another dozen or so at tables. In the back a group of four men played forty-two, snapping dominoes against the table as they laid down their pieces. Smoke hung heavy in the room. Men talked and laughed, creating a dull roar.

Mayor Lon sat off to one side puffing on a cigar, and across from him, Jim nursed a beer. Inside the door, Zeb Cain rested his elbows on the bar. Pap Caldwell stood next to him, and as I passed, Cain nudged Pap in the ribs and nodded in my direction.

Right then I knew there would be trouble. I should have walked out, but if I had, people would have seen it as a cowardly act. Worse, I would have seen it that way. Fear nestled inside my chest, making it hard to breathe, but I passed the beer pail to Ernie.

Ernie shifted his eyes up and down the bar before he held the container under the tap. His hands shook, and beer spilled over the rim. At last, he handed me the pail, and without a word I stepped for the door.

Zeb Cain blocked my path. I doubt he had passed the point of sobriety, but his breath stank of beer. He stood so close that I could see the grain in his yellow teeth, and I realized that they were false. Most people with false teeth took them out at night to sit in a glass of water, but Cain must not have put much store in the practice. "I want to know why you're helping that nigger."

Except for the scrape of boots or chairs against the floor, the room was silent.

"Like I told you before, it's none of your damned business," I said.

The back of his hand came up fast, my head snapped

back, and the pail flew out of my hand, beer spraying those nearest to me. Before I could regain my balance, he backhanded me again, slamming me against the bar.

Jim started out of his chair, but Lon Barron reached across the table, grabbed his arm and shook his head. Jim sat back.

My head was spinning. I touched my lip with my tongue, felt the split on the right side, and tasted blood. If Cain had been nearer my own age, I might have jumped him, despite his size, but the plain fact was he scared me. He was a good head taller than I and wide as a barn door, and I doubt he had much fat under his overalls and shirt.

I reached down, picked up the empty beer pail and lid, and handed them once more to Ernie. Ernie refilled the pail and sat it on the counter, snapping the lid in place. In a shaky voice, he said, "Go on, Davy. Get out of here."

The bar remained quiet except for my boots making muted thuds in the sawdust. This time Cain made no move to stop me.

My lip continued to bleed, and blood spotted my coat. Hoping to avoid Aunt Esther and Uncle Marsh, I walked around to the back stairs that led to our kitchen. I found both sitting at the kitchen table. Uncle Marsh had on a nightshirt, but he still wore his trousers and suspenders. He had stayed up waiting for his beer.

The moment she saw me, Aunt Esther jumped from her chair, almost tipping it over. "Goodness, Davy! What happened to you?"

She rushed over, took the beer pail from my hand and set it on the kitchen counter. She led me into the light for a closer inspection. Pulling a towel from a drawer, she held it under the pump while she worked the handle. Once she'd wrung out the excess water, she dabbed the cloth against my lip.

I tried to figure out a way to tell them without getting Uncle Marsh riled—in his condition, he didn't need that— but the longer I thought about it, the more I realized that only the truth would do. Sooner or later, they would hear the whole story from one of the townsfolk. "I sassed Zeb Cain."

Aunt Esther stopped dabbing my lip. "What could you possibly say that would make that man do such a thing?"

I meant to end it there, to accept my responsibility and not say another word, but Uncle Marsh gave me that look.

"He asked me what I was doing out there with Daniel. I told him it was none of his damned business."

Aunt Esther, her eyes ablaze, glared at me. "That mouth of yours is always getting you into trouble. First school, now this. By now I would've suspected you had learned that silence is golden." She brought the wet towel back to my lip, her anger getting the better of her, and she rubbed the area like she was trying to remove the lip. I caught her hand and took the towel. She said, "That Cain is nothing but a bully, Marsh. We should get the law on him."

"The law was there and saw the whole thing," I said. "Jim Kennison was about to step in, but Lon Barron stopped him."

Uncle Marsh leaned down and began to lace up his boots. Aunt Esther said, "What are you doing, Marsh?"

Standing, he stomped first one foot and then the other. He marched past me and out the door, a solid blast of cold wind blowing in his wake.

"Marsh!" Aunt Esther said. We heard his boots on the stairs. "He's too sick for this, Davy. Go after him, you hear. You go after him right now!"

Tossing the bloody towel onto the table, I dashed out the door. By the time I reached the landing, Uncle Marsh was already rounding the corner of the building. I flew down the stairs two at a time. As I made the street, I saw Uncle Marsh pause in front of Wiggins General Store, reach into a barrel, and pull out an ax handle. He placed that handle on the boardwalk and leaned on it as if to rest while he gathered his strength. I caught up to him there.

"What do you think you're doing, Uncle Marsh?" I said.

He looked at me with unfocused eyes and stepped past. I reached out to grab his arm, but my hip banged against the barrel, tipping it on its side so that it was ready to topple. By the time I set it back in position, Uncle Marsh was in front of the saloon, and I dashed after him.

Thrusting the ax handle forward, he plowed through the swinging doors. I reached the saloon as the doors swung back. Catching one, I held it open and watched, mesmerized by what followed.

Uncle Marsh took two steps, the ax handle coming in a wide arc over his head. Cain looked up from his beer and saw my uncle reflected in the mirror behind the bar, but by then, it was too late. The thick pine cracked into Cain's left shoulder, the wood against bone as loud as a shotgun blast. Cain screamed and the left side of his body went limp, as if it had simply stopped functioning. His knees buckled.

All along the bar men scurried away, startled at the sudden violence. My uncle's face was reflected in the mirror. The wild look in his eyes frightened me, too.

Uncle Marsh gripped the ax handle so tightly his knuckles bulged like they wanted to break free of the skin, his hands quivered, and the end of the handle bobbed like a fishing pole. He whirled on the crowded room, but he discovered no resistance, no threat. He spotted Lon and Jim still sitting at their table. "Lon Barron, you ain't worth a gob of spit." He shifted his glare to Jim. "But you! You're a deputy sheriff. It's your job to protect people."

"You assaulted a man," Lon said. "Jim could arrest you." His voice broke like an adolescent boy, and a couple of men laughed. Lon looked to the right and left trying to identify the culprits, but the room fell silent once more.

Jim adjusted his spectacles to get a better view of Cain. "You hit him pretty hard, Mr. Marsh. Looks like you could've busted his shoulder."

Uncle Marsh glanced down at Cain. "He'll get over it."

With that Uncle Marsh laid the ax handle across his

shoulder and marched toward the door. I jumped aside as he pushed through. I followed all the way to our stairs before he knew I was there. We stood in the dark between buildings, the chill wind cutting right through us. "You saw?" he asked.

"Yes, sir," I said.

His voice was tight, and I could tell he still carried his anger. "Cain won't bother you no more—least not for awhile."

"No, sir, I suspect he won't," I said.

"Listen, Davy, he's a mean one, and he makes two of you. You stay out of his way."

Uncle Marsh started up the stairs when he realized he still carried the ax handle. He held it out to me. "Put this back in that barrel in front of Wiggins' store. I'll thank him tomorrow for its use."

By the time I deposited the ax handle and walked home, I discovered Uncle Marsh already in bed, coughing and spitting into a handkerchief. He appeared tired, bags under his eyes, his jowls drooping, and I felt a rush of guilt for having caused the setback.

My guilt lessened when, after a couple of days and more tonic from Sister Rose, Uncle Marsh recovered to his previous condition. However, the incident made me realize that while Uncle Marsh appeared more robust and healthy, in reality he suffered if put under any strain.

As for Zeb Cain, I saw him the next day coming out of Doctor Gibbs' office, his left arm in sling. When he spotted me, his face twisted into his usual sneer. I was on my way to school, my book bag thrown over my shoulder, and I guess I could have walked past and said nothing, but when he gave me that look, I walked right up to him.

"I want to apologize, Mr. Cain," I said.

"Yeah? Well you should," he said.

"Absolutely," I said. "I should never have walked out of Ernie's last night. No, sir, I should have stayed right there and had it out with you toe to toe. Now, when you feel up to it and want to continue our discussion—well, sir, I promise my uncle won't object. My solemn word on that."

"I'll break you in half, you little bastard," he said.

He was right, of course. I was no match for him, but regardless of the consequences, I wouldn't put Uncle Marsh in a position where he would have to face Zeb Cain again. If I had to take my licks, I would do so, outmatched as I was.

11

Saturday I was on the old river road when I spotted Rachel a hundred yards behind me. While I waited for her to catch up, I tossed rocks at a log floating in mid-stream. Four times I found stones as big as my fist, and four times I sent one flying out over the river. Each time it flew straight and thudded against the water-soaked wood. I was so good at rock throwing that I didn't even have to take aim. It was one of those talents I fostered because I was a loner unused to friendships.

Dust covered her bare ankles and shoes, and the wind waved the bandana she used to tie back her hair. As she drew up beside me, my heart beat a little faster. "You're awfully good at throwing rocks," she said.

"It's my one physical accomplishment."

"Why did you wait for me?"

"We're both headed for the same place. We can walk together for a while."

"That's not a good idea, Davy."

"People in town already know I'm out here," I said. "They think we're building a church."

She chewed her lip, her forehead creased in worry. We failed to speak for several minutes, until I asked, "Are you frightened of being seen with me?"

She studied my face. "I don't know many white boys."

"Do I make you nervous?" I said.

"Some, I guess."

A gust of cold wind came off the river carrying with it the smell of mildew and waste. She hugged her coat tighter and cast her gaze upon the road ahead. I noticed then an old book sticking out of her pocket, the corner chewed away by the teeth of a dog.

"You're reading *Pudd'nhead Wilson*," I said. "That's the same exact copy both Daniel and I read. Miss Pilgrim loaned it to you, too."

"You can't tell anyone. If you do—"

"I've kept Daniel's secret. I'll keep yours," I said, but I could see doubt clouding her eyes. I was white, and like Daniel, she held little trust in white people.

Once more she became silent, and I figured it would be that way all the way to the Squires place, but she surprised me when, as we left the river road and headed toward the woods, she asked, "What happened to your lip?"

With my gloved hand, I touched the cut. "My mouth gets me in trouble sometimes." I shrugged away her concern. "Tell me about the book. Did you like it?

Her head down, she nodded but said nothing. "Don't you want to talk about it?" I asked.

"I ain't—" she began, halted and began again. "I never talked about a book before except to Daniel and a little bit with Miss Pilgrim."

Classic Miss Pilgrim, I thought. She was a stickler for the word 'ain't', and whenever any of the kids at school used it, she would say, "You say 'ain't' and people will always know you're an uneducated cracker." I could see she had impressed that idea upon Rachel, too.

"But you and me—we could talk about it," I said.

"I might say the wrong thing. You might think I'm dumb."

"Why would I think that?"

"You must know a lot of people who read books. They've got to know a lot more than me."

"Other than you, I know three people who read books: Daniel, his mother and Miss Pilgrim. Most of the people in town have never read a book in their lives, except maybe the Bible, and I doubt many have read all of it. I don't think that book learning is everything, but it takes a bright person to read a book, especially a person like you or Daniel."

"Because we're colored," she said, and a note of bitterness crept into her voice.

"It's harder for you and Daniel. You've got to want it a lot more than most white people."

She looked at the ground, her eyes avoiding me. "You're really smart, aren't you, Davy?"

"Not always. Ask Daniel. He'll tell you that sometimes I'm as dumb as a dead snail."

When we reached the clearing, we saw Daniel framed in the doorway, a claw hammer in his fist. The way he eyed us, all steel and flint, made me a bit uneasy. "What are you two doing?" he asked.

"We ran into each other on the river road," I said.

Rachel held out her hand, and my friend lifted her up beside him. I threw my bag of tools into the house and jumped up, too.

"If people saw you two together—" Daniel said, then let the thought trail off. But he couldn't leave it alone. "Look, working out here, probably nobody is going to bother us. But if we make a spectacle of ourselves—if we push white folks faces in it—all hell could break loose."

Rachel had warned me, but I wanted so badly to be close to her that I ignored her fears. Now I saw the danger through Daniel's eyes. What if someone like Cain or Pap Caldwell had seen us? Would they have conjured up the notion that I was sparking a colored girl? If that rumor spread, it could unleash all sorts of consequences for all of us.

I said, "It won't happen again." To Rachel I said, "I should've heard what you were saying. I'm sorry."

Her eyes widened. "You're the first white boy—the first white person—who ever apologized to me for anything." She laughed, and Daniel and I laughed with her.

In reality the situation contained little humor, unless you consider the human condition itself a source of humor. I suspect that we laughed because it was better than crying or whining.

For the next couple of hours we worked without stopping, Rachel to my left, Daniel to my right, the three of us ripping up and replacing the last of the warped floorboards. I kept sneaking glances at Rachel. She was so damned beautiful, all dark chocolate, soft and round, eyes full of innocence and intelligence. Once, when she caught me looking, she smiled, and I averted my eyes, my face hot with embarrassment.

A little past noon we paused for lunch and shared sandwiches prepared by Sister Rose, all three of us washing our food down with water from a single mason jar. We had finished eating, and I was packing up my lunch pail when I heard brush rustling off to the east of the house. At first I thought it was a possum or coon, but when I stuck my head out, I saw nothing. The wind stirred the tops of the trees, and the hair on the back of my neck stood straight. Was someone out there spying on us? Or I was imagining things? The warnings of Rachel and Daniel had spooked me.

But for the rest of the day, including my walk home that evening, I imagined an unseen presence behind every tree, ready to leap out and bash in my skull. No matter how much I told myself my fears were foolish, I couldn't shake the dread that hounded my steps all the way into town.

I no sooner crossed the old wooden bridge that spanned the Trinity than I spotted Tommikins, the mayor's son. He stood beside the wall of the bank, eyeing me, his face glistening with sweat like he had run a distance, his mouth twisted into a snarl. When I stopped and stared back, he sauntered to the rear of the building, his heavy boots kicking up dust.

12

*I*n early April a new storm blew in, and with it, Orvie Blaylock.

The storm, like the previous ones that winter, came straight down from Canada, crossing the Great Plains and the Texas Panhandle before roaring into Twin Forks. The morning it arrived, the sun shone and not a cloud dotted the sky. Then, around noon, a whole bank of dark, heavy clouds rolled in from the north, and the temperature plummeted fifteen or twenty degrees during the first hour. Uncle Marsh glanced out the store window. "Another bad blow coming," he said.

That afternoon, the Sunshine Special, on its way from St. Louis to El Paso, made another stop in Twin Forks. Three men waited on the platform, each huddled inside his coat, each with a hat pulled low over his eyes to protect his face from the cold wind.

Zeb Cain, an empty sleeve flapping in the wind, the arm in a sling under his coat, stood beside Lon Barron who chewed on his cigar and peered up the tracks for the first sign of the train. At his side, Preacher Joyner blew on his gloveless hands. They waited for Orvie Blaylock.

Blaylock had left town more than three years before. Stories varied as to the actual circumstances, but as far as I can tell, the events occurred something like this:

One Saturday night, Orvie caught the interurban at Hollister and rode over to Dallas. In a bar near Deep Elm, the colored district, he proceeded to get drunk on Lone Star. In no time the beer fueled his temper, and he got into a ruckus with another drunk, breaking a bottle over the fellow's head before the bartender pulled a gun and forced Blaylock to leave.

He went looking for trouble, which he found a block later where he confronted a colored man, his wife and their young boy of seven. When it was all over, the colored man was dead, his wife dying and the little boy suffering a cut across the face that would leave its mark for the rest of his life.

The Dallas Police arrested Blaylock on the spot, the knife still in his hand, bloody streaks across his denim trousers where he'd wiped the blade. They held him in jail until his trial three weeks later where the judge, before sentencing him to three years in Huntsville for manslaughter, slammed his gavel and said, "It gives Dallas a bad reputation when strangers come into our town and kill and maim our Nigra citizens."

In those days, good behavior mattered little in Texas prisons, and Blaylock served his entire three years. Now he rode the Sunshine Special as it rounded the far bend. I can't say what the three men who waited thought—I lack the ability to look into the seeds of time and see which will grow and which will not—but each must have harbored doubts and hopes. Cain must have wondered if prison had changed his friend, made him less a man, broken him. Lon Barron must have considered the possibility that Blaylock, now a convicted felon, might cause trouble that, since Lon was the mayor, he would have to deal with. Preacher Joyner must have prayed that he could restore and rejuvenate the immortal soul of his former parishioner.

The train puffed its way to the platform, cars rattling together as it rolled to a stop. Orvie Blaylock stepped off the train, a grip clutched in his left hand. The conductor blew his whistle, and the train lurched forward, heading to Austin, San Antonio and points south.

Orvie shook hands with each man, and they could see that indeed he had changed. He stood five-eight or nine, about my height, but his body, always compact, had grown more solid, more muscular. But what he'd gained in one area, he'd lost in another. His hair had receded until he was almost completely bald. Yet, his face had suffered the greatest change. The whole left side drooped to the point that it appeared he had gotten too close to a fire, and it had melted. At first the men believed he had suffered a stroke, until they saw the long scar that curved around the left side of his balding head. Later all he would say was, "A nigger cold-cocked me." When people pressed him for details, he would add, "That nigger ain't cold-cocking nobody no more."

The small group walked a block and a half to Ernie's, pushing through the closed doors into a room warmed by a potbellied stove in a far corner. Half a dozen men, having heard of Blaylock's homecoming, lined the bar, and the moment he entered, they rushed to shake his hand. When Ernie set a mug of beer before him, Blaylock held it up to the light then blew away the foam and drank the entire contents in one continuous gulp. Finished, he slammed the mug on top of the counter. "When I was inside, I missed two things—beer and women. I think I've got time for one more beer." That brought a roundhouse of laughter and backslaps.

Ten minutes later as Blaylock finished his second beer, the front door opened and Jim, his deputy's badge pinned to his coat, came in from the cold.

Lon Barron waved Jim over to the bar. "Jim, come over here. I want you to meet someone."

Lon introduced the two men, who didn't bother to

shake hands. "I heard you were on your way, Mr. Blaylock," Jim said.

"I figured you did."

"I guess you're glad to be home," Jim said. "I guess Huntsville ain't much of a pleasure spot."

"A guy can get used to most anything." Blaylock's tone grew hostile. "You got something important to say to me, deputy? Or is this a sociable call?"

"I'm not here to cause trouble. I'm here to make sure trouble doesn't get started."

Lon Barron held up a hand like a cop directing traffic. "I invited you over here to meet Orvie, not to hassle the man. He's had a hard three years. He needs to blow off a little steam. Ain't that right, Orvie?"

"I got no argument with a man howling at the moon," Jim said, "as long as it doesn't disturb the peace. I'm sure you can understand that, Mr. Blaylock?"

Blaylock refused to answer, his face an open book of hostility, and the mayor, puffing out his chest, said, "Forget it, Jim. Come on and have a beer. Orvie was a pillar of the community before he left. Ain't that right, Brother Joyner?"

The preacher who stood on the edge of the crowd nodded agreement. "Mr. Blaylock was a member in good standing in my church."

"I'm sure he was." Jim removed his Stetson, running his hand through his golden hair. "Sorry I can't have a beer right now, mayor. I promised Susanna I'd be over in a while. So I guess I'll be saying good night. Nice to have met you, Mr. Blaylock."

After Jim left, Blaylock said, "When did the county start hiring four-eyes for deputies? They that hard up?"

"Jim's a good man," said Lon.

"So why's he messing with me?"

"I'll have a little talk with him. You don't have to worry."

"I ain't the worrying kind." Blaylock motioned Ernie to

draft another beer. He leaned forward and looked at himself in the mirror behind the bar. "Just keep that deputy out of my face."

As the day wore down and men drifted home, Preacher Joiner approached Blaylock. "Will we see you in church on Sunday, Brother Blaylock?" he asked.

Blaylock, already bleary-eyed, regarded the preacher as if he were a stranger. "You'll be seeing me in a lot of places. I ain't sure church will be one of 'em."

The last to leave that evening were Zeb Cain and Orvie Blaylock. "You stay at my place," Cain told him as they pushed through the swinging doors. "We got things to discuss."

13

*D*aniel showed up before I left for school. We heard footfalls on the stairs leading to the landing and then a knock. When I opened the door, he stepped into the kitchen, his hands deep in his coat pockets, his head half-buried in the fur collar. He hurried to the stove, hands extended.

Aunt Esther stood at the sink, wiping her hands on her apron. "Where's your mama this morning?" she asked.

Daniel unbuttoned the top of his coat and pushed the collar from his face. "Mama's down with fever, but she sent me to bring the ingredients for Mr. Marsh's tonic." He patted his right pocket.

"Who's with your mama now?" Aunt Esther asked.

"I told her I should stay with her, but she wouldn't have that," Daniel said.

"Then you go right back and take care of Sister Rose. She needs you more than Marsh and me." When Daniel started to protest, Aunt Esther said, "I'll not hear another word on the subject. You give Marsh his tonic and be off. Marsh can do without a person fussin' over him all day. I declare, that man's getting downright spoiled."

Daniel took the herbs and roots, grinding them into a paste and dissolving them in water. I followed as he carried the homemade brew to Uncle Marsh, who sat on the edge of the bed. By now he showed every sign of recovery from the incident in Ernie's Bar. His cheeks glowed with a healthy pink, and the combination of Sister Rose's tonic and the daily draughts of beer had added more weight to his frame.

"Esther told me your mama's ailing." Uncle Marsh leaned over and grabbed a boot, stuffing his right foot inside it and stamping it against the floor. He slipped on the other boot before taking the glass from Daniel. He downed the contents in two quick swallows.

"Anything else I can do for you, Mr. Marsh?" Daniel asked.

"Well, I'd like your mama to read some more of that book." He snapped his fingers as he tried to remember the title. "What's it called, Davy?"

"*Great Expectations*," I said.

"I can stay and read a bit," said Daniel. "I can read pretty well. Not as good as Mama, but pretty well."

"That'll keep until your mama is better." He waved Daniel toward the door. "Go on now, get out of here."

Daniel and I left the room, and I said, "We can walk a ways together."

I slipped into my coat, threw my book bag over my shoulder, and we were out the door. A blast of north wind caught us halfway down the stairs, the cold stinging my nose and cheeks, and like Daniel, I flipped up my collar and pulled my cap low. Dark, heavy clouds rolled across the sky. The bitterness of the cold far surpassed those days when snow hugged the ground and icicles hung from every roof. Then the wind stirred the trees, but it never held the power of that cold morning when it roared in our ears and blew dust and grit in our faces, forcing us to duck our heads to protect our eyes.

I was walking that way when, in front of Wiggins

General Store, I collided with Orvie Blaylock. He must have seen me coming and placed himself in my path. He stood braced, his feet wide apart, his hands on his hips, and I bounced off him, my head snapping up. Behind him, and to his left, stood Zeb Cain, a grin twisting his thick lips.

"You ought to watch where you're going, kid." Blaylock spoke in a low grumble. "You're liable to get hurt if you don't."

"Sorry," I said and tried to step around, but he put a thick hand on my chest.

"So, you're Marsh Langdon's brat," Blaylock said. "You were a snot-nosed kid when I left. Ain't changed much, have you?" He cast his eyes on Daniel. "Who's he?"

"That's his nigger friend I was telling you about," said Cain.

Blaylock breathed through his open mouth, exposing teeth that showed brown creeping from the gums. As close as we stood, I could smell the stale beer on his breath. His misshapen left eye appeared to stare from an oblique angle, and the left side of his mouth pulled downward, all of which made him appear more than a little sinister.

Perhaps Blaylock intended to push things further. Right then he gave every indication of doing so, and I felt myself go cold with fear. I held no illusions that in a fight I could prevail. Blaylock was solid muscle, and the scars on his head and knuckles showed clear evidence of past encounters with men far more adept at fighting than I.

All the while, Daniel edged away until he stood next to the barrel full of ax handles, the same barrel from which Uncle Marsh had borrowed one the night he busted Cain's shoulder. Without looking, Daniel reached back until his hand curled around the wood.

A voice coming from behind me ended whatever confrontation was about to take place. "What's the problem?" Jim came to stand beside me, and for the first time in my life, I was truly happy to see him.

Blaylock scratched the side of his face, his fingernails digging into his dark stubble, flakes of dried skin peeling off. "Me and this boy getting acquainted."

Jim smiled. "Davy needs to get along or he'll be late for school." Without taking his eyes off Blaylock, he said, "You better hurry, Davy, or you're likely to get a scolding from Miss Pilgrim."

As I stepped past Blaylock, he said, "Maybe you and me will get another chance to talk, kid."

Neither Daniel nor I spoke before we reached the edge of town. There we paused. "Don't fool with that man." Daniel huddled inside his coat, the collar covering most of his face, his cap pulled low, but I could see his eyes, pinched in worry. "It wouldn't be a fight, Davy. It'd be a massacre."

I started to tell him I knew how to fight—hadn't I beaten the stuffings out of Tommikins?—but I kept my mouth shut. Daniel was right, and I knew it.

With that, Daniel headed for home. I watched for a moment before I headed toward the schoolhouse a hundred yards away where Miss Pilgrim stood on the front steps bundled in a long coat and clanging the bell for first call. On most days the yard would be filled with kids running and playing, but the weather had driven them inside. I picked up my pace, and Miss Pilgrim waited, holding her hat as the wind tried to swipe it from her head. When I reached the steps, she rang the bell one last time and followed me inside.

For the rest of the day, I never quite shook the fear that coiled inside my chest whenever I thought of Orvie Blaylock.

14

I spent part of the morning helping the first and second graders—all half dozen of them—with their handwriting, making sure their printed letters stayed within the lines. At noon recess, with the wind outside howling like a thousand ghosts, all of us, including Miss Pilgrim, remained inside to eat our lunches. I sat in a far corner eating my peanut butter and banana sandwich and washing it down with a mason jar of water. Every so often, I'd catch Tommikins focusing his beady little eyes on me, and when I stared back, he dropped his gaze and concentrated on his food. I wondered if he needed another thumping. I was all ready to give it to him, and this time I wouldn't need a reason.

I think Miss Pilgrim spotted us and grasped my feelings. Even before I finished my water, she came from her desk, and in a gentle but firm voice, sent me to the back room to do my reading. A couple of days before, she had assigned me *Don Quixote*. I read for a little over an hour, and as I came to the passage where the old knight confronts the windmill, the door to the storeroom opened and Miss Pilgrim entered followed by Aunt Esther. Aunt Esther had never once come to school, and my first thought was that Uncle Marsh had taken a turn for the worse. Miss Pilgrim moved aside, and I saw the iron pot my aunt carried, so heavy that she listed to port. I took the pot, placing it on the floor.

Miss Pilgrim closed the door, leaving us alone.

"Uncle Marsh?" I asked.

"He's minding the store. He'll be fine 'til I get back." Deep impressions of the pot's handle lay embedded in her gloves. Aunt Esther rubbed her hands together in an effort to restore circulation. "This morning after you and Daniel left, I made chicken soup. I want you to take it to Sister Rose. Miss Pilgrim said missing half a day won't hurt as long as it doesn't become a habit."

Forgoing my reading, I hefted the pot and strode out into the cold, dark afternoon, a sense of exhilaration my companion. I doubt that, presented with such an opportunity, I was any different than most boys my age. As much as I loved school, I longed to escape the humdrum of the classroom, and Aunt Esther had delivered me just such a gift. I would not have wanted every day without school, but for one day, or part of a day, I could enjoy a taste of freedom.

Even with my heavy load, and with the cold wind cutting through me, I whistled as I made my way along the river trail. By the time I reached the heights above the river and walked among the shacks, the first drops of rain plopped onto the dry ground. The place appeared deserted except for a small colored boy who stared out from behind a window. I recognized him. He was the kid Tommikins had picked on the day Uncle Marsh had come home. I smiled and waved, but his expression remained one of suppressed anger, as if I were to blame for the bad weather that had driven him inside.

Lightning flashed and thunder broke so close that the electrical charge belted me like a fist to the head. I threw both arms around the pot to keep the lid on and the contents from spilling. Reaching the house, I kicked the door, and when it opened, the wind jerked it from Daniel's hand. I stepped inside, and Daniel leaned against the door, sliding a chair under the knob.

Deep shadows filled the interior. Sister Rose reclined in the bed, a quilt pulled up around her neck. Her skin was stretched tightly over her cheekbones, her eyes a glassy sheen.

Less than a year before the great influenza epidemic had carried off a dozen people in and around Twin Forks, and she reminded me of those who'd come down with the illness. For a while that winter, and following spring, the town council forbade people to gather in public places, shutting down the movie theater and the church and the school. Even Ernie's Bar closed until the epidemic passed. During that stretch I had seen four men carry old Mrs. Toddhaven on a stretcher from her house to the makeshift hospital on the edge of town. Compared to her, Sister Rose appeared downright healthy. Of course, Mrs. Toddhaven died the day after I saw her.

Sister Rose managed a smile. "Why, Davy, what brought you out in such weather?" She sounded more tired than sick.

I placed the pot on the table. "Aunt Esther sent chicken soup. She said she hoped you were feeling better."

"That's kind of Miss Esther." As if that little conversation were too much, she closed her eyes and appeared to fall asleep.

Outside the rain arrived in force, pounding the roof and north side of the house, and I glanced out a window. The structure next door was a blurred outline, and as I watched, two pieces of the tarpaper roof peeled away and disappeared. We remained dry and warm. The ceiling showed no leaks, and the old wood stove in the corner, alive with a few coals, put out enough heat so that I unbuttoned my coat.

"Come over by the fire." Reaching down, Daniel retrieved a log from the woodpile, opened the grate and stirred the coals. He dropped in the log, and it blazed up. He appeared thoughtful and even a bit morose.

"You're not thinking this is charity, are you?" I said, "Your mother has been kind to our family. This is my aunt repaying that kindness. That's not charity."

"I'm worried about Mama," he said. "I've never seen her take to bed in the middle of the day."

"What about her tonic? The one she gives Uncle Marsh?"

"It helps her rest, and that's good."

Thunder shook the house, and before it faded, I heard footsteps splashing outside. A moment later the knob rattled, and the chair propped against the door prevented the person from entering. Daniel stepped to the door, pulled the chair back, and threw it open. The wind swirled in the rain, and with it, Rachel.

Once more Daniel leaned into the door and stuffed the chair underneath the knob. Rachel stood next to him, pushing wet hair out of her eyes. She glanced first at the bed then at me, her expression one of mild surprise. "I came to see how Sister Rose was doing, and I got caught in the rain." She laughed, her white teeth flashing, her voice soft music.

Daniel helped her off with her wet coat. Her dress showed dark where the rain had seeped through at the neck, and her boots were caked in mud. Daniel led her to the stove, and she held out her hands to gather in the warmth. Dancing shadows played across her face, and she smelled of rain, and at that moment I could not remember a time since we'd met that she had looked more beautiful. Our eyes met and held until Daniel draped her coat over the table and said, "Davy brought chicken soup from Miss Esther."

"That's real nice of your aunt," she said. "And you, too, for coming all the way out here."

I blushed. Aunt Esther or Miss Pilgrim passed along such praises, and once in a while, Uncle Marsh might throw one my way, but never from a person my own age. I should have said something—thanked her—but frankly, I didn't know what to say.

Chilled, Rachel wrapped her arms around her chest. I slipped off my coat and held it out it to her. "Won't you be cold?" she asked.

"I've got a heavy wool shirt and an undershirt," I said. "I'm warm as can be."

She cast a furtive glance at Daniel, wondering, I suppose, what he would think. When he failed to react, she swung the coat around her shoulders.

Once more, lightning flashed followed by thunder, and rain washed over the ground in undulating waves, as fierce as I can ever remember. "Looks like you two are going to be here awhile," Daniel said.

"I'm fine," I said, which caused Daniel to raise an eyebrow.

Rachel stared at the fire as if it held the answer to an obscure riddle.

For the next hour, rain and wind beat the house as if trying to break in. Sister Rose woke once to ask for water, and Daniel filled a glass and lifted his mother's head enough for her to drink. Daniel pulled the blankets up around her chin. When he sat back with us, he said, "She's sweating now. The fever's broke. I got to keep her warm."

By four-thirty, the combination of black clouds and pouring rain brought on an early darkness. "I guess you two are spending the night," Daniel said. "Rachel can take my bed. You and me can sleep on the floor."

Later, Daniel placed the pot on the stove. Every five minutes or so, he removed the lid and stirred the soup with a long wooden spoon. Sister Rose awoke and sat up. "My, that smells good," she said, her voice a weak whisper.

She and Daniel owned two bowls, so she and Rachel ate first, then passed their spoons and bowls to Daniel and me. My aunt had loaded the pot with chicken, carrots, peas, and broth, and even after we finished, the pot remained half full.

After dinner, Sister Rose fell asleep. As the night grew colder, Rachel, Daniel and I huddled around the ancient pot-bellied stove. "It's going to be a long night," he said.

"It'll pass fast," I said and looked across at Rachel, whose eyes reflected the firelight. Once again I marveled at her beauty. No, marveled is the wrong word. I was stricken by her beauty. When I'd first met her, I put my attraction down to the exotic. She was colored, I white. Since then, I had come to realize that beauty had nothing to do with the color of one's skin. She was beautiful, and that was all there was to it. Yet there was more to her than that, a lot more.

She drew my coat tighter, and in doing so, her hand struck an object in my right pocket. Curious, she pulled out a slim volume that I had carried around for several days. She held it to the light so that she could read the spine. "William Shakespeare," she said and looked at me.

"An English playwright and poet," I said.

"I know who Shakespeare is." Daniel sounded irritated as if he thought that I'd talked down to them. Perhaps I had.

Rachel said, "Well, I don't know who he is. What's this book about, Davy?"

"Those are his sonnets, a type of poem. They're called sonnets because of the way they're structured."

"I've got no use for poetry." Daniel waved his hand as if to dismiss the subject.

"I thought that, too, at first." I took the book from Rachel. "Then Miss Pilgrim gave me this. She said these poems might be on the exams I'll take to get into college. Once I started reading them, hating them about as much as I ever hated anything, I discovered something I didn't expect."

"What was that?" Rachel asked.

I opened the book, flipping to a page that I had dog-eared. "I discovered that this Shakespeare fellow felt the same as me about a lot of things. I mean, well, he lived over four hundred years ago, yet he said things I'm feeling right now." I tapped the page. "Here, let me read this. Maybe you'll see."

Extending the book to catch the light, I began to read Sonnet 127. "'In the old age black was not counted fair, / Or if it were, it bore not beauty's name.'"

I read slowly, trying to accentuate the right words, and when I'd finished, I studied Rachel's face, anxious to see her reaction. She knotted her brow, and then shook her head. "I don't understand all the words. Once or twice it sounded like you were reading in a foreign language, but I think I understood some. Did this Shakespeare really say those things? Did he really feel that way?"

"He wrote the words, so yeah, I guess he felt that way." I passed the book back to Rachel. "You can borrow it, if you want. I've read it twice—every poem—and some I've gone over so many times that I've almost memorized them."

"Miss Pilgrim—" she began.

"Miss Pilgrim gave me the book. It's mine," I said. "Now I'm loaning it to you."

She flashed a grateful smile. "I'll read it. I promise. Every last poem, even if I don't understand them."

"Most I didn't understand the first time either," I said.

Daniel snorted. "How can you like what you don't understand?"

"I like you, Daniel," I said, "and I don't always understand you."

After everyone had gone to bed, I sat against the wall next to the stove, my knees drawn up, trying to keep warm. Rachel had given me back my coat before she climbed under the covers, but the pinewood floor embraced the cold. Outside the rain continued, pausing every now and then as if to gain more strength, and then began again with renewed fury.

Daniel fell asleep right away, his head propped on one

arm, his body curled into a fetal position, but around one or one-thirty he awoke and came to the stove where he shoved in another log. Closing the grate, he sat beside me. "Can't sleep?" he asked in a whisper.

I shook my head.

The log in the stove caught fire, and flames illuminated Rachel's face. I stared at her, all the time a pressure building in my chest that made it hard for me to breath. I wanted to cross the space that separated us and touch her cheek, her hair, her lips. I wanted to explain to her my hopes, my desires, my fears. I wanted her to whisper her secrets to me, I wanted her to hold me, I wanted her to want me. The more I thought of these things, the greater the pressure grew in my chest.

"There's no future in it, Davy," Daniel said.

His words awakened me from my reverie. "What?" I asked.

He spoke so low that I had trouble hearing. Or maybe I didn't want to hear. "There can't be anything between the two of you. You know that. There's nowhere it can go."

I started to tell him he was mistaken, that I didn't harbor those kinds of feelings, but he saw the truth, and any denial on my part would be meaningless. I retreated inward, saying nothing. Up to that point, I had fantasized that if I ever got the nerve to approach Rachel—and she liked me in the same way that I liked her—that we could find a way to be together. Now Daniel's words forced me to see myself for who I was, a deluded adolescent blinded by feelings of self-importance.

For the first time since we had known each other, Daniel laid a hand on my shoulder in an effort to comfort me. I lowered my head between my knees so that he couldn't see how close I was to tears.

15

*B*efore first light, and trying not to wake anyone, I pulled on my boots and left the house. Outside I discovered Boonesville quiet and empty, everyone still asleep. I set off toward home. I'd walked less than ten paces when Daniel caught up to me. He had left his coat behind, and when he spoke, a frosty cloud blurred his lips. "Are you mad about what I said last night?"

"What you said is the truth. I know that."

"You were leaving without saying goodbye."

"I've never been away from home all night. Uncle Marsh and Aunt Esther must be worried sick." I smiled even though I didn't feel like it. "If I don't get home soon, they're liable to send a posse looking for me."

That mollified him, and with a quick nod, he went back inside. As I descended the path from Boonesville, I walked into the face of a cold drizzle. When I reached the river trail, I discovered that overnight the Trinity had risen so that the current, most days so slow you could hardly tell it was moving, rushed by, carrying with it brush and small, uprooted trees. I found myself identifying with that old river that lacked the power to stop or change course.

I reached home past seven. I climbed the back stairs

and entered the kitchen where Aunt Esther stood at the stove cooking breakfast. Uncle Marsh sat at the table already on his second or third cup of coffee.

Aunt Esther paused long enough to offer me a cursory glance. "I figured you'd be dragging in about now; though another hour and we'd have come looking for you."

She scooped a bit of bacon grease in with the eggs and stirred with passion. Uncle Marsh pointed to the chair across from him. "Get any sleep?" he asked.

"Some."

The coffee pot sat on the table, and I poured myself a cupful. I blew on the steaming liquid, sipped it, and felt it collide with my empty stomach. A moment later, Aunt Esther laid before me a full plate of eggs and biscuits and gravy. I dug in, far more hungry that I thought. When I finished eating, I stood, intending to change for school, but with a nod, Uncle Marsh sent me back to my chair. As if he'd passed Aunt Esther a signal, she left the kitchen. "Tell me what's going on," he said.

"Nothing."

He laid the coffee cup in the same water ring where he always set it. "Your face says different."

I guess I could have protested further, but Uncle Marsh could see through me even when no one else could. And perhaps I needed to talk, needed someone to listen, so I told him about my feelings for Rachel and about Daniel's warning. He listened without speaking, without even changing his expression, but his eyes never left me. He leaned forward, placing his elbows on the table. "Sad thing to say, but in this kind of situation, feelings don't count for much."

"It's not fair."

"Never said it was." Standing, he pursed his lips as if looking for something else to say, some pearl of wisdom that would make me feel better. At last he said, "A man always has to make hard choices. That's the way life works. Knowing that don't make it any easier."

"Will it always be like this?"

"You mean the way people treat each other?" He shrugged. "When I was in France, color of skin didn't seem to matter as much to those folks. But a war was going on. I don't know how things are now. Still, it makes a fellow think that things could change."

They made me stay home from school. Aunt Esther said that she heard the influenza might be coming back, and I shouldn't take a chance on running myself down. Most of the morning I buried myself in my room, thinking I should lie down and sleep awhile. Instead, I dug in my book bag and pulled out *Don Quixote*. In the late afternoon, my eyes grew heavy, and I dosed off. The next thing I knew, Aunt Esther was shaking me. I opened my eyes to find the room dark. I had slept right into night.

"There's someone at the back door. Don't keep them waiting." My aunt held out my coat.

I shoved my feet into my boots, crusty with dried mud, and slipped on my coat. As I hurried through the house, I wondered who would call at this time of night. When I stepped out onto the landing, I thought my aunt mistaken, that no one was there, then dark figures emerged from the shadows on my right.

"Hello, Davy," Rachel said. Her grandfather stood behind her.

"You give the boy his book, and say what you have to say." Solomon went down the stairs, the wooden planks groaning under his boots.

Rachel held out the book of Shakespearean sonnets.

"I told you it was a loan. That you could keep it as long as you needed it," I said.

"I read it all, like I said I would."

I reached for the book, and our fingers touched. We clung to the book longer than necessary until she released her grip.

In the kitchen, Aunt Esther or Uncle Marsh lit a lamp, which cast its faint glow through the window, and Rachel became more than a shadow and a voice. Now I saw her face, her eyes, her hair. The light also reflected our frosty breaths, which merged like eager lovers.

"Daniel told me what he said to you." She dropped her eyes as if she couldn't bear to look at me. "He had no right to say those things. I know you don't feel that way."

I wanted to tell her sure, I felt that way, but I couldn't bring myself to do that. Daniel had made it clear and Uncle Marsh had reinforced the idea that together Rachel and I had no future. If I told her how I really felt, I might well be messing up my world as well as hers. "Even if I did, what could we do about it?" I said.

She lifted her eyes to study my face. "Most white boys think colored girls will do anything a white boy asks. Some do, I guess, but not anyone I know. You understand what I'm saying, don't you, Davy?"

My face burning, I said, "I only meant that there are no options, regardless of what we feel. Anyway I don't feel that way. Daniel was wrong."

Without another word, she hurried down the stairs. I wanted to call her back and tell her the truth, but that would have ruined everything. She joined her grandfather in the dark alley, and the two disappeared into the night.

16

For most of the week I debated whether or not I should return Saturday to the old Squires place to help Daniel. I feared I might run into Rachel. I believed we had said all that could be said, and yet I could not stop thinking about her. One evening, while Aunt Esther closed the store, I found Uncle Marsh alone at the kitchen table reading the newspaper, and I voiced my feelings. I told him, under the circumstances, I wasn't sure I could help Daniel any more.

He laid the paper flat against the table, smoothing out the wrinkles while he considered my plight. "Finish what you began, Davy."

I had not seen Daniel since I'd left his house that previous Monday. I supposed that he'd stayed home to care for Sister Rose. So Saturday morning I packed up my bag of tools and set off for the old Squires place. The sky remained leaden, mirroring my mood.

The moment I stepped outside, I spotted Zeb Cain pulling up in his wagon in front of Wiggins General Store. Using his good arm, he reined in the team, his two bays snorting heavy white clouds in the brisk morning air. His other arm remained suspended by a sling. Beside him sat

Orvie Blaylock, who cast a hard stare at me. I should have walked on, not said a word, but something wild and unpredictable made me cross the street so that I passed right by the wagon. "Good day to you, gentlemen," I said, placing a bit of emphasis on 'gentlemen.'

I continued on out of town where I picked up the river trail, all the time wondering what had gotten into me. Not content to let things alone, I had, to use the old expression, stirred the waters. Yet I had provoked no response, so I whistled a happy tune and thought well of myself. I had faced the demon and survived quite nicely—and I hadn't needed Jim Kennison to rescue me.

The ground had dried, and the Trinity rode lower. The banks showed where the once heavy current chewed away great chunks of earth and left the roots of trees exposed. Off in the woods a flock of pigeons took flight, and in the tall grass, male cicadas sang their shrill songs. An occasional cottontail sprang ahead on the trail before disappearing in a blur. Far ahead a pack of buzzards circled over a sandbar where an animal had crawled to die.

Leaving the river trail and passing the path to Boonesville, I came at last to the clearing and caught sight of the Squires place, discovering much to my surprise that in the intervening week, Daniel had begun the front porch and added steps. The building needed a coat of fresh paint, but other than that, most of the exterior work appeared completed.

The front door was closed, and I stepped up onto the porch, my weight testing the boards. I knocked. Inside I heard footsteps cross the room, and I feared that Rachel was inside; my heart raced. The door opened, and Daniel moved aside. I stepped inside and discovered that Daniel was the only occupant. A bitter feeling of disappointment rushed through me.

The interior was now filled with a dozen old school desks and a chalkboard nailed to one wall. The room smelled of paint, and the east wall glowed with a fresh, white sheen. "You've done a lot this week," I said.

Daniel closed the door, and the room grew warmer. "I stayed with mama until this morning. Solomon and Rachel did all this. They finished the steps and brought in these desks and the board. The only thing left is whitewashing the walls."

"All this came from Miss Pilgrim," I said.

"Hand-me-downs she kept in a storeroom," Daniel said. "It's better than nothing, which is what we had before."

"She could get in a lot of trouble for this," I said.

"Solomon did all the moving last night." Daniel walked across the room and picked up his brush, ready to resume painting. "Nobody saw him." He dipped the brush in the bucket, and then laid the brush to the wall, making long, even strokes. "I'm glad you came, Davy."

"No reason not to." I wanted to ask about Rachel, whether she would be coming by or not, but even the thought of her name hurt. Instead I said, "What do you want me to do?"

"Still a few loose floorboards. You might see to nailing them down."

For the next hour or so, I went around the room checking each board and pounding home those that were loose. Within minutes I worked up a sweat, and opened my coat. At noon we paused to eat. I laid my hammer on top of one of the desks, dug into my satchel, and pulled out sandwiches and water. We sat with our backs propped against a wall and ate.

The wind came up again, stirring the trees and brush, and the cold at last penetrated the thin walls to chill the unheated room. We buttoned our coats and pulled up our collars.

Because of the wind, neither Daniel nor I heard the boots on the stairs.

17

*T*hat morning after I left Twin Forks, the world began to fall apart. This is the way Jim, who pieced it all together, told me it happened:

Blaylock sat in the wagon box and watched me walk away. The horses stirred in their traces as if they feared his anger, and Cain pulled back on the reins trying to control them with his one good arm. With a snort, one of the horses reared, and the wagon jerked, throwing Cain off balance. The horses might have bolted, but Jim came from the store, his long legs covering the distance in two quick steps. He grabbed the bridle. "Whoa there, girl." His soft voice calmed the bay, and it settled.

Cain wrapped the reins around the brake and watched as Blaylock, showing surprising agility for a man with such a thick body, jumped to the ground. "You ought to learn how to control that team, Cain. Take a whip to 'em if you have to."

Jim stroked the nose of the bay one last time before releasing his hold on the bridle. "No need for a whip."

"They almost threw me out of the wagon." Blaylock growled as if issuing a challenge.

"Kind of hard trying to control a team with only one arm. Ain't that right, Mr. Cain?" Jim said.

"Damn near impossible," Cain said and climbed down from the wagon to stand beside his friend.

"Might have been better had you taken the team, Mr. Blaylock," Jim said.

The long scar across Blaylock's bald head wrinkled into an angry, thick worm. "Never handled a team."

Before Blaylock had gone off to prison, he had worked in and around town as a carpenter, doing occasional odd jobs. More often he'd worked for Ernie, moving kegs of beer from wagons into the saloon, or for old man Wiggins unpacking crates for the general store. Once in a great while the lumberyard to the north hired him for a day or two. Other times he mucked stables or cleaned sumps. Such jobs never called for the use of a wagon and team, and those who knew Blaylock would never have entrusted him with such. All too often he showed up for a job hung over and mean-tempered. He lost wages to colored people who took the jobs when employers fired him, and Blaylock resented every lost dollar. And he resented every person who had ever tried to order him around, and he resented Jim because Jim wore a badge. I think he would have loved to rile Jim into a fight, but at that moment, Mayor Lon Barron and his daughter Susanna stepped out of the general store.

"Good morning, gentlemen," Lon flashed his best mayoral smile.

Susanna slipped her hand through Jim's. "I did promise to walk you home, didn't I?" he said, and touched the brim of his Stetson. "So I'll say good day, Mr. Blaylock, Mister Cain."

With that, he led Susanna toward her house. A gust of wind swirled up the street creating a small twister that engulfed them before it subsided.

Blaylock spit. "I told you to keep that deputy away from me."

Lon Barron dropped his smile "I'll speak to him again."

"Maybe he's your boy, and maybe he ain't, but I got a feeling me and him are going to butt heads soon."

Lon blanched, fearful of any talk of violence in his town. "There's no need for that kind of talk."

"The deputy came out to help with the team," Cain said. "He didn't mean nothing by what he said."

Blaylock threw a piercing gaze at Cain that told his companion to shut up.

"You seem to be in a foul mood this morning, Mr. Blaylock," Lon said.

"It's Davy Stoneman's fault," Cain said. "He set out to rile us."

"Davy Stoneman?" Lon Barron reached inside his coat pocket and pulled out a cigar. He bit off one end and spit it into the street. "I'll see Marsh about this. You can rest assured on that. And I'll have a talk with the boy myself. Where is he? I'll have a talk with him right this minute."

"He's headed out to the old Squires place," Cain said. "He goes out there every Saturday."

Lon pulled a match from his vest pocket and struck the tip on the heel of his shoe. "The Squires place, huh?" He put the lit match to the cigar, puffing to keep it lit.

"Him and his nigger friend are building a church." Cain snickered and shook his head.

Lon flashed an indulgent smile. "A church?"

"That's what the nigger told Pap Caldwell and me." Cain narrowed his eyes. "You saying that ain't so?"

"Maybe they'll use it as a church—I don't know about that, " Lon said, "but I heard that Sister Rose has been wanting to set up a school for all the colored children."

Cain slammed a fist against the wheel of his wagon. "I'll be damned! If I'd known what those two was up to, me and Pap would have put a stop to it right then and there."

The mayor blew smoke at the sky. "Now I don't know for sure. Let's be clear on that point."

Blaylock scratched his dark stubble. "Exactly how do

you feel about such a school, Mr. Mayor?"

Lon removed the cigar and stared at the tip. "Educating coloreds breeds unrest. It gives them a false sense of possibilities."

"So if something happened to that school," said Blaylock, "say it burned down?"

"An accident like that would be fortuitous...as long as no one got hurt, mind you," Lon said. "We wouldn't want that."

"No, we ain't wanting that," said Blaylock.

Lon left the two men standing in front of Wiggins General Store, and the moment he was out of earshot, Blaylock said, "Let's me and you pay them boys a visit."

"We got supplies to buy." Cain reached into his pocket for the list. "No time to go traipsing all the way out there."

"Won't take long." Blaylock scratched his cheek, his fingernails making a grating noise against the stubble. "I told you I'd handle this Stoneman kid and his uncle. I owe you for putting me up."

Cain had the list in his hand. "The supplies—" he began

"—will keep," said Blaylock.

Meanwhile, much to Jim's chagrin, Susanna Baron, in no hurry, sauntered along, maintaining a tight grip on his arm. "Papa told you Mr. Blaylock doesn't mean anything, that if you don't pester him, everything will be fine."

Jim broke into a wide grin. "Do I look like the kind of man who would pester anybody?"

"The way he looked at you with that eye of his—" She leaned her cheek against his arm. "—the one that looks straight at you while the other looks away. He scares me. And you were talking to him like it didn't mean anything, like he was a regular person and not some...some—"

"—ex-convict," Jim said, finishing her thought.

She broke away, forcing Jim to face her. "Daddy says Mr. Blaylock got thrown in jail because the judge was a Red trying to overthrow the social order."

"Mister Blaylock got thrown in jail because he killed a couple of folks."

"Coloreds," said Susanna.

Jim removed his Stetson, running his hand along the inside sweat band, but the silk was dry to the touch. The wind stirred his blonde hair. "He killed two people."

"Papa said Mister Blaylock was only defending himself."

He took her by the arm. "I need to get you home."

"I don't want you talking to Orvie Blaylock," Susanna said. "You hear me, Jim Kennison. I don't want you talking to him."

"I can't pick and choose who I need to talk to."

"He's none of your business." A note of desperation crept into her voice.

"He is as long as I wear this badge."

"But he's dangerous. Even I can see that, regardless of what Papa says."

He glanced over his shoulder and saw Cain's wagon heading toward the river trail. He guided Susana into her yard and up to the front door. "I'll see you this evening, along about supper time," he said.

He waited until she was inside and then hurried after the wagon.

18

The door burst open, the wood frame splintering in a dozen places. Startled, neither Daniel nor I moved; we both froze against the wall. Across from us stood Orvie Blaylock, and behind him Zeb Cain cradling a shotgun under his good arm, a knife in a frayed scabbard attached to his belt.

Hands on hips, Blaylock looked around the room. "See those desks and that chalkboard. Looks like a schoolroom to me."

Daniel pushed himself to his feet, and I stood, too, telling myself to calm down and not let these two see my fear. "You got no right to come busting into our house." I infused my voice with a sense of righteous anger.

"Our house?" Blaylock mimicked my tone. "You hear that? *Our house...*"

Cain snickered. "Sounds like these boys are in love."

I tensed, my fear forgotten. "You're a real sonofabitch, Cain," I said.

"No Davy—"

But Daniel's warning came too late. In three quick steps, Blaylock was upon me, swinging for my face. I flung up one arm in defense. Even so, the blow knocked me against the wall. Blaylock reached out to grab my coat, and I threw a wild uppercut that bounced off his chin, inflicting little damage, but it surprised him. He released his grip, his guard dropped, and I shot a right that caught him above the eye, the thin skin erupting in a shower of blood. Enraged, he renewed his attack, his huge fists pounding my head and neck and shoulders. Covering up, I went down on one knee, and he kicked me in the ribs, sending me sprawling onto my back. He was over me then, his boot diving for my face. The heel scraped my cheek, the skin ripping like wet newspaper. I covered my head, and the solid toe of his boot slammed into my ribs, making me gasp. I dropped my arms to protect my middle.

Blaylock raised his boot, intent on driving the heel straight into my face, but before he could deliver the blow, Daniel launched himself at the ex-convict, the charge sending both flying into a pile of desks that tumbled about in a cascade of cracking wood. I rolled over onto my side and tried to get to my feet, but stunned by the ferocity of Blaylock's attack, I could only watch.

At first I saw only arms and legs entangled with the desks. Then both men sprang to their feet, and I saw the open knife in Blaylock's hand. Daniel jumped left trying to avoid the thrust, but Blaylock was faster than he looked. The blade buried itself into Daniel's side.

Then the hammer came up, my hammer, the very one I had brought that morning, clutched in Daniel's hand, the broad side cracking against Blaylock's skull. Daniel stepped back, giving himself room for a wider swing. This time the hammer came in an arc, slamming onto the top of Blaylock's bald head and spraying blood in all directions. Without a sound, Blaylock collapsed like a puppet whose strings had broken.

Cain shifted his grip on the shotgun, struggling to draw back the hammer, but with one arm in a sling, he had trouble lifting the weapon that swayed first right, then left.

I put my arms under me and tried to get to my feet, but the pain in my side drove me back to the floor gasping in pain, and all I could do was watch as the shotgun swung toward Daniel.

Footsteps pounded on the porch, and Jim burst through the open door. I don't think Cain heard him because he never took his eyes off Daniel, and as he jerked the trigger, Jim came under the gun and forced it up. The shotgun exploded, rocking the interior of the schoolhouse like it was an earthquake, and parts of the ceiling rained down and swirled dust and debris round us.

Cain, who was as tall as Jim and wider, fought to control the gun, but with only one good arm, he lacked strength and balance. Jim wrestled it away with ease. Cain took a step back and threw a wild roundhouse left that glanced off the side of Jim's head and sent his Stetson flying halfway across the room. Cain drew back for another swing, and Jim drove the stock of the shotgun into his gut. Cain doubled over and dropped to his knees.

Jim stood over Cain, his face red, his hands gripping the shotgun. In the year that I had known Jim, I had never seen him angry, not once. Despite the fact that he was a deputy sheriff, he was the easiest going guy I knew, but at that moment, his anger was ready to boil over. He shifted the shotgun, and I thought he was about to drive the stock into the back of Cain's neck. Instead, he broke open the gun with an angry snap and pulled out the shells, slipping them in his pocket.

Cain shifted his weight and tried to get to his feet, but the blow had taken too much out of him. With a groan, he fell back to a sitting position, gripping his belly as if to keep his guts from falling out.

Jim tossed the shotgun out the door. It clanged once against the edge of the porch and bounced out of sight. He cast a last glance at Cain before he crossed the room, kneeled beside Blaylock, and felt for a pulse. By that time, I managed to grasp a chair, and using it for leverage, pulled myself to my feet. "Is he dead?" I asked, although I already guessed the answer.

"They don't get any deader," Jim said.

He stood, stepped around the fallen desks and found Daniel, the knife buried in his side. Daniel let the hammer slip from his grip and made a weak effort to pull the blade free, but Jim leaned down and stayed his hand. "Leave it be. You pull it out, and you're liable to bleed to death." Jim motioned for me to give him a hand. "We need to get him to town."

"He can't walk far with that knife in him," I said.

"Mister Cain left his wagon and team where the river trail ends. I passed it on the way here. Between the two of us, we can carry the boy that far." Jim hoisted Daniel to his feet, and I took the other arm. Daniel grunted with pain, and blood seeped down the front of his overalls. "Two hundred yards at most; think you can make it?" Jim asked.

Daniel cast a last glance at the dead man. "I got him, Davy. I surely did." He spoke barely above a whisper, but Jim heard him as well as I did, and his brow wrinkled, his eyes narrowed. Looking at me, he shook his head.

Cain remained on the floor, his face white, his mouth pinched, his one hand over his belly. "You takin' the nigger and not me? What about me?"

Jim didn't bother to look at Cain. "I'm not putting you and this boy in the same wagon. You stay here with your friend. I'll be back for both of you in a while."

We found the wagon and team where Jim said it was, and I threw down the gate, climbed onto the bed, and helped Daniel to lie down. I spotted a couple of horse blankets in one corner, and I draped them around Daniel, careful not to let them come into contact with the knife. I looked into his eyes, the whites now gone gray, the pupils dilated. "I'm scared, Davy." His voice was weak and unsteady.

With my back against the wagon, I held him, hoping I could absorb some of the blows of the road. "You'll be fine," I said.

Jim jumped into the box and unwrapped the reins from the brake. "We can't go too fast. We don't want to open that wound more than it already is. You understand, don't you, boy?"

Daniel closed his eyes and pressed his lips together. Jim flipped the reins, and the pair of bays stepped off. For the next half hour, Jim guided them around potholes and ruts as best he could while trying to avoid the brush and trees that closed in. The wagon wheels dipped and teetered, the wagon rocking side to side with each jolt. Daniel gritted his teeth to fight the pain. I glanced down at the knife in his side, praying that the wound didn't widen, that the bleeding would stop. Already the whole lower half of his overalls was soaked in blood.

So concerned for Daniel, I forgot my own pains, and we were halfway to town before I felt the sting in my left cheek. When I touched my face, I brought away blood on the tips of my fingers. In addition, each breath brought a sharp pain, and I figured I had at least one cracked rib. Other pains radiated around my head and shoulders, but nothing serious. I had gotten off lucky, all because Daniel risked himself to save me. Now he lay in my arms, his life seeping out in red.

When we reached town, Jim flicked the reins and the horses broke into a slow trot, their hooves kicking up dust that trailed behind us. We passed our store, and I saw both Uncle Marsh and Aunt Esther through the plate glass window. I wanted to call out, but what help could they have given us? Daniel appeared in a stupor so deep that when I spoke his name, he failed to respond. I held him tighter.

On the far edge of town, we pulled up to Dr. Gibbs' house. Tossing the reins around the brake, Jim leapt from the wagon and dashed inside. Moments later he came back with Doc Gibbs. Even before he reached the wagon, I smelled the whiskey on the doctor's breath. Rumors floated around town about his imbibing, but no one ever claimed to have seen him downright drunk. His drinking had started the previous year after the Spanish Influenza carried off his wife. Since then, his hair had turned white, and he now walked with a stoop.

When he pulled up to the tailgate and saw me holding Daniel, he shook his head. "If I saw to every colored boy who got in a knife fight, I'd have no time for anything else." He waved us away. "Take him to his mother. I hear she has all sorts of cures. Let her patch him up." He started back up the walk.

"Orvie Blaylock did this to Daniel!" I shouted at the retreating form, and Doc Gibbs stopped and looked back. "Daniel didn't have a knife. We were fixing up the old Squires place, and Zeb Cain and Orvie Blaylock showed up. They started it."

The doctor studied my battered face. "You're a little rough for wear yourself, boy. Orvie Blaylock do that, too?" Without waiting for a reply, he said, "Yeah, that's something that sonofabitch would do."

"Will you help Daniel?" I asked. "Please. He's going to die if you don't."

Jim said, "He's right, Doc. The boy will die if we have to take him all the way back to Boonesville."

Dr. Gibbs stroked his chin as he debated the problem. "Who's going to pay if I fix him up? The county going to pay?" Jim shrugged, and Doctor Gibbs said, "Yeah, that's what I thought."

"I'll get the money," I said. "I'll work it off. I promise."

The old man pursed his lips and shook his head. "Hell, boy, you're too stove up to walk five feet."

"When I'm better..." I gasped, the pain in my side cutting off my words.

"I'll pay," said a deep, resonant voice, and there stood Uncle Marsh. He had seen us pass and followed the wagon up the street.

Doc Gibbs raised an eyebrow. "Hard cash or barter?

Let me tell you straight off, Marsh, I don't need no clothes."

"Cash. Now get the boy inside and patch him up." Uncle Marsh spoke with a tone that said he would brook neither insolence nor procrastination.

"Bring him in," said Doc Gibbs.

Jim grabbed Daniel's legs. I slid forward, then doubled over. Uncle Marsh moved to help me, but I shook my head. "I'll be all right. Let me catch my breath."

Uncle Marsh and Jim carried Daniel into the house. I managed to inch my way to the lip of the wagon bed where I lowered myself to the ground. Pressing my hands into my side, I stumbled to the porch and through the front door, entering as Jim and Uncle Marsh came out of Doc Gibbs' office. Uncle Marsh rushed over and helped me to a chair. He kneeled so that he faced me on my level. "What happened, son?"

I explained as best I could. I told him I didn't know what would have happened if Jim hadn't arrived when he did, and Jim, the brim of his Stetson rolled in his hands, said, "If I'd gotten a sooner start—"

"You knew this was going to happen?" Uncle Marsh stood, facing Jim.

"I had a feeling those boys were up to no good, but I give you my word, I didn't have any idea where they was headed. Even when I stumbled on Mr. Cain's wagon, I didn't know. I had a suspicion they was up to no good. I followed after them as soon as I could."

Jim pushed at his golden hair and flopped the Stetson onto his head. "Maybe I should go see to Mr. Cain. He seemed in a bit of pain when we left."

"I'll go with you," Uncle Marsh said, and the hard set of his jaw told both Jim and me what he had in mind.

"Best you stay right here, Mr. Langston. See to it that Davy and that boy in there get what they need." With that, he left us in the waiting room.

For the next hour, Uncle Marsh sat with me. At last

Doctor Gibbs, smelling of ether and carbolic acid, came from his office wiping his hands on a towel. Through the open door, I could see Daniel on a table covered by blankets.

Uncle Marsh said, "Well?"

"The knife was buried mostly in flesh and muscle here." Dr. Gibbs tapped his left side. "As far as I can tell, no vital organs were damaged. I stopped the bleeding, cleaned the wound, and stitched him up."

"He looks bad," I said,

"Colored boys have strong constitutions. They survive what'll kill an ordinary white man." He must have seen my reaction, and he said, "Documented fact. Medical journals all say the same thing."

"See to Davy," said Uncle Marsh.

I sat on a chair next to Daniel, whose heavy breathing filled the confines of that small room. Doctor Gibbs cleaned the deep gouge in my cheek and placed a heavy bandage across it, instructing Uncle Marsh to change the dressing at least once a day. He told me to remove my coat and shirt, but when I tried to lift my arms, the pain bent me double. With the aid of Uncle Marsh, I undressed, and bare-chested, watched as Dr. Gibbs wrapped my ribs so tightly that I thought he would crush the breath out of me. "You're going to be in some pain, boy." From his desk he produced a bottle of laudanum and passed it to Uncle Marsh. "This will help."

Uncle Marsh stared at the label. "I knew men in the trenches who couldn't live without this stuff."

"Yeah, I hear that can happen. Give the boy a tablespoon every couple of hours. Ease off in a day or so. No more by the end of the week."

Uncle Marsh stuffed the bottle into his pocket and leaned over to help me out of the chair.

"Hang on there." Doctor Gibbs held out a hand to stop us. "You said you'd pay me...in hard cash. You owe me—" He glanced at Daniel, then at me. "—five dollars.

That includes the laudanum."

Uncle Marsh pulled out a couple of bills and some change, counting it out and dropping it in a heap on the doctor's desk. He slipped his arm around my waist and helped me to my feet.

"You ain't leaving this colored boy here, are you?" Dr. Gibbs said.

"You let me know when he's awake, and we'll move him to our place," said Uncle Marsh.

"Your place?" The suggestion that Daniel would find refuge with us shocked the doctor, but when he looked into Uncle Marsh's steely eyes, he knew better than to argue. "If that's what you want," he said.

The word must have spread around town, for when Uncle Marsh and I stepped outside, we discovered the street was full of people standing in front of their houses or stores, all eyes on us. We walked slowly, every step sending a jolt of pain through my side. A few people greeted us with nods, but otherwise they stared in silence.

Chewing on a dead cigar, Mayor Lon Barron stood in front of the bank, his face dark with anger. He watched as Jim guided the wagon down the street and passed us on the way to Doc Gibbs' place. Zeb Cain sat beside him, bent at the waist and still holding his belly. The dead man's boots stuck out from under a dark blanket, jumping each time the wagon struck a rut.

Uncle Marsh stopped, his eyes burning into Cain, who, so caught up in his own problems, never saw us. I think Uncle Marsh intended to issue a challenge, but I laid a hand on his arm. "Jim gave him what was coming to him."

He focused those intense blue eyes on me in a long look of appraisal. "You're a good boy, Davy," he said, and added, "though after today, I don't guess I can call you a boy. More's the pity for that."

19

*D*oc Gibbs proved to be correct about the pain. For the rest of the day, it grew until each breath stabbed me so fiercely that I feared taking the next. I put off the laudanum, trying to make it to bedtime, and in an effort to anesthetize myself, I buried my nose in a Zane Grey novel.

Aunt Esther kept looking in on me, and before dark, brought Uncle Marsh with her. "You're white as snow." She put her hand to my forehead to judge if I had a fever.

"I'm hurtin' some," I said, and even those few words sent lightning through my ribs.

Uncle Marsh held out the bottle of laudanum. Aunt Easter measured a spoonful and fed it to me. I put up no argument. The drug tasted bitter, but ten minutes later the pain began to ease, and my breathing settled into a more normal rhythm. I found myself better able to concentrate on the book, and when Aunt Esther called me to the table, I managed to eat most of my food.

I waited until all had finished eating before I asked, "What about Daniel?"

Uncle Marsh wiped his mouth with the napkin and laid it aside. "Haven't heard a word. I'll walk over to Doc

Gibbs' and see how he's doing."

"What about his mama?" I asked. In all my pain and confusion, I had forgotten about Sister Rose.

Aunt Esther, washing plates in the dishpan, said, "LeRoy was in town, and I sent him to fetch Sister Rose."

LeRoy had been the first to greet Aunt Esther and me that time we had gone to Boonesville to see Sister Rose, but mostly I knew him as a patron of Ernie's who hung around the back room reserved for coloreds.

Uncle Marsh said, "LeRoy likes the sauce a little too much."

"He appeared to be sober when I saw him," Aunt Esther said. "He headed straight out of town."

"And I suppose you kept an eye on him to make sure." Uncle Marsh winked at me.

"All the way to the river trail." Aunt Esther wiped a plate, set it on the stack, and faced us. "Just what are you saying, Marsh Langston? You saying I'm a busybody?"

Uncle Marsh smiled. "Well, you always seem to know what's happening."

She laid a hand on his shoulder, her wet fingertips leaving damp spots on his shirt. "A person has to keep abreast of things, you know."

He reached up, his hand caressing hers. They remained that way, neither wanting to disturb the moment, each content to remain close to the other, both staring across the room at nothing in particular. They seldom displayed such affection in front of me, so I kept my mouth shut, not wanting to disturb the moment.

The scene ended with the sound of feet on the stairs followed by a knock on the door. Without thinking, I started out of my chair, and a sharp pain stabbed my side. I gasped, and Aunt Esther waved me back and went herself. As she swung open the door, a blast of cold air entered the room. Sister Rose stood on the landing wrapped in her heavy coat. "They've arrested my boy," she said. "Jim Kennison came right into the doctor's house and took

Daniel away. I tried to see him, but they wouldn't let me. The mayor told me Daniel's been charged."

"Charged?" said Uncle Marsh. "Charged for what?"

"Murder," she said.

20

*A*ccording to Jim, this is the way it happened:

All the way up the river trail and into town, Jim listened to the sounds of the wagon, a litany of protesting wood and metal. The racket did little to improve his dour mood, and his only consolation was that Cain, who sat next to him, kept to himself.

Jim felt the weight of guilt. If he had put a stop to it that day in Ernie's Bar when Zeb Cain had slapped me, then maybe none of this would have happened. Jim could have blamed Lon Barron—after all, it was he who had kept Jim in his seat while Cain bullied me—but Jim refused to allow himself an easy excuse. He was the deputy sheriff, and it was he who should have acted.

He drove the wagon to the storehouse of the Dallas Metropolitan Ice Company. Often, when people passed on, the city placed the bodies there to keep until burial. Using the fireman's carry, he hauled Orvie Blaylock inside where he laid him in a far corner, arranging a blanket to cover the face and torso. Here the body would keep until either a family member or the town got around to burying him.

When he came out, Cain and the wagon were gone. Instead, Mayor Lon Barron stood chewing on an unlit cigar. Lon asked, "Is it true what Cain said? That Sister Rose's boy killed Orvie Blaylock?"

"Don't rightly know, Mr. Mayor. I got there after it was all said and done."

Lon Barron shifted the unlit cigar from one side of his mouth to the other. He took a match from his vest pocket and struck it on the bottom of his shoe. Applying flame to weed, he puffed until the tip glowed. Tossing the match aside, he said, "Arrest the colored boy. I'll get Cain to fill out the complaint later."

"What charge?" Jim asked.

"Murder, of course."

Jim hooked his thumbs in his belt and regarded the mayor with a skeptical eye. "Looks to me more like the boy was defending himself. He's the one that got belly stuck."

"And Orvie Blaylock's dead. You ain't the jury here, Jim. Now do what I tell you. That's an order, not a suggestion."

Lon walked away, his small feet kicking up a whirlwind of dust that swirled into Jim's face.

PART III
TRIAL BY FURY

21

"I'm going to see about this." Uncle Marsh reached for his coat on the back of the chair.

I stood, gritting my teeth to fight back the pain. Aunt Esther reached across the table and grabbed my hand. "Marsh can handle this without your help."

I slipped one arm through my coat but I couldn't reach around to get the other sleeve. "See what I'm telling you," Aunt Esther said. "You're in no shape to go anywhere."

"I don't need a coat," I said.

Rather than put up more arguments, Aunt Esther came around the table and held the coat for me. "You get back here as quick as you can. You need to be in bed."

I followed Uncle Marsh out the back door and down the stairs, every step bringing a jolt that reminded me of Blaylock's boot pounding my ribs. As we reached the bottom, Uncle Marsh stopped short, and I almost ran up his back. "Who's there?" he said.

From underneath the landing emerged two dark figures, specters in the night, and for a moment, I felt a touch of fear. Then my eyes adjusted. "Rachel?" I said

Her grandfather stood behind her, one hand on each of

her shoulders. He said, "We couldn't let Sister Rose come alone."

"Why didn't you come upstairs with her?" asked Uncle Marsh.

"We don't mean to disturb you," Solomon said.

"I'd like for the two of you to go sit with Sister Rose and my wife until Davy and I get back." Before Solomon had a chance to object, Uncle Marsh added, "The women need the company. You'd be doing me a great favor."

Solomon nodded, and he and Rachel passed so close that I could see her dark eyes, caught in the light from our kitchen window. I smelled her, too, a mixture of roses and river bottom.

Uncle Marsh held to a slow pace in deference to my injuries, but still my feet dragged in the dust, and by the time we reached the jail, I was breathing hard. We pushed through the door as wind whipped down the street.

Jim stood next to the potbellied stove warming his backside. I suspect he had seen us through the front window as we approached, and his expression was grim. I closed the door, shutting out the cold wind, but before either Uncle Marsh or I spoke, Jim said, "I'm sorry, Mr. Langston. There was nothing I could do." Unable to look Uncle Marsh in the eye, he found solace by pushing at his glasses and staring at the floor. "The mayor convinced Zeb Cain to file charges. I was only doing my job."

"You were there. Why didn't you speak up?" A note of rising anger infected my uncle's voice.

"I didn't get there 'til it was all over. I didn't see a thing."

"You got Davy's word," Uncle Marsh said.

"And I got a statement from Mister Cain that goes against Davy's version."

"Zeb Cain." My uncle spit out the name like he was saying something dirty. "You taking his word over Davy's?"

"No sir. I'm not taking nobody's word. I'm only doing

what I was told to do."

I sensed Uncle Marsh's frustration—it mirrored my own—and I heard it in his voice. "Why the hell did you keep Sister Rose from her son?"

Jim's mouth twitched like a bee had stung him, and I thought he was going to defend his position. Maybe I even thought he was going to call us 'nigger lovers' or some such nonsense—certainly Zeb Cain or Lon Barron would have—but truth be told, I had never once heard Jim use the word 'nigger.' And frankly, except for that time in the bar when he and Daniel had had their run-in, I can't remember any time he tried to bully a colored person. Even then, he had only called Daniel 'boy,' and white people applied that term to every black man no matter his age. Did Jim harbor such feelings as Lon Barron and the rest of the town? I can't say for sure, but the only white people I knew who seemed untainted by such prejudices were Uncle Marsh and Aunt Esther. Even I, as I had come to discover, was infected by it. After all, we lived in Texas, where you probably couldn't find a hundred white people that felt the same as Uncle Marsh and Aunt Esther.

Whatever Jim felt, he showed more gumption than I thought possible. He lifted his eyes from the floor and looked Uncle Marsh squarely in the eye. "It was wrong of me to tell Sister Rose she couldn't see her son. You send her right over. She can see him any time she wants."

Jim's surrender took us by surprise. I think Uncle Marsh and I both figured he would follow Mayor Barron's orders to the letter, even on this point. Uncle Marsh said, "In that case, I'll fetch Sister Rose."

"Can I see Daniel?" I asked.

Jim waved me toward the solid oak door that led to the cells in back.

"Daniel," I called.

His reply was weak and throaty. "Davy?"

He sat on the lower bunk, encased in shadows and little more than a shadow himself. He leaned into the light coming from the office. He had removed his bloody shirt and thrown a blanket around his shoulders to keep off the chill. The white bandage that circled his waist was in stark contrast to his dark skin. The area around his eyes crinkled like that of an old man, and his eyes were half closed like he had gone a couple of days without sleep. Even the skin on his face sagged as if all his muscles had gone flaccid.

I started to ask him how he was before I realized the stupidity of such a question. Instead I said, "They've got no right to do this to you."

He raised his lids, and the whites of his eyes were gray. "They mean to do me in, Davy."

"I'll tell them what happened. I'll make them believe." My words were those of a green and foolish kid, but I wanted to shore up Daniel's courage—and perhaps my own. The attempt proved fruitless. He knew as well as I the lack of power we shared. He was a Negro and I an orphan. Who would listen to me defending him?

His fingers touched the bandage above the wound where red seeped through. "I killed a white man," he said, and for him, that summed it up.

I said, "Uncle Marsh has gone for your mama. He persuaded Jim to let her see you."

"Mama?" Daniel drew the blanket tighter, his expression listless, his shoulders slumped.

I could find no words of comfort, and I said, "I'll come by tomorrow and see how you're doing."

He failed to answer, and I left him huddled in the dark, alone and afraid, probably more afraid than he had ever been in his life. As I stepped into the office, the front door opened and Sister Rose entered followed by Rachel.

Jim shook his head. "That girl can't go in there. I didn't agree to that."

I held open the door to the cells. Once Sister Rose passed, her face lined with worry, I closed it to allow mother and son some privacy. Jim didn't object.

"You and the girl better wait outside." Jim shuffled

through papers pretending to search for something so that he wouldn't have to look at us.

I crossed the room, took Rachel by the arm and led her outside. The light from the windows cast a wide arc, and although the street appeared empty, I guided her around the corner of the building where we found protection from the cold wind as well as prying eyes.

"I'm sorry you couldn't see Daniel," I said.

"I came to keep Sister Rose company."

We stood so close that when she spoke, her breath warmed my face. She reached up and touched the bandage, her fingers tracing the path from my ear almost to my mouth. "Does it hurt?"

"Other things hurt more," I said.

I could no longer help myself, and I reached out to caress her cheek. The touch of her flesh sent a shock wave through my whole body, and the muscles in my belly shook like an earthquake. When I spoke, my voice trembled. "I lied," I said.

I didn't need to explain. She knew what I was talking about. I leaned forward, she rose on her toes, and we kissed.

This was no kiss of mythical proportions, the kind you read about in stories of romance and great deeds. As a matter of plain fact, it was a bit awkward. We came at each other a little too fast. Our teeth clicked, and we never figured out what to do with our hands.

Ten seconds, I figure—ten seconds or less, and then we broke apart, no longer even touching. "We can't," she whispered. "You said so yourself."

"That doesn't keep me from thinking about you all the time," I said.

22

Sister Rose came again the next morning, a Sunday, to bring Daniel a fresh set of clothes. I found her with Aunt Esther and Uncle Marsh sitting at the kitchen table sharing toast and coffee. The moment I entered, Sister Rose laid the coffee cup aside, stood and gathered up a bundle of clothes from the floor.

With nothing more than a sip of coffee in my belly, I shuffled down the back stairs after her. The laudanum from the previous night had worn off, and I had grown stiff in my chest and side. The wind had faded to a slight breeze, still chilling to the bone, and I hugged my jacket to my chest, my hands stuck deep inside my pockets.

As we crossed the street heading toward the jail, Lon Barron, Susanna and Tommikins approached from the opposite direction dressed in their Sunday-go-to-meeting clothes. I knew the moment I spotted them that this was trouble. I almost suggested to Sister Rose that we come back later, but the determined set of her jaw said nothing would deter her.

We reached the jail ten paces ahead of the mayor, and I threw open the door for Sister Rose. Jim was slumped forward on his desk, his head in his arms, and with our entrance, he sat up straight and peered at us with eyes still full of sleep. His hair was tousled, his shirt wrinkled. "Lon Barron's coming," I said.

He stood and ran his fingers through his hair and pressed his palms over the front of his shirt. Lon paused at the front door and told Susanna and Tommikins to wait outside, and that he would be only a minute. He stomped into the office, his round cheeks glowing with anger, and slammed the door. He glared at Sister Rose. "What's she doing here?"

"I came to bring my boy fresh clothes." Sister Rose clutched the bundle to her chest as if she thought the mayor might rip it out of her hands.

"Leave them with the deputy. Now you and this boy get out of here."

"I want to see my son," Sister Rose said.

"I told her she could see the boy," Jim said.

The mayor raised a speculative eyebrow and stared at Jim for a good long while. "That's not wise, Jim. Feelings are running high."

Jim removed his wire-rimmed spectacles, pulled a handkerchief from his pocket, and wiped the lenses. "I gave my word."

"That boy killed a white man." Lon put emphasis on the word 'white'.

At this point I could no longer hold my tongue. "Orvie Blaylock was the one that pulled a knife. Daniel was only protecting himself."

The mayor shifted his eyes to me. "Yeah...I expected you to say something like that."

"You think I'm lying?" I asked.

"Sure, you'd lie to save your nigger friend, though why you'd go against your own kind, I can't figure. You got nigger blood in you that nobody knows about?"

I started to call him a bastard—I even considered taking a swing at him—but I recalled my aunt's caution.

Why was I angry? That he had suggested I might have colored blood in my veins? Why should that make me angry? I willed myself to remain calm, and I said, "You believe what you want."

He wanted to anger me, but my calm confused him. He whirled on Jim. "You didn't give your word to this kid, did you?" When Jim shook his head, the mayor said, "Then get him out of here. Now!"

"Best you step outside, Davy," Jim said.

Sister Rose cast pleading eyes in my direction. I think she feared if I wasn't there, the mayor would keep her from seeing Daniel, but Jim said, "You go see your boy now, Ma'am."

With the door shut, I started back home, but the front window was cracked a couple of inches so that I had no trouble hearing their words, and I could see the two men as clearly as if I were in the room with them. Jim stood behind his desk, the mayor on the other side pointing an accusing finger. "You best remember your place, Jim." Mayor Barron removed a cigar from his breast pocket, bit off the end, and spit it on the floor. He stuffed the stogie into his mouth but didn't bother to light it. "I told you not to let the old woman in here, but you went against me. Now why would you do that?" With each word, his cigar bobbled like a cork on water.

"She's a mother needing to see her son," Jim said. "It didn't seem right to keep the two apart."

Lon took a deep breath and expelled it, his features relaxing, his anger fading. "I warned you once about that streak of kindness. In times like these, that ain't such a good thing, not for a man who wants to move up in the world." He paused, waiting for his words to take effect. "You do want to move up in the world, don't you?" Jim nodded, and the mayor said, "Let me hear you say it."

"Yessir, I want to move up," Jim said.

Lon reached into his vest pocket, drew out a match, and struck it against the desk top, leaving a long scar. He applied the flame as he rotated the cigar and puffed until the tip glowed red. He shook out the match and tossed it onto the floor. Taking the cigar from his mouth, he blew smoke at the ceiling. "I'll smooth this over with folks. Tell people you're being fair, so no one can point fingers later. They'll buy that. So let the old woman see the boy a couple of times a week. Give her ten minutes or so and then send her on her way. Don't let nobody else in—especially Davy Stoneman."

"What about Dr. Gibbs? Blaylock gave the boy a pretty nasty wound."

"Yeah, we want to keep that boy healthy for the trial." Lon Barron laughed, his anger completely gone now. "After we find him guilty—and we will find him guilty, have no doubt on that point—we'll ship him off to Huntsville. There they'll strap him in that newfangled electric chair and fry him up real nice." He nodded again, pleased with himself. "Yes sir, we'll make sure none of them Northern newspapers can disparage us over the way we treat our colored folk." He puffed on the cigar until a white cloud surrounded his head like river bottom fog.

I was so furious that, if I'd had a shotgun, I might have gone right back in the office and filled Lon Barron's backside with birdshot. But I didn't have a gun, and even if I had, such action would not have helped Daniel.

Just then Susana and Tommikins came out of Wiggins's General Store. The moment she saw me, she marched right up to me and said, "What's gotten into you, Davy Stoneman?"

I faced her and her brother. Susana, holding a parasol to shade her face, wore an ankle-high dress with an open neck line, exposing a hollow of white skin. The dress was heavy on soft browns and clung to her in a way that outlined every curve. She wore white gloves, and a small hat pinned to her thick, blonde hair.

Tommikins stood behind his sister, her petite frame acting a shield between us. "Looks like you got your comeuppance." He stuck his thumbs in his belt trying to appear tough, and he screwed up his mouth like a snarling dog. The fact that he was dressed in his Sunday finery, long pants and all, did nothing to mitigate his ugly face, misshapen because he needed to show how tough he was. However I knew, as probably most of the town knew by now, he was a dog without much of a bite.

I took a step toward him, and his snarl vanished. "Go on, now," I said.

He tried to stare me down, but his weak little eyes flinched, and when I took another step, he spun away, his heavy boots making solid thumps against the boardwalk. "Yessir, you got your comeuppance," he shouted. With that, he increased his pace to a fast walk. He had no idea how stiff and sore I was from Orvie Blaylock's beating or he wouldn't have feared me one bit.

Susanna stomped her foot to draw my attention back to her. "Gallivanting around with that colored boy—and then standing up for him after what he's done."

"After what he's done?"

"My daddy said—"

"Your daddy wasn't there," I said.

"And what are you going to tell people?" she asked.

"The truth. Would you have me say anything different?"

Her eyes narrowed. "Mr. Cain said they paid you a friendly visit, and you started a fight for no reason."

"If you know Mr. Cain, then you know he didn't drop by for a friendly visit. And as for Orvie Blaylock—" I touched the bandage on my face. "He might've killed me if Daniel hadn't stopped him. No, Mr. Cain is a damned liar."

She fought to hold to her father's version, but the shadow of doubt crossed her face. "Good day, Susanna," I said, and stepped off the walk.

Susanna called after me. "He's only a colored boy..."

I didn't bother to look back.

23

The county set the trial for April first—April Fool's Day. The county seat was over at Hollister, but because the courthouse had suffered a recent fire, they scheduled the trial at Twin Forks Baptist Church, Preacher Joyner's church. As for Daniel, he had no counsel. A person charged with a crime had to provide his own lawyer or do without. Neither Sister Rose nor Daniel nor any of the people in Boonesville had money to hire one. Daniel would have to defend himself, an impossible task.

Uncle Marsh and Aunt Esther didn't have much money either, but that didn't keep them from making plans as they did that Monday night after Daniel's arrest. The clock read eight, a good half an hour after Uncle Marsh usually went off to bed. I heard them talking in the kitchen, but I was much too absorbed in writing an essay for Miss Pilgrim to pay much attention. Still, when Uncle Marsh called my name I laid my work aside. I found both he and my aunt sitting at the table. Uncle Marsh held a warm glass of milk in one hand and a pencil poised over a sheet of paper in the other. He pointed me to a chair. The paper was filled with numbers and other scribbling. "Esther and I have been discussing an important matter, one that concerns you."

"Yessir?" I said, puzzled at his meaning.

"We've been going over our finances." He tapped the paper with the point of the pencil.

"Is the store in trouble?" I asked.

He shook his head. "No, the store's fine. We've been looking at our reserves. Since you've come to live with us, your aunt and I have been putting a little away every month. In addition, I got back pay from the army for those days I spent in the hospital. All told, we've got close to a thousand dollars."

"Yessir?" I said, still confused.

"You understand, don't you, that Daniel will get no help from anybody, not unless we help?"

"Yessir, I know that."

"We've got enough to hire a lawyer for Daniel, that is if we can find one that will take his case."

Without a lawyer, Daniel was doomed. Even with one, his chances were slim. Then it occurred to me that at some point they might need their reserve. Neither was really old. They each could expect to live another twenty years or more, and except for Uncle Marsh's war injuries, they both appeared spry and in good health. But that reserve—if they used it and a crisis followed, what would happen then? "That money is yours and Aunt Esther's nest egg," I said.

With a quick wave of his hand, he vanquished my objection. "Some of that money is what we set aside for your college. If it's not there when the time comes, we may not be able to send you, even if you do get a scholarship." He tapped the paper again, drawing my attention to the hastily scrawled figures. "This is your future we're talking about, Davy. We couldn't make a decision without consulting you first."

I hesitated a moment, trying to see all the angles, but then I realized there was really only one angle. "Helping Daniel comes first," I said.

So on Tuesday morning Uncle Marsh traveled to the county seat in hopes of finding a lawyer to represent Daniel. I accompanied him, even though it meant I missed another day of school. He rented the Liberty Motor car from Misener's Livery. Mr. Misener rolled out the automobile, the motor chugging away. The running board was littered with hay, and the leather interior smelled of horse sweat.

We climbed inside, Uncle Marsh behind the wheel, me in the passenger seat. We sat there for fifteen minutes while Mr. Misener, his foot on the running board, instructed my uncle on driving the vehicle. Uncle Marsh listened patiently even though he had driven lorries during the war. Once he'd said all he could think of, Mr. Misener stepped away, his face pinched in worry, as if he had forgotten a very important point but couldn't remember what it was. Instead he said, "Still got that Winchester I traded you?"

"As soon as I get some time, I plan to take the boy hunting. Maybe you'd like to come, too."

Mr. Misener pulled at the brim of his hat as if to keep the sun from his eyes even though we were still inside the barn. "I thank you, but best I say no. Your offer is appreciated."

"You know," said Uncle Marsh, "any time you want that piece back—"

"Got no time for shooting. Now you all have a good day."

We drove south out of Twin Forks. The clouds hung low and dark, threatening rain. The wind whistled into the interior through cracks and crevices around the canvas top, and I huddled in my heavy coat, my cap pulled low, the flaps covering my ears, my gloved hands stuffed deep inside my pockets.

For the first ten miles we bumped along a dirt road, kicking up dust that trailed in our wake. Every time the wheels dipped into a rut or a pothole, the blow sent pain shooting through my wounded side. Perhaps I should have taken a dose of laudanum before we'd left, but the drug had a way of dulling my senses, and I wanted to be as alert as possible when we met the attorney. I looked over to see how Uncle Marsh was holding up and found him intent upon the road, gripping the steering wheel with knuckles rising like small mountain peaks.

Just east of Ennis we hit the macadam surface. Where before we had passed a couple of horse-drawn wagons, now we encountered automobiles traveling in both directions, some at speeds reaching thirty miles an hour. But Uncle Marsh drove so cautiously that the speedometer seldom rose above fifteen. As a result, a line of automobiles piled up behind us. Every so often, when traffic in the other lane allowed, a vehicle pulled around us and sped away, the driver glaring at Uncle Marsh.

At last we entered the outskirts of the county seat, passing frame houses that lined both sides of the road. At one point, we intersected with interurban tracks laid right into the street and followed them into the middle of Hollister where we found the courthouse, a large ornate stone building, the upper floor scarred with soot from the fire and ringed with scaffolding. Uncle Marsh drove around the courthouse, which formed the center of the town square, until he found an empty space not occupied by either another automobile or a wagon and team. With much pulling forward and backing up, he maneuvered the Liberty against the sidewalk.

As we stepped out of the automobile, a gust of cold wind threw grit in our faces. Uncle Marsh bent over the hood and hacked away for a good minute before he straightened and wiped his mouth with a handkerchief. The exertion of the drive as well as the biting wind had taxed him, and the healing sores on his face glowed pink, all of which proved a reminder that Uncle Marsh, while he appeared healthier and more robust, was still far from recovered.

Another blast of wind tore into us, and I pulled my coat collar up around my face. Leaning into the wind, we headed up Main Street to the corner drug store where we ducked inside. The bell above our heads rang as we entered. The druggist had his back to us, but looked over his shoulder at the sound of the bell. He was a tall, thin man dressed in a white jacket, the left sleeve of which was rolled and pinned above the elbow. "What can I get you gentlemen this morning?"

"Information is about the only thing we need," said Uncle Marsh.

"Got plenty of that, and it's all free," said the druggist.

"Looking for a lawyer by the name of Stokes. Leonard Stokes."

The tall man gave Uncle Marsh directions: Lawyer Stokes kept an office above the Hollister Bank and Trust. My uncle thanked him.

"Where did you get it?" the druggist asked. The question confused my uncle at first, and the man said, "It's easy to spot guys who got it over there. Those spots on your face—they're healing nicely, but I've seen their like before."

"Château-Thierry," my uncle said.

The man touched his empty sleeve. "Me, too." His voice was void of bitterness, but I did detect a tone of regret. "We'll never get it back, will we? The way we used to be?"

"Once a thing's gone, it's gone," said Uncle Marsh.

"Like my arm."

"Like your arm, like my lungs." My uncle smiled, looking at me. "Like our youth. But that's life, isn't it? We're always losing things one way or another."

"I guess you've got a point there," said the man.

We walked the few steps to the bank and climbed the inside stairs to the second floor and the office of Leonard Stokes, Attorney-At-Law. Few white lawyers—and those were the only kind, as far as I knew—would defend colored people, but Stokes was young and trying to make a name for himself. A month before, he'd defended a colored man accused of robbing a store. Even though the thief made good his escape, a policeman went looking for him. All he had for a description was that the colored man wore a green jacket. Two blocks from the store, the policeman had arrested a colored man wearing a blue jacket. The storeowner identified the man as the one who, at knife point, robbed his store. At the trial, however, Lawyer Stokes brought in a dozen other colored men, all about the same size as the defendant, all wearing bib overalls and plaid shirts like the defendant. He mixed them together, and when they came apart, he asked the storeowner to pick out the man accused of the robbery. When the storeowner picked the wrong man, the prosecutor, an assistant district attorney, cried foul, but the judge threw out the case and released the defendant.

We found the door with a frosted glass insert on which was painted 'Stokes' in bold, black letters. Uncle Marsh knocked, and a voice said, "It's not locked."

We entered a small office. A bookcase filled with a law books sat against one wall, and above the bookcase hung a degree from the University of Texas that stated Leonard Stokes had graduated from their School of Law. Behind the desk sat a young man not many years older than I, who in an effort to disguise his youth, wore a great handlebar mustache, the kind that men proudly displayed fifteen or twenty years earlier. He rose, stepping around the desk, and extended his hand. Despite the fact that he wore boots, I doubted he stood much over five-three or four. We introduced ourselves, and he searched our faces with dark, intense eyes.

"We need help," Uncle Marsh said.

"Of course you do," he said, and guided us to chairs.

He seated himself behind his desk, and reaching into his breast pocket, brought out a pen. As Uncle Marsh explained the reason for our visit, he made notes, once or twice nodding. When Uncle Marsh had finished, the lawyer said, "I read about it in the paper. They didn't make it sound too favorable for this boy."

"No one ever asked me," I said. "I would've told them what really happened."

"Davy." My uncle spoke my name in that tone that told me to be quiet. To Stokes, he said, "We don't know no lawyers who might help us—who might help Daniel. We only heard your name, that you defend colored people."

"I defended one colored man—probably the case you heard about—and I took it because I was desperate for a client—any client. It was also a case I thought I could win. But taking another case involving a colored—" Stokes shook his head and ran one stubby hand through his hair. "On top of that, I hear that Caleb Mactierney is the prosecutor."

I had seen District Attorney Caleb Mactierney once when he came through Twin Forks stumping for votes, a tall aristocratic looking individual with a sweeping mane that reminded me of portraits I had seen of Henry Clay. He delivered his speech with an Old Testament fire and damnation presentation, a quality that no doubt helped him in court.

"Are you saying there's no hope?" Uncle Marsh asked.

"From what I've read and heard, that boy's convicted already."

"The truth—" I began.

"—doesn't count for much," Stokes said. "He's a colored boy accused of killing a white man. Once in a thousand times a boy like that might be found innocent, although to be quite frank, I can't cite a single case where it's happened. Add the fact that he's going to be tried in your town with Mactierney as prosecutor—well, that shrinks the odds somewhere south of zero."

"Then you won't take the case," Uncle Marsh said.

Stokes smiled. "It would be a David and Goliath match. If I won, it would certainly be a feat people would remember." His smile faded, and his mustache drooped. "Unfortunately, I don't have a slingshot, not one I could take into court. No sir, if I took money to represent the boy, I'd be taking it under false pretenses."

"If you're right—if Daniel doesn't have a chance—" I leaned forward, my hands on the desk, "—then what does it matter if you take the money to defend him? At least if he's got a lawyer, his side of the story gets told. Maybe somebody other than us would believe him."

"It may well be, as you say, the boy is innocent. But I have a few white clients now who I'd like to keep. If I take this case, my presence in this town—in this county— would no longer be tolerated." He drummed the desk as he regarded me. "It pains me that I have to refuse, but I feel I have no option. I'm sure you see my point."

I touched the bandage on my face. "See this? Orvie Blaylock did this to me. And he cracked a couple of my ribs, too. He would've killed me if Daniel hadn't stopped him." I pushed myself out of the chair, gritting my teeth against the pain. "No sir, Mr. Stokes, I don't understand. I don't understand one bit."

He escorted us to the door, telling us once more how sorry he was to refuse us, but by the time we stood outside his office we were no better off than before we'd come. In fact, we were worse off. At least we had come to Hollister with a glimmer of hope, and now Stokes had crushed that.

"What'll we do now?" I asked, my voice echoing down the empty hallway.

"Go home and try to figure things out," Uncle Marsh said. "Though at the moment, I'm at a loss."

"What'll we tell Sister Rose and Daniel?"

"The truth. It's all we've got."

We were at the stairs when Lawyer Stokes came out of his office and called for us to wait. For a moment I hoped he'd reconsidered. "I have a suggestion, if you would care to hear it, sir," he said to my uncle.

Uncle Marsh showed no sense of renewed hope, but

his expression said he was willing to listen.

"A person can ask for representation from anyone." When neither my uncle nor I quite understood his meaning, he said, "In other words, the boy could ask you, Mr. Langston, to represent him. I gather that there is no one else who would be willing to help."

"I know nothing of the law," Uncle Marsh said.

"I understand. But perhaps there is a way." He held out a hand motioning us back toward his office. "Let me explain."

He claimed that as soon as the door closed and we were gone, the idea came to him. "Like a message from the Almighty himself," he said. An obscure Texas law, held over from frontier times when lawyers were a scarcity, stated that when a defendant had no representation, he could authorize anyone to speak for him. Since the legislature had never removed the law from the books, it still held force. If Daniel asked for my uncle to represent him, the county would have no choice but to allow it. "Caleb Mactierney is a stickler on points of the law," Stokes assured us. "He won't refuse you, but the boy, Daniel, has to ask for you. That's the sticking point."

I said, "But we still don't know anything about the law. Neither of us has ever been to court."

Stokes smiled and said, "I won't take the case—I've stated my reasons—but I will give you advice. You must, however, promise to keep my name free of the proceedings. If that's acceptable, I'll give you as much time as possible. I have a few cases pending, but I can spare a couple of hours each day for the next few weeks. I could help you understand some fundamental proceedings."

"I'm a storekeeper," my uncle said. "Davy's the smart one here. This boy reads more than anybody I know."

"I'm afraid the court would not allow a boy to represent anyone."

Uncle Marsh flushed angry. "Davy's more man than most I know."

I laid a hand on Uncle Marsh's arm. "He's talking about my age. Not who I am."

"I meant no disrespect." Stokes looked at me. "I can see you're a smart one, Davy. I like intelligence in a young man. That's the kind of quality that will take you a long way. Still, you're what—sixteen, seventeen? You understand, don't you, that no court in the world would let you represent anyone, even this colored boy?"

"My uncle is not a well man," I said. "If he takes on this job, he's going to need a lot of help. Maybe I couldn't represent Daniel, but I could act as my Uncle's assistant. Nothing wrong with that, I suppose."

Stokes laughed and said to Uncle Marsh. "He is a bright young man, Mr. Marsh. Real bright."

We left Stokes for the second time that afternoon with our glimmer of hope restored, although I believe that Uncle Marsh must have felt many of the same misgivings as I felt. How could he not? Despite the fact that Lawyer Stokes promised to tutor us, we felt incompetent and unprepared.

We spoke little during the drive back, the rattle and rumble of the automobile making talk nearly impossible. After we dropped off the motorcar at the livery and were walking to the store, Uncle Marsh said, "The odds are stacked against us, Davy."

He never made another negative statement about our chances, but in those few words he expressed his fear, not for himself but that another person's life depended upon us. Uncle Marsh meant to throw himself into the battle with all he could muster—he was that kind of man—but already the responsibility weighed on him. I could see it in the slump of his shoulders and in his gaze that seemed to look beyond the present and forward into a dark, ominous future.

24

On her next visit to the jail, Sister Rose carried our plan to Daniel.

She found her son with Doctor Gibbs, who was in the process of attending the wound. She saw the gash in her son's side, white thread against the dark skin, the two sides swollen like bloated lips and discolored to a reddish brown. Doctor Gibbs placed his fingers on either side of the wound, probing it, and dark fluid leaked from the stitches.

Daniel stared at the ceiling. He had lost weight. His cheekbones appeared sharp and protruding, and the whites of his eyes still possessed a gray pallor.

Doctor Gibbs reached into the black bag and pulled out a jar filled with yellow powder that he sprinkled over the wound. "Sulfur," he said. "Can't do harm, might do some good. He's running a fever, but I don't suspect he's in much pain. How 'bout that, boy? You in pain?"

Daniel gave no evidence that he'd heard. Dr. Gibbs replaced the cap and dropped the bottle into the bag, closing it with a snap. He snatched the handle and stepped to the cell door. "Jim! Jim Kennison! Get me out of here!"

Jim came from his office, unlocked the door and stood to one side as Dr. Gibbs stepped past him while mumbling something about ingratitude. Sister Rose entered the cell, waiting until Jim retreated to the outer office before she spoke in a soft whisper. "Daniel, I got something important to say, and I want you to listen real careful." She sat on the bunk, and he shifted his body to give her room. "Are you listening? You need to pay attention now." Sister Rose laid a gentle hand on her son's chest, her fingers sensing the steady beat of his heart. "You've given up. I can see that—and maybe you have good cause—but Mr. Marsh and Davy have taken steps."

She explained our visit to the lawyer. When she finished, he rolled his head back and forth. "I heard the mayor tell the deputy what they had in mind. They mean to send me off to prison and have me executed. Nothing anybody can do to stop them."

Sister Rose could see the defeat in his face and heard it in his voice. "You don't want to do this for yourself. I see that," she said. "But you need to think of other people now. Mr. Marsh and Davy went to a lot of trouble to help you."

She had brought a paper bag with her—one that Jim had searched before allowing her into the cell block. She brought out clean clothes, placing them at the foot of the bed. She reached back into the bag and drew out a copy of *Don Quixote*. The barred window to his cell sat a good seven feet above the floor, and if Daniel kept repositioning himself, he could find five or six hours of reading light each day. "Davy said it might help you pass the time. Now, what should I tell the sheriff?"

Daniel held the book in his lap, a hand covering the title. "I don't like beholding to a white man, even if he is Mr. Marsh."

"If we could do this on our own, then I would say more power to us, but the only hope we've got is Mr. Marsh."

"Mr. Marsh means well, I know that, but—"

"You'll let Mr. Marsh try, won't you? You'll do it for your mama?"

He released a long, pent-up sigh as his resistance faded. "All right, Mama, for you..."

Sister Rose called for Jim, who came with jingling keys in hand. Daniel said, "I want to see Mr. Marsh."

Jim unlocked the cell door and held it open to allow Sister Rose to exit. "Mayor said only your mama and Doctor Gibbs can see you."

"I want Mister Marsh to speak for me." When Jim appeared not to understand, he added, "I want him to speak for me in court, like he was my lawyer."

"He's no proper lawyer." Jim twisted the key with a loud clang.

"I want Mr. Marsh to speak for me," Daniel said. "I got a right. You call the people over at the county seat. You ask for Mr. Mactierney. He's the one going to prosecute my case, isn't he? He'll tell you I have a right."

Once Sister Rose left, Jim went to see Lon Barron and discovered the mayor inspecting a set of papers scattered across his desk. Although he appeared peeved at the interruption, he motioned Jim to a chair.

Jim removed his Stetson and sat, crossing his long legs. "That boy asked for Mister Langston to represent him. Said he had a right. Claimed the county prosecutor would back him up."

"We'll see about this." Lon charged around his desk to the phone on the wall and cranked the handle. The mayor talked for a good ten minutes, his face growing more and more red. At last he slammed the receiver on the hook and stared at the black phone as if it had betrayed him. He dropped back onto his overstuffed chair, slapping the desk with his open palm and sending papers flying. "This is what comes of your overdeveloped sense of kindness, Jim. That old lady, Sister Rose, got the word to her son. Passed along from Marsh Langston, no doubt. I knew that he and that boy of his were up to no good when they drove over to the county seat." He waved an accusing finger at Jim. "This wouldn't have happened if you'd kept that old woman from her son like I told you."

"Then the boy has a right to see Mr. Marsh," Jim said.

Tight-faced, Lon leaned back in his chair, the leather folding itself around his heavy body. "I don't suppose it will make any difference. What the hell does Marsh know about the law?"

"Then you shouldn't worry."

"Of course I should worry," Lon snapped. "When something unexpected happens, you should always worry. Now the question is: What are you going to do, Jim?"

"I don't see the point in doing anything. The trial's coming, and that's that."

"We can't let this boy get away with killing a white man," Lon said. "If he does, pretty soon every buck this side of the Mississippi will think white men are fair game in this town. Orvie Blaylock will be only the first."

"It don't follow that because the boy asked for Mr. Langston to speak for him, he'll go free. Even if he does— and under the circumstances, that seems pretty far-fetched—I can't see colored folks rising up and killing us in our beds."

Lon shook his head even before Jim finished. "You don't know these people. You don't realize what they're capable of. They're only a few years separated from the jungle. Trust me on this; I know what I'm talking about."

"Yes, sir, I suppose you do," Jim said. "Still, I don't see what I can do about it. I jailed the boy, and I'll hold him for the trial. Other than that, things are out of my hands."

Lon took a long time studying Jim before he said, "You're an honest man, Jim."

"What's your point, Mayor?"

"Honesty sometimes gets in the way of doing what's necessary," Lon said.

25

*F*ifteen minutes later, Uncle Marsh and I sauntered over to the jail. We found the door locked. Uncle Marsh knocked but got no answer. I looked through one of the barred windows, but the interior was dark and empty.

"Davy..." Uncle Marsh drew my attention to the bank where Jim stepped into the street, and we both knew he had reported to Lon Barron. I can't say his actions surprised me, but I was disappointed. I wanted Jim to be made of sterner stuff.

Jim waited for a motorcar to rattle past, and he crossed the street, a handkerchief covering his mouth. Once the dust cleared, he removed his eyeglasses and wiped the lenses. I don't think he saw us until he reached the front door. "What is it you want, Mr. Langston?" he asked.

"I know that Daniel has asked for me," Uncle Marsh said.

Jim repositioned his spectacles. "Yessir, and I guess I've got to let you see him. But you can't take Davy with you. I mean, you're speaking for him, not Davy."

"Davy's my assistant," Uncle Marsh said, and when Jim hesitated, he asked, "Do you need to check with Lon on that, too?"

Jim shifted his weight from one foot to the other. "Look, I've only been here a little over a year now, and I've never dealt with anything like this. I'm not sure what I should do."

"That makes two of us," said Uncle Marsh.

Jim withdrew the keys from his pocket and unlocked the door. Once inside, he said, "I guess you can take as long as you need."

Jim shut the oak door that led to the cells, giving us privacy, but in doing so, cut off all light except that which filtered through the bars high in Daniel's cell window. Daniel rose from his bunk and came to the bars, reaching through to grasp my Uncle's wrist, not in a savage way, but so that my Uncle would look at him and know he was serious. "You've got to promise me one thing," he said.

Uncle Marsh laid his hand over Daniel's. "What's that, Son?"

"You got to promise you won't let those white men lynch me."

"Nobody's going to lynch you," Uncle Marsh said.

"Promise me."

"I promise."

Daniel released his hold and managed to look at me. "Thanks for sending *Don Quixote*. Maybe I'll read a bit, when I get to feeling like it. Right now, I can't seem to concentrate."

"It's yours to keep," I said.

"I'm as good as dead. I guess I don't see any point in reading a book."

Shadows molded themselves to Uncle Marsh's face, filling in hollows and crevices, but his eyes caught the light, holding it like tiny spots of fire. "Let's not talk of dying. We got a ways to go yet."

"We have this lawyer over in Hollister willing to coach us," I said. "We're not going into this thing blind. We've got a chance."

"If you say so," Daniel said.

I wanted him to feel a sense of hope, the possibility of a future, and his listless response angered me. I started to lash out, to tell him he was an ungrateful soul, that we were doing everything in our power to set things right. I caught myself. What right did I have to complain to Daniel about anything?

We didn't stay long. We had come to see how he was and to give him the word that we would defend him to the best of our abilities. We told him we would be meeting with Attorney Stokes the next day, and we would be back with more information and strategies. Before we left, he asked, "Have you seen Rachel and her papa, Davy? They've been real good to Mama and me. Might let them know what's happening." He stared at me with those intense eyes. "She's a good girl. She doesn't deserve to be hurt."

"None of us deserves that." I should have said more. I wanted to say that he was my best friend in the whole world, that I'd never had a friend as good as him, but as so often happens, the words remained unspoken, causalities of male insecurity. Boys weren't supposed to say those things, especially to other boys. So Daniel and I nodded to each other, and Uncle Marsh and I left.

Jim sat behind the desk but said nothing as we passed. Outside a cold wind greeted us. We started to cross the street to our place when a half dozen men led by Zeb Cain stormed out of Ernie's Bar and marched straight toward us. Standing in front of the swinging doors, his hands on his hips, Lon Barron watched. They must have seen us enter the jail and waited for us to come out. Had we continued on, we would have met them in the middle of the street, but Uncle Marsh touched my arm, and I followed him two doors down to Wiggins' General Store where he reached into the barrel of ax handles, choosing one at random. For all I knew, it was the same one he had used on Cain that night in the bar. He tapped his open palm with the oak as if to test its strength.

Cain and his crew drew up short of the boardwalk. Cain narrowed his eyes and spit. "We want to have a word, Marsh Langston...to you and this boy here."

"How's your shoulder?" My uncle kept his voice low and without emotion.

Cain touched the sling, holding his left arm. "Mending."

"No. I mean the other one."

Cain's brow knitted in question. "Nothing wrong with it."

"There's about to be something wrong with it if you don't get out of our way," Uncle Marsh said.

Cain knew, as the others knew, that he had crossed the line with Uncle Marsh. The others began to edge away as though to distance themselves if trouble began. Cain shifted his eyes from side to side, but he tried to remain brave. "We came to talk," he said.

"When I want to talk to you, I'll let you know." Uncle Marsh pointed the ax handle in the direction of Ernie's Bar. "Now get back where you belong before I get riled."

I could see by their faces that they had no stomach to face Uncle Marsh, not with him holding the ax handle and looking like he wanted to use it. Even Cain could not muster enough courage to say another word. The men shuffled back in the direction of Ernie's, their boots kicking up little clouds of dust that the wind whisked away. Uncle Marsh called out, "Cain!" They stopped and faced us. "If anything happens to my store—as much as a broken window—I'll figure you're behind it. Understand?"

Once again Cain screwed up his features and exposed his yellow teeth in an effort to face down Uncle Marsh. Uncle Marsh stepped off the boardwalk, and I thought he was going after Cain, who must have thought so too, for he growled a quick, "I understand."

We watched until they disappeared into Ernie's. Disgust written all over his face, Lon waited until the last one passed, then followed them inside. Uncle Marsh replaced the ax handle in the barrel.

Old Mister Wiggins, his skin wrinkled like wadded tissue paper, stood in the doorway of his store, a smile lighting his ancient face. "You know, Zeb Cain might be a reasonable feller if someone was around to bust his shoulder every day of his life."

Uncle Marsh motioned toward the ax handle. "If I keep using this, you'll have to charge me rent."

"It's yours," the old man said. "If I was you, I'd keep it close for a while. Might just discourage Cain and anybody else dumb enough to listen to him."

That night, Uncle Marsh went into his fishing tackle. He pulled out his old knife with which he had gutted many a catfish, its wooden handle stained dark with dried blood. He sat at the kitchen table late into the evening carving into the oak ax handle. Aunt Esther sat across from him, not speaking, only rocking and sewing. He whittled away, the chips and sawdust dropping onto an open newspaper, until on opposite sides of the handle the words "truth" and "justice" stood out in clear relief. When I asked him why he'd carved those words into the handle, he said, "I want them to know what I stand for."

"Don't they already know?" Aunt Esther asked.

"They might have heard the words, but they don't know what they mean. Not yet." He blew on the ax handle, clearing away the last residue of dust.

I had a feeling that before this whole mess was over Uncle Marsh would drive home the meaning of those words to those boys, even if he had to bash in every one of their skulls to do so.

26

One Saturday in mid-March, I packed up my tools and headed for the old Squires place. More than a week had passed since the incident with Orvie Blaylock and Zeb Cain, and I feared that if I didn't get back there soon, the vines and creepers would again assume control. In addition, storm clouds rolled in from the Gulf, and I wanted to make sure the windows and door were sealed. The last storm exposed leaks in the roof that had caused the floors to warp. Texas weather has a way of destroying wooden structures if left unattended. A person must always be alert for wood rot and termites and general weathering or else a good strong wind will send a house or barn or outhouse tumbling to the ground. Daniel and I, Solomon and Rachel, and Sister Rose had put too much effort into the new school to neglect it now. I didn't want to let our efforts go to waste.

I carried my slicker over one shoulder, my bag of tools over the other. The pain in my ribs slowed me somewhat, but not enough to prevent me from continuing. I left our place well before seven that morning to avoid running into anyone. A light shone in Wiggins' General Store, and I saw young Mr. Wiggins moving about, but the rest of the town still slept or stayed inside because of the impending rain.

No one saw me leave—I was pretty sure of that—but as I reached the halfway point on the bridge, a team and wagon reached the other side, the hooves and wheels clattering against the boards. The driver was Zeb Cain, and he spotted me about the same time that I spotted him. The width of wagon allowed a space no more than three or four feet between its sides and the railings.

I stepped to the right, giving him plenty of room to pass, but Cain, his mouth twisted into a cruel smile, gave the reins a tug, and the team and wagon came straight at me. I crossed to the other side. Right away, Cain shifted the reins, and the two mares changed direction.

Now I knew his intention. I waited until the two mares were within six feet or so, and in one motion, I swung the sack of tools from my shoulder, the hammer, saw screwdrivers and nails rattling together, loud and discordant. I never meant to hit the mares, although the bag passed within inches of the their noses, and they reared back in their harnesses. With his one good arm, Cain fought to hold the team under control. I stepped aside and reached the rear of the wagon before he quieted the mares. I was at the opposite end of the bridge before I heard his feet thud against the wood planks. I stopped and faced him.

His right hand gripped the hilt of the knife stuck in his belt, an old serrated blade that he used to gut fish, the teeth dirty with dried blood. He took a step toward me, his massive bulk filling the space between the wagon and the bridge railing. I dropped the sack, stooped and reached into it. When I stood again, I held a hammer, long and heavy, and that gave him pause. He could not help but remember Blaylock's fate. Yet if he knew how frightened I was, he might still have come at me. I did my best to remain calm, but my belly shook, and my mouth was dry.

We stood facing one another for a good thirty seconds

before he took his hand from the knife. His fingers touched the sling that cradled his left arm. "If I didn't have this," he said, "I'd gut you from belly to chops."

"I suppose you'd try," I said.

His eyes narrowed. "I'd do a lot more than try, boy."

He climbed back onto his wagon, unwrapped the reins from the brake handle, and gave them a flick.

All the way to the Squires place, I kept looking over my shoulder. Only when I reached the house and jumped inside did my heart rate slow. Soon I lost myself pounding nails into loose boards. Afterward, I righted chairs and tables. In one corner stood an old broom, the handle worn of varnish, the straw ragged, and I began to sweep up the dead leaves and dirt. Right then I heard footsteps on gravel, and my heart started up again. I laid the broom against the wall and retrieved my hammer.

Even before I reached the landing, a brown hand gripped the door jamb, and Rachel peered inside. I breathed more easily, although my heart continued to pound, but now for an entirely different reason.

"Davy," she said. "I wasn't sure—"

I took her hand and pulled her beside me. We stood so close that her breasts pressed against my chest.

"You're alone?" I said.

"I came over to straighten up the place." She looked beyond me to the room. "I guess you've taken care of that."

"Your grandfather?" I asked.

"His rheumatism is bothering him. It's the change in weather. He's taken to bed."

"I am sorry," I said.

I felt badly for her grandfather—what I'd seen of rheumatism sufferers, the pain was often excruciating—and yet, I could not feel badly about being in the house alone with Rachel. Since the day I'd first met her, I'd dreamed of such a time.

She noticed the hammer in my hand, and her brow

knitted. "Who did you think I was?"

"I had a run-in with Zeb Cain as I was leaving town." I held up the hammer. "He backed off when he saw that I wasn't going to take any of his guff." I dropped the hammer onto a desk.

"Mr. Cain is dangerous, Davy. They say he stabbed a man over in Dallas."

"I've heard the stories. He would have taken a knife to me this morning if he'd thought he could get away with it."

Concern pinched her eyes, and she reached up and touched the bandage on my cheek. "You shouldn't come here. You're taking too many chances." Her fingers slipped from the bandage to my face where they lingered. "I've never touched a white boy like this. I've never touched any boy like this."

"Rachel." I spoke her name in a dry, hoarse voice that didn't sound at all like me.

"Yes?"

I swallowed, and when I next spoke, the words were so heavy in my throat that I had trouble getting them out. "I think about you all the time."

She dropped her hand, grasping it with the other, and stared at the floor. Her pose reminded me of a picture I had seen in *National Geographic*, an African carving, a very famous one, of a black Madonna. "It's not right; we're different," she said.

"Do you ever think of me?"

She took a long time to answer. When I thought she wasn't going to, she lifted her eyes and said very softly, "I can't help myself."

"It's the same with me."

I reached out and took her hand. She leaned into me, her head raised, her lips parted, and I kissed her. This time we avoided our teeth clicking together. Our mouths open, our breaths mingling, we lasted for fifteen seconds or so before she pulled back. She said, "What we're about to do—they got laws against it."

My voice was still not my own. "What do I care about laws made up by the fat old men down in Austin. They don't know us."

I took her by the shoulders and led her away from the open door. She put her back against the wall. Her bosom rose and fell, and she began to shake all over. Outside the wind picked up, swaying the trees. She said, "I've never done this before."

"Neither have I."

I pressed my body against hers, and I realized for the first time that I was shaking, too. "We shouldn't," she said.

"I know."

Our mouths found each other again, and I cupped her breast in my right hand. Her jacket was open, and under it she wore a cotton dress, so thin it felt as if she wore nothing at all.

Perhaps it was a bold move on my part, perhaps I was taking far more liberty than she intended, yet I experienced no guilt, no sense of shame, and when her hot breath filled my mouth, when she moaned, I knew she was experiencing the same pleasure as I.

We slid to the floor, fumbling, exploring each other through our clothes. I suffered a momentary sharp pain in my side, and then forgot all about it. She drew up her legs, and her dress fell across her stomach. I caught a glimpse of white panties, and when she didn't try to hide herself, I slipped my thumbs beneath the waistband. Together we got them off and they tangled around her ankles. The next thing I knew she was fumbling with the wood buttons of my pants, and reaching inside, she seized my penis. We both gasped, and when she pulled it free, I exploded, my white seed spilling on the inside of her dark thigh.

I was only a kid, and I didn't know much about sex, but I had wet dreams, and every time it happened, I messed my nightclothes. That was nothing to the embarrassment I felt now. And, too, when it happened at night, I dwindled back to my normal size within a minute or so, but Rachel held on, her grip tight, and I remained rigid. I rolled over between her legs, but frankly, I had no idea what came next. I knew boys and girls were different, but exactly what the difference was, I had little idea.

Rachel guided me home. I slid inside her only part way, then I shoved, something gave, and she let out a small yelp. I rose up on my elbows, afraid I had hurt her, but she threw her arms around my neck and drew me down. I lasted maybe seven or eight minutes, and at the end, she buried her face in my shoulder, stifling a scream.

When I rolled off her and stuffed my limp penis back into my pants, my fingers came away stained with blood. "I hurt you," I said.

"A little." She leaned into me. I slipped my arm around her, and she cradled her head in the hollow of my shoulder where I couldn't see her face. Her hair smelled of lemon and rainwater. "Girls bleed their first time; it's normal."

"What'll we do now?" I asked.

"Just hold me." She encircled my chest with her arms, squeezing with such fierce abandon it was as if she wanted us to merge as one. She held me that way until her strength began to ebb. By then I tilted her head back and kissed her over and over again until I rose up, once more insistent. "Can we do it again?" I asked.

Much later, when the light outside indicated that it was nearly noon, we stood and straightened our clothes as best we could. "Can we meet here again tomorrow?" I asked.

"It's not safe." Rachel ran the palm of her hand across the lap of her dress trying to straighten the wrinkles, but they were too deeply embedded. She looked up, and she must have seen the disappointment register on my face. "You more than anyone has to know how dangerous it is, Davy. What if white men come snooping around again? What if they found us?"

"I want to see you, Rachel. I need to see you."

Her unruly hair curled about her head, a smudge of dust streaked her left cheek, and she gave off a slightly musky odor. At that moment, I thought she was more beautiful than ever, and I said, "I love you."

She lowered her eyes, and I took her in my arms. She buried her head against my shoulder and cried. I held her tightly, not ever wanting to let go.

Of course, sooner or later a person has to let go. We kissed goodbye, and she dropped off the stoop and ran toward the trees. I thought she was crying. I called her name, but she didn't look back before she disappeared amidst the undergrowth.

Then I remembered her warning, and fear crept up the back of my neck. I scanned the woods but saw no one. I went back inside, packed up my tools, and headed home, all the while feeling a presence lurking out of sight. Only when I reached town and climbed our back stairs did I feel a sense of relief.

The rest of the day I spent reading *Great Expectations*, which Miss Pilgrim had assigned, but I had trouble focusing on the words. Past ten that evening, I fell into bed exhausted, but sleep did not come easily, and when it did, Rachel haunted my dreams.

The next morning, groggy from my restless night, I climbed out of bed, dressed and was out of the house before Uncle Marsh and Aunt Esther were up and about. This time I made it to the old Squires place without incident. I spent most of the morning stacking the furniture in one corner, and afterward I whitewashed two of the walls. All the time I expected Rachel to show up, but by noon I knew she wouldn't come. I went home with a sick ache in the pit of my stomach.

27

*W*e met with Lawyer Stokes twice more before the trial began, and he instructed us on court procedures and gave us several options for handling the case. I took notes, and at night when I should have been doing my schoolwork, I sat with Uncle Marsh at the kitchen table discussing strategies. Often we didn't get to bed until past midnight, and the next day I had trouble concentrating at school. A couple of times I nodded off at my desk, and once Miss Pilgrim took me into the back room. I suspect my classmates thought she was going to give me a tongue lashing, but instead she told me to sit and put my head on the desk. "A little nap right now will do a lot more good than solving algebra problems," she said.

She barely had closed the door before I was fast asleep. When finally I emerged an hour later, some of the kids, including Tommikins, snickered and passed knowing smiles. I let them think what they wanted. Before I took my seat, I cast a malevolent glare at the mayor's son, which wiped the smile off his chubby face. He must have thought I intended to jump him after school, because the moment Miss Pilgrim dismissed us, he swept up his books and bolted for the door. I waited until everyone had left, and then thanked Miss Pilgrim.

Sitting at her desk, she studied me through her thick lenses that made her eyes appear as large as silver dollars. "The trial starts day after tomorrow, doesn't it?"

"Yes ma'am."

"I think it would be best if you stayed home until this thing is over."

"That's not fair, Miss Pilgrim."

"This is not a punishment, Davy. You're carrying a big load, an awfully big load."

"I can handle it," I said, my tone defiant, surly.

I had never spoken to Miss Pilgrim in such a way, but my temper was short, and she was inflicting on me a punishment I didn't deserve. I expected a retort in kind; Miss Pilgrim had a sharp tongue and brooked no insults or insubordination. Instead, her usually stern expression softened. "You and your uncle have taken on a herculean task. You should welcome the time to prepare." She rose and came around her desk. Deep wrinkles etched patterns in her cheeks, and she pulled her iron gray hair into a tight bun, which only accentuated her advanced age—she must have been fifty if she were a day—but I doubt there was another townsperson, other than my aunt and uncle, who I respected more. She laid a hand on my shoulder. "Your studies will keep until this is over."

Since the trouble began, few people had shown me such kindness. I could think of little to say, but I managed to stutter a few words. "Daniel is my friend."

"Of course he is," Miss Pilgrim said, her voice soft, soothing.

"The color of his skin doesn't matter."

"Of course it doesn't."

"He was protecting me when he killed Orvy Blaylock."

"That's what friends do. They look after one another."

"What this town—what Mayor Lon and the others are doing to Daniel—is unfair. He doesn't deserve it."

"No, he doesn't deserve it. Neither do you."

I lowered my eyes and looked at the desktop where nameless boys had carved initials and letters into the wood. When I spoke, my voice sounded far away, as if it weren't mine at all. "It's all so complicated."

"My boy, we're always trying to make sense of a world that seems beyond our understanding."

As Miss Pilgrim had suggested, I stayed home the next two days, which was a Friday and the following Monday. I worked right through the weekend, spending time going over my notes and drawing up a series of questions for both our witnesses and those of the prosecution. We didn't know everyone Mactietrney would call, but we could be sure of two: Zeb Cain and Jim.

Tuesday, April first, arrived all too soon, and I felt we were woefully unprepared. I arose that morning and dressed in my one suit and tie. In the kitchen I found my aunt and uncle already waiting. Like me, they were dressed in their best clothes. When I sat at the table, my aunt asked, "Did you get a good night's sleep, Davy?"

"Not really," I said.

"I suspect none of us got much sleep last night," Uncle Marsh said.

Despite his words, Uncle Marsh looked healthier than he had since returning home. He had shaved, and his cheeks held a ruddy glow. In addition, those spots on his face had faded into light discolorations. With the help of Sister Rose's tonic, he had put on weight, although he was still twenty pounds lighter than before the war.

Aunt Esther laid a hand on his shoulder. "You'll do fine. I know you two. You're bulldogs when you set your mind to a purpose."

"That doesn't mean we know what we're doing," Uncle Marsh said.

"You'll find a way." She smiled, but her unbridled optimism did little to quell my fears.

We ate breakfast in near silence until Uncle Marsh

pulled the watch from his pocket and flipped open the case. "Half past seven. Best we get down to the church. The doings start at nine."

I gathered up our notes and met Uncle Marsh on the landing. Aunt Esther stayed behind to clean the kitchen, promising to be along in a few minutes. Before he shut the door, Uncle Marsh said, "Don't take long, Esther. I suspect the church will fill early."

We descended the stairs and rounded the building to find Sister Rose waiting for us. My uncle tipped his hat. "Morning, Sister Rose. We would be honored to walk with you."

She carried a slim volume of the New Testament, the edges frayed, the pages tattered. The strain of the past weeks showed on her face. Deep furrows worked their way from the corners of her eyes and mouth, and gray strands streaked her black hair. As she walked, she dragged her feet, creating dust that blew away in the early morning breeze. Black clouds rolled across the sky, and with them, the smell of rain, heavy and immediate.

So the three of us emerged from the alley beside the store and made our way down the street to Brother Joyner's Baptist church. It was a wood building with a spire that made it the tallest building in town, and the spire held a bell that hadn't sounded in ten years, at least not since I'd come to town. The exterior white paint had faded and peeled in spots, and the clear glass windows, now open, carried a film of dust.

Already the street was alive with people moving in the same direction, and a crowd of more than thirty waited at the doors. About everybody in and around Twin Forks had come for the show. Mr. Egbert Jenkins, the telegrapher, stood among the crowd as did Old Man Wiggins, his son and family. Lon Barron and his daughter huddled with Zeb Cain and other denizens of Ernie's bar. Even the druggist we spoke to in Hollister, the one who'd lost his arm at Chateau Thierry, was there, his long face hanging above the heads of most of the other men. No one smiled, no one talked, but they all watched us approach.

Fifteen or twenty yards from the church and gathered under an elm older than the town itself, stood a dozen inhabitants of Boonesville, the dark leafless branches in harmony with their dark skins. Solomon stood at the head, his grizzled hair and beard setting him apart from the rest, but Rachel was not with him. They all watched us, too, and said nothing, but I noticed that their eyes held an expression I had not seen in the townspeople. I think that expression was one of gratitude. I doubt that any one of them believed we could get Daniel off, but we were two white people willing to defend a colored man.

We marched right up the stairs of the church where a burly deputy sheriff met us, his arms crossed over his chest, his jaw jutting forward. "You can't go in," he said, his voice raspy, his tone gruff. "It ain't time."

Uncle Marsh cast a smile that I can only describe as half-friendly, half-indulgent. "I'm representing the defendant. Davy here is my assistant."

The big man narrowed his eyes and scrutinized us before he reached back and opened the door. We started past, but he laid a beefy hand on Sister Rose that swallowed her whole right shoulder. "I didn't say nothing about her..."

"She's the boy's mother," said Uncle Marsh.

"No coloreds inside. Those are my orders."

"What's she supposed to do?" I asked.

"There's windows. People can see in as well as out."

He noticed the New Testament that Sister Rose held to her chest. He removed his hand from her shoulder, and when he spoke, his tone was apologetic. "It's not my doing. Just my orders."

Sister Rose gave the deputy a smile that said she understood. "It's all right; I'll be watching."

The deputy ushered us in and closed the door behind

us. The interior was only fifteen rows of pews facing the front, each row holding about ten or twelve people. At the front of the auditorium, the lectern had been removed, and in its place rested a judicial bench. In front of the dais sat two tables replete with chairs. District Attorney Caleb Mactierney sat at the table on the right, Daniel sat alone at the table to the left, the chains to his handcuffs nailed to the floor and secured by a heavy lock. His expression blank, Jim stood behind his prisoner and stared forward.

Macteirney rose, his hand extended. His long hair contrasted with his dark eyebrows. "You must be Mr. Langsdon," he said in a deep, rich bass. Uncle Marsh took the hand, and Macteirney said, "I've heard quite a bit about you."

"I bet you have," Uncle Marsh said.

"Taking the cause of this boy hasn't earned you any friends."

Uncle Marsh dropped the handshake. "It's not friends I'm interested in."

"And what are you interested in, if I may ask?"

"Defending an innocent boy."

Macteirney raised a dark eyebrow. "I'm afraid you've been misled, Mr. Langdon. The witnesses we have paint a very convincing story. Now, if you would like to withdraw..."

"Thank you kindly for your concern, but right now, we need to talk to Daniel."

Uncle Marsh walked away.

I started to follow, but Macteirney said, "You must be Davy."

"I'm helping my uncle."

He glanced at the thin sheaf of papers under my arm. "I'd say your defense looks a bit flimsy."

"It may well be," I said, "but we've got the truth on our side."

"Ah, yes, the truth. You see it one way, the state sees it another. That's why we have trials, to see which truth prevails." His eyes blazed with a fiery zeal, although his voice remained calm, steady. "I understand that you and the defendant were friends. I've also been told you're an intelligent lad. You must have known only trouble would come from your association with a colored boy."

"Why should the color of his skin have anything to do with it?" I asked.

For the first time, a faint smile touched his lips. "That's a right smart question, young man. Right smart, indeed. I could try to point out the innate inferiority of the Negro, but frankly, I don't believe that malarkey any more than you do. The reality is that we live in a world where color does matter. We—you and I and everyone in this room— must abide by its rules, whether we like them or not. Otherwise it's anarchy."

"Maybe a little anarchy is what we need," I said.

Macteirney's smile, if it was that, vanished altogether. "I don't believe you know what you're saying, Davy. Look what's happened in Russia: the collapse of government, the killing of innocent women and children, starvation rampant. Now we hear stories that Germany and Hungary may be headed that way. It's because of events happening over there that we must be especially vigilant here. No one, and I believe that includes you, my boy, would like to see us follow examples such as those."

I joined Daniel and Uncle Marsh at our table. "What else did Mactierney have to say?" asked Uncle Marsh.

"He wants to make sure the world stays as it is," I said.

"That means convicting me," Daniel said, his tone bitter and bleak.

Uncle Marsh laid a hand on Daniel's arm. "We're going to do our best to make sure that don't happen."

"Mr. Marsh, I know you'll do your best." Daniel looked across at Macteirney, who sat at his table going over his notes. "But no matter what you say or do, people have already made up their minds. I'm a colored boy who's killed a white man. That's all there is to say."

"Daniel, look at me." Uncle Marsh squeezed his arm until Daniel took his eyes off Macteirney and focused on him. "If you don't show some courage, then you're letting them win before this trial ever begins."

Daniel sat straighter and forced a smile. "You do your best, Mr. Marsh. I won't let you down."

At that moment, the guard opened the door and people flooded into the church and raced for the pews nearest the front. Heavy boots and shoes pounded the hardwood floor. I looked for Aunt Esther among the crowd, but she was not there.

Once all the pews had filled and people had lined the walls, the guard closed the door and came forward to act as bailiff. The residents of Boonesville gathered at the windows, among them Sister Rose. Beside her, amidst the sea of dark bodies, stood Aunt Esther.

"All rise," said the bailiff, and everyone inside the church came to their feet. A door to the vestibule opened and out stepped a man dressed in a black robe. "The court is now in session, the honorable Judge John J. Weatherford presiding."

The judge was a short man, no more than five-five, and he sported a long beard that covered his cheeks and neck. Several years before he'd almost died when his house had caught fire. Two of his servants had managed to pull him to safety, but not before he'd suffered disfiguring facial burns. He grew the beard to hide the scars, although a few showed through the growth. This, along with an unruly mop of black hair and wild eyes, made him appear as if he were ready to be hauled off to an insane asylum.

He took his place behind the bench, and the bailiff told us to sit.

Even though it was early and the weather pleasant, the interior of the church was already warm from so many bodies. A buzzing arose behind us, and Judge Weatherford slammed his gavel once and the room went silent.

"Before we get started, let me make one thing perfectly

clear." He spoke in a slightly high-pitched voice. "I will brook no insolence, no disruption, from anyone, whether Negro or white. At the first sign of such behavior, I will clear the court and the surrounding grounds and conduct the proceedings in private." He glared at the crowd as if he expected a challenge, and when none came, he ordered the bailiff to read the charges against Daniel. Once the deputy uttered that word 'murder', applause rippled from the white audience. The colored folk at the windows stirred but said nothing. The judge banged his gavel, and the auditorium quieted.

Next the judge ordered the bailiff to draw names for a jury.

The bailiff shook a jar filled with slips of paper. Reaching in, he drew out the first name: Egbert Jenkins, the man who brought us the telegram from the army. Others followed: Ernie, the bartender; Mr. Misener, the owner of the stable; Mr. Waltzer, the theater owner; Young Mr. Wiggins, whose father owned the general store; Mr. Emery, an employee in the bank; Mr. Adamson, whose body was so ridden with arthritis that he had to be helped to his jury box by his son; and five farmers from the outskirts of the town that I knew only by sight, all male and all white.

The judge asked Uncle Marsh what questions he would like to ask the jury. Uncle Marsh rose to his feet and faced the twelve stern faces. He seemed to study them for a moment, before he said, "These are mighty good fellows. I don't have a problem with any one of them."

"Are you telling me you accept the jury as it's composed?" the judge asked.

"Judge, that's what I'm saying."

Uncle Marsh and I had discussed this option. Whichever twelve men the bailiff chose would probably be no better or worse than any other twelve, and we figured a few might even be favorable to us before the trial started. It also put Macteirney in a bind. If he questioned the jury and dismissed those he thought unfit, he might well incur the wrath of the community, which at the start, was solidly behind him. He, too, accepted the jury as it was.

The judge called for opening statements, and Macteirney rose and addressed the jury. He spoke in his deep bass for well over an hour. He started slowly, letting his points build one upon the other, but he soon gathered passion until he waved his arms and pounded a fist into the palm of his other hand. His hell and damnation delivery was straight out of the pulpit of Jonathan Edwards, and like all those in attendance, I couldn't take my eyes off the man. He invoked the Bible and Texas law and the needs of society. When Daniel killed Orvie Blaylock, the boy committed a crime for which there could be no forgiveness. "This is a crime against order, a crime against society." His voice rose in a crescendo. "The defendant set himself above man, above God, and for this the state asks—no, the state demands—conviction. It demands a life for a life."

Behind us, the audience broke out in thunderous applause. By then I had begun to feel as downcast as Daniel. How could we hope to compete against a man who held the power to mesmerize with the mere sound of his voice?

Judge Weatherford banged his gavel until everyone settled down.

Uncle Marsh pushed himself to his feet, his cheeks aflame with color. He looked into the face of each juror before he spoke. "You men all know me, and you know I wouldn't defend a man I believed guilty of murder." His voice was steady and strong.

Macteirney leaped to his feet. "I object, your honor!"

The judge leaned forward and pointed the gavel at my uncle. "Mr. Langston, you will not address the jury on personal terms. They are not your friends."

"They're not my friends?" Uncle Marsh tilted his head to one side as if he didn't fully understand.

"No sir, for this trial they are not," said the judge. "Do you understand what I'm saying, Sir?"

Uncle Marsh nodded politely. "I'll do my best not to think of them as my friends."

A smattering of laughter flittered through the room, and the judge glared at Uncle Marsh. Uncle Marsh held up one hand as if he were taking an oath. "You let me know when I've done something wrong, Judge, and I won't do it again."

The judge leaned back in his chair and told Uncle Marsh to get on with his opening statement. Uncle Marsh faced the jurors.

"I can't preach a sermon like Lawyer Macteirney. He's got a silver tongue, and words roll out of his mouth like they're straight from the Almighty. But they ain't. He's got a lot to say about Daniel, as if the boy is in league with the Devil himself, but he leaves out a heck of a lot, and he twists certain facts so they really ain't the facts at all. Since I ain't much of a speaker, I guess that's about all for now." Uncle Marsh started back for our table when he stopped and again faced the jury. "Maybe I got one more thing to say. This case is about evidence. It ain't about the color of Daniel's skin."

I think right then Macteirney intended to object again. He was half out of his chair, his mouth open, but he must have had second thoughts. After all, if he objected, he would be telling the jury that Daniel's skin did have something to do with this case. He couldn't bring himself to admit that, at least not openly, although he had said as much in his opening remarks. His fingers beat an irregular pattern on the table.

The judge pulled a watch from underneath his robe, opened the case, and seeing it was nearly noon, adjourned the court until two o'clock. The auditorium cleared quickly. We had only one eating establishment in town, a dining room at the Dolan Rooming House where Ma Dolan served meals family style, although Ernie's Bar provided cold cuts with every beer. Most of those in attendance either headed home to fix lunch or went off to their wagons and cars for food they'd brought with them. Sister Rose and her people wandered off under a couple of weeping willows where they sat on the grass and chewed on home-made jerky and corn cakes.

Once the auditorium emptied, Jim dropped to one knee, inserted a key into the lock and opened it. Daniel stood, and his wrist and ankle chains clinked like discordant chimes. Leading Daniel by the arm, Jim took him out the back door and off to his cell.

By the time we got back to our place, Aunt Esther was already putting food on the table: ham, black-eyed peas, and warmed over biscuits and gravy. We didn't have much to say. Uncle Marsh moved his food around with his fork, eating very little, although he finished three cups of coffee. We were getting up to go when Aunt Esther said, "You did fine, Marsh. I know you don't think so, but you did."

"I had so much to say," he said, "but when I got up before the jury, I couldn't think of a thing."

"That Macteirney is a long-winded jackass." Aunt Esther ran her hand over her mouth. "Sure his words were pretty, but he tired the jury out. You could see it in their faces. Now you said what you had to say and sat down. They appreciated that."

"I feel like I'm letting Daniel down. I feel like I'm letting you and Davy down, too. I tell you, Esther, I'm not smart enough. It should be Davy arguing the case rather than me."

"People respect you, Uncle Marsh," I said. "They wouldn't listen to me. They'll listen to you."

His brow came together. "I hope you're right. I surely do."

28

*E*very pew was filled, and dark faces crowded every window. Precisely at two, the bailiff called the court to order, and Judge Weatherford strode into the room, his black robe flowing behind him. Taking a seat behind the bench, he instructed District Attorney Macteirney to call his first witness. Macteirney called Jim, the bailiff administered the oath, and Jim took his seat on the witness chair.

In order to fit his hips in the confined space, Jim shifted his holster and pistol until it rested in his lap. He gripped his hands together, thumbs on top, and glanced at Uncle Marsh and me, his expression one of confusion and dismay. He liked and respected Uncle Marsh, and I was pretty sure he liked me, too. But he was a witness for the prosecution.

Macteirney rose, came around the desk, and stood off to one side so the whole auditorium had a clear view of Jim, yet the district attorney remained less than three steps away, as if to remind the witness that this was his courtroom, so pay attention. Most of Macteirney's early questions established Jim's identity and put him at the scene of the crime. As in his opening remarks, he began slowly, his questions deliberate and precise. When he reached the point in the story where Jim arrived on the scene, his voice became louder, more bombastic. "And at this *schoolhouse*—" His emphasis on 'schoolhouse' made the word sound dirty. "—exactly what did you find?"

"Fact is, I found a lot of things."

"Did you find a body?"

"Not at first, no sir. First, I found Zeb Cain pointing a shotgun at the defendant."

"He was holding the defendant under arrest?"

"No sir. He was about to blow his head off."

A sprinkling of laughter made its way around the courtroom.

"Surely you don't know this for a fact, Deputy."

"He had the hammer cocked when I knocked the gun aside. As it was, he blew a hole as big as your head in the roof."

"Isn't it possible that Mr. Cain never meant to shoot the defendant? Isn't it possible that when you knocked the gun aside, you caused the weapon to discharge?" When Jim didn't answer right away, Macteirney said, "Isn't that possible, Deputy?"

"I guess it's possible."

"And Mister Blaylock? What of him?"

"He was dead."

"And how did he die?"

"I don't rightly know for sure. I wasn't there."

Mactierney's dark eyebrows came together. I think he expected more cooperation from Jim who seemed reticent to answer questions the way the district attorney wanted them answered. "Did Mister Blaylock have visible wounds?" he asked.

"The top of his skull was bashed in."

"By what?"

"A hammer, I suppose."

"And why do you believe it was a hammer?"

"The defendant had one in his hand. There was blood on it."

"Did the defendant have anything to say about what he had done?"

"He said, 'I got him.'"

A stirring went round the pews, and the judge banged his gavel. I glanced at the jury to see what impact Jim's words had had, and I didn't like what I saw. Every one of them, including Mr. Misener, whom I thought of as a good man, appeared angry or outraged.

Macteirney asked half a dozen more questions, which continued Jim's story and ended with the delivery of Daniel to Dr. Gibbs' office. All during the testimony, I took notes and formed questions that Uncle Marsh might ask. I slid the paper over to him, and he read as he stood. He was still reading a minute later when the Judge said, "Mr. Langston?"

Uncle Marsh looked up, a sheepish smile lining his mouth. "Sorry, Your Honor. I'm trying to figure out a few things. Now, let's see, Deputy..." He scratched the back of his ear and appeared perplexed. "I don't recall Mr. Macteirney asking you about Daniel. You took him to Dr. Gibbs after the incident at the schoolhouse. Is that right?"

"Yes, I did."

"Why?"

"He had a knife stuck in his side. Stuck in pretty deep."

"Whose knife was it?"

"Mister Blaylock's; I'd seen him with it earlier that day."

"Was this when you stepped between Mr. Blaylock and Zeb Cain as they were about to start trouble with Daniel and my nephew Davy?"

Macteirney jumped to his feet. "Objection, Your Honor. He's leading the witness, and his statement is prejudicial in the extreme."

"Objection sustained," Judge Weatherford said. "Rephrase your question, Mr. Marsh."

Uncle Marsh scratched the back of his head. "I'm sorry,

Judge. I didn't know so few words could stir up so much trouble."

Laughter erupted from those at the windows, which gave me time to scribble a question on a piece of paper. Uncle Marsh took the paper and read as he faced Jim. "Tell us about the incident where you saw Mr. Blaylock with his knife."

Jim told the story of Blaylock and Cain confronting us on the street. "And Mr. Blaylock and Mr. Cain—you thought they meant to make trouble?" said Uncle Marsh

Mactierney jumped up to object on the grounds that what Jim thought was immaterial. Uncle Marsh said, "The prosecutor is a right objectionable person, Your Honor." Laughter again. "But he was the one who asked all about Jim's work. It only seems fitting that we give Jim a chance to explain himself."

"You are asking for the deputy's opinion, Mr. Marsh. Opinion is not evidence."

"No sir, it's not. But it does tell us why Jim followed those two men out to the schoolhouse. He must have thought it was part of his job."

Judge Weatherford considered the point before he said, "You may answer the question, Deputy."

"When I stepped between Mr. Blaylock and Davy, I believed Mr. Blaylock wanted to start a ruckus. When I saw them trailing after Davy and the defendant, I figured he was still looking for trouble."

"Why Blaylock?"

"I knew his reputation. He had just been released—"

Mactierney rose and objected again. "Mr. Blaylock is not on trial here." His deep bass resounded throughout the auditorium. "His reputation has nothing whatsoever to do with these proceedings, any more than Mr. Marsh's reputation."

Uncle Marsh waved his hand for Mactierney to sit down. "There you go objecting again. A fella can't get a word in edgewise with all your objections."

The judge banged his gavel. "Mr. Marsh, you will address your remarks to the bench, not the prosecutor." The judge cast a stern eye at my uncle. "As for the objection," he focused his attention on Macteirney, "I have already ruled that the deputy can testify as to this point. Now allow him to do so." To Jim he said, "Go on, Deputy."

"Mr. Blaylock had just been released from Huntsville. I wouldn't exactly say I anticipated trouble, but his actions, especially around Davy and the defendant, seemed pretty hostile."

"Why was Blaylock in Huntsville?"

"He knifed a colored man and a colored woman over in Dallas."

"Did he kill them?"

"Yes, sir."

Some already knew of Blaylock's past but many didn't, and a buzzing arose from the room. The Judge banged his gavel for quiet. Uncle Marsh said he didn't have any more questions, and the judge dismissed Jim. I cast a furtive glance at Mactierney, and while the testimony would seem to have weakened his case, he appeared unruffled and confident. He called his next witness, Doc Gibbs, and with his dark, intense eyes watched the older man come forward to take the oath.

Mactierney's early questions established Doc Gibbs' credentials, including the length of time he'd practiced medicine in Twin Forks, which was twice as long as I had been alive. Twenty minutes after Doc Gibbs took the stand, Mactierney finally got around to questions concerning Daniel and Blaylock.

"Now, Doctor, much has been made of the defendant's condition when he was brought to you. Would you please tell us the extent of his injuries."

"He did have a knife stuck in him. Lower left side. That blade was buried a good six inches, but he was in no real danger unless he'd pulled that pig sticker out. If he had, he might have bled to death."

"So he wasn't hurt badly."

"No, sir, not bad at all."

"Now, as for Mr. Blaylock, did you examine the body, Doctor?"

"I went to the ice house and took a look."

"And what did you find."

"The victim had been struck on the head, twice."

"Twice?"

"Yes sir, twice."

"The weapon?"

"Judging from the shapes of the wounds, most likely a hammer."

"And what about the wounds themselves?"

"The first caught Mr. Blaylock toward the front of the cranium." Doc Gibbs placed a finger above his forehead. "This would have been enough to knock the man unconscious. The head would have dipped." He lowered his chin against his chest. "The second blow struck the rear of the skull, here." He placed his fingers on a thinning bald spot. "That was the blow that killed him."

"So the first blow incapacitated him. At that point, he would have been unconscious. Is that correct?"

"It is."

"So the second blow, the one that killed Mr. Blaylock, occurred when the man was unable to defend himself. Is that also correct?"

"It is."

Once more the crowd buzzed, and an expression of triumph lighted Mactierney's face. "Your witness, Sir," he said to Uncle Marsh.

Uncle Marsh looked down at my notes, studying for a minute before he rose and approached Doc Gibbs. "Now, Doc, what I understand is that you weren't at the schoolhouse when all this took place?"

The Doc snorted like a rooting hog. "Now, Marsh, you know I wasn't."

"So you only saw Blaylock after he was dead?"

"That's right."

"There's one thing I can't understand. How can you be sure that first blow knocked Blaylock unconscious? A blow that might knock me flat might not have the same effect on a guy with a thicker skull. Isn't that right?"

Doc Gibbs leaned forward, his hands gripping his knees. "Well, Mr. Blaylock—"

"Whoa there, Doc. My question is not about Blaylock. I'm asking if different people would react differently to a blow on the head, assuming it was applied with the same force?"

"Yes, it's possible. But in Mr. Blaylock's case—"

"Can you be one hundred percent sure that Blaylock was unconscious with that first blow?"

"Well, not one hundred percent."

"So, that first blow might not have knocked out Mr. Blaylock. He might still have had the ability to hurt Daniel, even to kill him."

Doc's dark eyebrows came together to form one continuous bushy line. "I find that highly improbable."

"But not impossible."

"No." Doc Gibbs spoke the word as if it were a sigh. "Not impossible."

Mactierney next called Zeb Cain to the stand. Cain rose from one of the back pews and came forward, his heavy body filling the small aisle. As he passed our table, he glared at us with the perpetual scowl that twisted his face into something ugly and frightening. He hadn't shaved in several mornings, and his dark stubble added to his menacing appearance. He wore tattered overalls and a plaid shirt frayed around the collar. His dusty boots had long ago lost their original color and scuffmarks crisscrossed the surface. He laced his boots with twine, the only part of his apparel that appeared new. He had discarded the sling that he had worn since his encounter with Uncle Marsh, although he leaned slightly to the left as if favoring the shoulder.

The bailiff administered the oath, and Cain took the witness chair, which strained to contain his bulk. He squirmed and fidgeted, unsure what to do with his hands and finally settled on gripping the arms of the chair, which made him appear smaller, as if he were drawing in on himself.

Mactierney's first questions concentrated on Cain's background. Yes, he owned a farm a few miles outside Twin Forks. Yes, he knew Orvie Blaylock before Blaylock went to prison, and yes, once Blaylock was released, they resumed their friendship. Blaylock had even moved in with Cain until his friend could find a job.

"It has been suggested that Mr. Blaylock was intent on causing trouble," MacTierney said. "Is this true?"

"No, it ain't." Cain shook his head, his black hair falling across his eyes. He swept his hair back with a toss of his head. "Orvie served his three years in Huntsville. He sure as hell didn't want to go back."

"When you and he encountered the defendant and David Stoneman on the street on that fateful day, what were your intentions?"

"We didn't have no intentions. We was in town to buy supplies when that Stoneman kid—" he nodded in my direction, "—sassed us both."

"So, you weren't the ones to instigate the trouble?"

"Instigate?" Cain obviously was unfamiliar with the word.

"You didn't start the trouble," Mactietrney said.

"Naw, it was them. They sassed us."

"Deputy Sheriff Jim Kennison said he believed that Mr. Blaylock was the one looking for trouble."

"He didn't get there until it was all over. He didn't see what happened."

"But you and Mr. Blaylock did follow the defendant and David Stoneman out to that schoolhouse."

"Yeah, we did that."

"For what purpose?"

"A while back, me and a friend, Pap Caldwell, stumbled on the old Squires place. We found them two working on the house, cleaning it up."

"And what reason did they give?"

"They said they were fixin' it up for a church."

"And were they?"

"Orvie and me heard that they was building a school for nigger kids. We wanted to see for ourselves. That's all."

"So, you didn't go out to the schoolhouse with the idea of causing trouble or punishing the defendant and his friend for, as you say, sassing you."

Cain shook his head, and his black hair again fell across his eyes. He brushed it back with a sweep of his hand. "No, that ain't the way it happened. We were there, friendly like."

"And what happened when you arrived at the schoolhouse?"

"We no sooner got inside than Davy Stoneman sassed us again. Called Orvie a sonofabitch. Told us to get out."

"And did Mr. Blaylock take exception to this?"

"I'd be a liar to say different. Orvie got good and mad. He slapped the kid. That's when that boy over there—" Cain pointed to Daniel, "—jumped Orvie."

"So it was the defendant who attacked Mr. Blaylock first...with a hammer?"

"He was swinging it like he was crazy as a hoot owl. If you ask me, that boy meant to kill us the minute we walked in."

For the first and last time that day, Uncle Marsh stood and objected. "Judge, I've got to object to Zeb Cain speculating on what was in Daniel's mind. Seems nobody in this room—hell, in this county—has that ability."

"That's a good point Mr. Marsh. Objection sustained." Judge Weatherford pointed his gavel at the twelve men seated to my right. "The jury will ignore that last remark concerning the defendant's state of mind."

Uncle Marsh retook his seat, but if he felt any sense of triumph in this small victory, he didn't show it.

On the other hand, the District Attorney nodded his acceptance but his arched eyebrows said he was peeved at the interruption. He said, "The defendant was wounded in this encounter. How did that happen?"

"Once the colored boy started swinging this hammer, Zeb pulled his knife all right, but that boy ran right at Zeb, ran right into the knife. Zeb never made one move to defend himself. That boy was willing to get stuck to get to Zeb. He knocked Zeb senseless, and then for good measure, hit him again. I figured I was next, and I wasn't going to let that happen."

"So you covered him with your shotgun?"

"That I did."

"And would you have shot him if Deputy Sheriff Kennison had not shown up when he did?"

"Not unless that boy came for me. I would've shot him then."

At that point, Mactierney handed over Zeb Cain to Uncle Marsh. I had written out a series of questions, but my uncle barely perused them before he stood and approached Cain, whose face twisted into a snarl befitting a rabid bulldog. Instead of meeting hostility with hostility, Uncle Marsh flashed a smile, catching the big man off guard. "How's that shoulder, Zeb?"

Inadvertently Cain lifted a hand to his injured shoulder then caught himself.

Uncle Marsh said, "I see you ain't wearing the sling anymore. Did it heal up nicely?"

"It's tolerable."

"How did you hurt that shoulder?"

"You oughta know." He growled the worlds as much as spoke them.

"You tell us, Zeb. Tell us how that shoulder took a beating."

"You laid a ax handle across it."

"Now why would I do a thing like that?"

"You're a mean sonofabitch."

At that point, Uncle Marsh dropped his affable approach, and his voice and face grew harder, more insistent.

"Mean or not, I must've had a reason. Not what would that be?"

"I don't know."

"Now, Zeb, I can call a dozen men who saw what happened. What would they tell this court?"

"How the hell should I know?"

"You slapped my boy, didn't you, Zeb? You slapped Davy."

"The little bastard sassed me."

"What did he say that was so insulting that you felt you had to discipline him?"

Cain clenched his jaw with such force that the muscles along each side stood rigid. "I don't recall."

"Was it because Davy had a colored friend? Was that the reason?"

"I don't recall." He mumbled the words, and his face reddened.

"You can't recall..." Uncle Marsh nodded. "Well, we all forget things we'd rather not remember. Let's see if you remember why you served four months in the county jail. You do remember that, don't you?"

"Yeah. So what?"

"Why did you serve those four months?"

"A guy pulled a knife on me. I defended myself."

"That's not what the court records say. I took a look at them when I was in Hollister last week. They say you pulled a knife first. They say you started the ruckus."

"I didn't start nothing."

"There were four witnesses that said you did. Are all four lying?"

Zeb scowled but said nothing.

Uncle Marsh said, "You know people in this town

think you're a bully, Zeb?"

Mactierney objected, but the judge said, "I want to hear this." Cain glowered at the judge, who said, "Answer the question, Mr. Cain."

"I ain't no bully."

"I got half a dozen people who have something to say about that. You want me to call them to the stand?"

As far as I knew, Uncle Marsh hadn't asked anyone to testify on that point, but Cain shifted his gaze to the audience. He must have been wondering who among us would have the courage to take the stand against him, and he also must have figured that enough people in town disliked him enough to do so. He said, "I got a short temper."

"Do you hold grudges?"

Cain gave another long pause before he grumbled an answer: "Sometimes."

With a hard intensity, Uncle Marsh said, "And you still claim you and Blaylock intended no harm when you went out to that schoolhouse?" He slammed the bottom of his fist on our table with such force the wood crackled and the legs shook as if it might collapse. "If you still claim that, you're a goddamned liar, Jeb Cain, and everyone knows it!"

Mactierney rose to object, but his voice was lost in the uproar of shouting and swearing.

It took a full two minutes for the judge to restore order. The effort brought beads of sweat to his forehead and an angry set to his eyes. He tore into Uncle Marsh for inciting the crowd, and Uncle Marsh took the berating without flinching. When the Judge finished, Uncle Marsh scratched the back of his head and once more played the country hick. "I'm sorry, Judge. I didn't mean to cause so much trouble, but Zeb Cain's lies got me angry." Mactierney objected, and Uncle Marsh shook his head and acted contrite. "I'm saying all the wrong things today, Judge. I'm real sorry."

The judge leaned forward so that part of his upper

body hung over his desk. "Mr. Langston, I accept that you are unfamiliar with court proceedings. But so help me, one more outburst like this and I will hold you in contempt of court and haul your backside off to jail. Do you understand what I'm saying?

"Yes sir, I sure do, and I promise it won't happen again. I don't know what came over me, except that Zeb got me so—"

"Stop right there, Mr. Langston. Not another word." The judge aimed the gavel at my uncle. "Not one more word!"

Still fuming, the judge pulled his watch from underneath his robe, and seeing that it was past four, adjourned the trial until noon the next day. The audience rose and filed out quickly, jabbering to one another like a murder of crows. Some looked back at us, none too kindly, and among them was Zeb Cain, his narrow pig eyes burrowing into me, and his mouth twisting into a sneer that, I believe, was meant to frighten me. Most walked two or three abreast, but Cain's bulk prevented anyone from passing him.

The judge had called Uncle Marsh and District Attorney Macteirney to his chambers—really only the vestibule behind the emersion tank where Reverend Joyner baptized new converts—so Daniel and I had the table to ourselves. He leaned toward me, the chains that linked his wrists and circled under his chair clanging discordant notes. "Davy, stay away from Cain," he said. "He would as soon cut you up as look at you."

"What makes men like him and Blaylock so hateful?" I asked

Daniel shrugged. "I think you have to be taught to hate like that. And whoever taught him, they were taught, too."

"So no one ever gets blamed?"

"They all get blamed as far as I'm concerned." Daniel slid his chair closer to me and added in a whisper, "You think I'm sorry I killed Blaylock? If I had a chance, I'd do it again. I'd do it every day of my life if I could."

There was a wildness in his eyes that unsettled me. He was a colored male talking about killing a white man, and even though intellectually I understood Daniel's feelings, his remark repelled me. Daniel must have seen the way I felt because he pushed his back into the chair and stared off to the front of the courtroom.

Uncle Marsh, his brow creased, his mouth tight, came back to the table and pulled his chair between Daniel and me. "The judge believes the trial will finish tomorrow. The prosecution will rest, then I'll call Davy."

"If Davy's all I've got—" From the sound of his voice, I understood that I had shattered the little confidence he had in us.

"I'll tell the truth, Daniel," I said. "I'll make them believe me. I will."

"They'll believe Cain. They won't believe you." He wasn't exactly angry at me, but I had disappointed him.

All this time Jim sat a few feet away, trying his best to appear disinterested, but now the bailiff came forward and signaled him to take Daniel away. Jim unlocked the chain under the chair. Daniel stood, and we stood with him.

Uncle Marsh gripped Daniel by the shoulder. "Don't give up."

"Can't give up what I don't have," Daniel said. "They've already heard enough to convict me, and they didn't need much."

Jim took him by the arm, but before he could lead him away, Daniel said, "No matter what happens, I thank you Mr. Marsh. You've been kind to me and my mother."

"Son—"

"It's all right, Mr. Marsh. I understand." Daniel looked past Uncle Marsh to me. "It's not your fault. None of this is."

I wasn't sure if he spoke these last words to me or to Uncle Marsh.

"Come on, Boy. Let's get you back to your cell." Jim

tugged on Daniel's arm, and together the two disappeared through the rear exit.

Uncle Marsh and I were the last to leave the house of judgment. All through the proceedings, the preacher stayed in his quarters, coming out only when the judge adjourned for the day. Now he stood on the dais looking down on us and offered a benign smile. He muttered a 'God bless' that sounded perfunctory rather than sincere.

As Uncle Marsh and I walked home, deep oranges and reds streaked the heavy clouds moving in from the Gulf. A slight wind swayed the tops of elms, their limbs waving in unison like somnambulant dancers. "A storm's coming, Davy," Uncle Marsh said. "Tonight or in the morning."

29

*T*he following morning, I rose, dressed and was out of the house before Aunt Esther and Uncle Marsh were up. I left a note to let them know where I was going. I didn't tell them face to face for fear they would try to stop me. I wanted to see Rachel.

Since that morning we made love, I thought about her more than ever. My mind conjured up images of her at the times most hostile to romance—as I carried out the trash, as I ate dinner, as I read *Great Expectations*. She was with me at night as I crawled into bed, and when I awoke to face the next day. Seldom did an hour pass that I failed to remember the heat of her lips, the curve of her body. I kept telling myself that we could find a way to be together, that the world couldn't be so cruel as to keep two people apart who cared for each other.

Even as I walked the river trail, I knew deep inside that my desires were nothing more than illusions. Yet, as much as I told myself that any dreams of a future that included Rachel were stupid as well as dangerous, I couldn't extinguish a spark of hope that drove each step. I think that, if I accepted the future as inevitable, I could never have made that journey, but hope, a tiny seed, gave me courage. Perhaps that is all that hope is, a way to instill us with courage, for without it, we would all be cowards incapable of action.

I left town under heavy gray skies that drained the color out of the river, the buildings, the earth itself. The Trinity flowed slowly, eddies swirling in the middle where the current ran deepest. As always, the water was dark with mud. A fish broke the surface, its mouth open, searching for water bugs that scurried this way and that like hyperkinetic skaters. At one point I surprised an unkindness of ravens pecking away at a dead possum, and they took flight, all except one that remained guarding its prize, refusing to surrender, ready to fight. Another time a hawk dropped from the sky, a blur that swooped to the grass and rose with a small rabbit caught in its talons, the tiny creature squealing as the knife-like points dug in. The hawk and captive disappeared among the tree tops.

The river smelled of decay and death, and I was glad when I forged inland toward the house a quarter mile away. Broken corn stalks and brown leaves littered the fields, but the house was so white that it surprised me. In Boonesville, the structures were little more than hovels. Even Sister Rose's place, as nice as she kept it, was a shack compared to our home. But this house rivaled any in Twin Forks, except for the Barron's, which was more mansion than house. The paint appeared bright and new, and not one shingle or board needed repair. On both sides of the front porch, rose bushes showed the very beginnings of new life, their crooked stems cut short, the new leafs scarlet in hue. Curtains covered the front windows, and smoke drifted from the chimney, carrying with it the smell of frying bacon. I had left home that morning before breakfast, and my belly rumbled with hunger.

Just as I reached the porch, the door opened, and Solomon's dark bulk filled the door frame, his expression one of disquiet. "What's the problem, Mr. Davy?" he asked.

I said, "I came for a visit."

His brow wrinkled, but he stepped aside and ushered me in. The aroma of bacon permeated the interior, and on the stovetop sat a pan full of biscuits. Rachel stood at the table holding a skillet filled with scrambled eggs colored brown with bacon grease. Our eyes locked for a moment, and then she looked away and scraped eggs onto a plate.

"I'm sorry to call so early," I said.

"That's no problem, Mr. Davy," Solomon said.

"I don't deserve to be called 'Mister'," I said. "Just Davy, please."

Rachel said, "You want breakfast?"

I could sense that her suggestion made Solomon uncomfortable. I suspected that, other than Miss Pilgrim, not many white people had sat at his table. Maybe not even her. "I don't want to be a bother," I said.

She set another plate on the table and served the rest of the eggs. She added a couple of pieces of bacon and a biscuit to each plate, and the three of us sat. While Solomon said grace, I bowed my head out of respect, but I watched Rachel and marveled once more at the richness of her skin, the silkiness of her hair, the dark eyes that examined me as I examined her. I noticed again the little ribbon of a scar on her chin, and wondered what accident or misfortune had caused it.

During breakfast, I explained that Uncle Marsh and I had spent the previous evening going over the testimony I would deliver later that day. Solomon and Rachel listened politely, but when I finished, Rachel said, "You and your uncle can't really believe it will do any good."

"Rachel..." Solomon spoke her name in much the same manner as Uncle Marsh would speak mine when he wanted me to be quiet.

"It's cruel, Papa," Rachel said. "Daniel's sitting in that jail knowing what's going to happen."

"Uncle Marsh and me—we won't give up without a

fight." My tone was full of bravado, but I feared she was right. Yet for the life of me, I didn't want her to believe the situation to be hopeless.

After breakfast, Rachel walked me to the river, both of us silent until we reached the road. There I dug into my pocket and drew out a slim volume, Elizabeth Barrett Browning's *Sonnets from the Portuguese*. "This is for you," I said, handing it to her.

She didn't take the book. "Don't you want it?" I asked.

She pointed to the river. "See those two islands." They weren't islands so much as sandbars with some scrub brush growing on them. One was situated at the far bank, one near us, separated by twenty yards of dark water. "That river is goin' to keep them apart forever, and one never going to reach the other."

I wasn't ready to give up. I tapped the book. "There's one poem, Sonnet forty-three, her most famous. She wrote it for her husband."

I had spent part of the previous evening memorizing the poem, and now I began to quote it word for word. "How do I love thee? Let me count the ways. I love thee to the depth..."

I didn't get past the second line before she slapped the book, and it flew from my hand.

"Take your book and go away. There's nothing for you here, Davy Stoneman. Nothing!" She whirled and fled toward her house.

For the next ten minutes, I stood there, the book at my feet, and stared at those sandbars and hoped she would come back. All that time, I thought my chest was about to split open and the very life of me spill out.

The walk home was long and lonely. I tried to tell myself that Rachel was gone from my life, and I should vanquish my pain and concentrate on helping Daniel. But we humans are too weak, too fragile. When we are in pain, we find it hard to concentrate on anything but that.

As I crossed the old wooden bridge that spanned the

Trinity and entered Twin Forks, a slight drizzle began, enough to dampen the ground. At that point, I sensed a difference, a stillness that seemed to mirror my emptiness. At first I put it down to the fact that I had projected my mood onto the town. Yet, as I walked down Main Street, I saw a couple of wagons and teams in front of Ernie's Bar, but not one soul strolled along the boardwalk, not one wagon or automobile rolled up in the street. No dog barked, no child yelled at play. Most of the storefront windows were shrouded in darkness, as if they had already closed even though it was still morning. For one frightening moment, I feared ghosts populated the town. But ghosts are imaginary and not to be feared. Real people inhabited Twin Forks, and it was those real people that I needed to fear.

As I reached our store the first drops of rain splattered upon the dirt. I had no sooner opened the door when Uncle Marsh came around the counter, holding the ax handle in his right hand. I think he had been waiting for me. "Come along, Davy. We need to get to the jail."

Aunt Esther stood behind the counter, shadows obscuring part of her face, but the worry lines around her mouth and eyes were deep. Without a word, I fell in step behind Uncle Marsh, my personal concerns forgotten, and I had to run to keep up.

Uncle Marsh started through the jail door but found it locked. He banged the ax handle against the wood. "Jim! Jim Kennison! This is Marsh Langston!"

The lock snapped, the door opened, and we stepped inside. Jim leaned into the door, slipping the lock back into place. Susanna Barron stood beside the desk, her lips pushed together, and her cheeks glowed angry red. She glared at Uncle Marsh and me as if she hated us.

"You know what's going on over at Ernie's?" Uncle Marsh asked. "A dozen men are talking lynching. Did you know that?"

The word 'lynching' sent a chill through me. Although I

had never seen one, I knew they happened all too often. Until this moment, I had not allowed myself to think of such a possibility, even though Daniel must have.

Jim ran his fingers through his hair. "Right now it's only talk."

"They're getting liquored up," Uncle Marsh said. "Sooner or later they'll come calling."

Jim looked to Susanna, and I realized then that she had come to persuade Jim not to interfere, to let the men at Ernie's have their way. "He's only a colored boy," she had said to me. Perhaps her father had sent her to smooth the way, perhaps she had come on her own, but regardless, her purpose was clear. Once I thought her the most beautiful girl in the county, perhaps the whole state, but when I looked at her now I saw that her lips were a bit too thin, her eyes too close together, her jaw too square. She wasn't pretty at all, I told myself, and I wondered how a girl could lose her looks in so short a time.

Uncle Marsh said, "You make the wrong choice here, and living with yourself is going to be right near impossible. If you want help, I'll stand by you."

Without asking permission, I stepped through the oak door leading to the cells. Daniel sat on his bunk, hugging the shadows. His shirt was open, his fingers probing the bandage. "I've been listening," he said. "They don't think I can hear, but I hear every word."

He remained so far under the top bunk and in shadows that he was a specter.

"They fear your uncle." Daniel leaned into the light, his elbows thrust forward upon his knees. Up until that moment, I believed him to be apathetic, that he had surrendered himself to his fate, but I saw now that I was mistaken. A fire burned in his eyes, not from fever, but from defiance. "They think he has tricks to get me off."

"We've got no tricks," I said. "All we have is the truth."

"I guess that's what they fear the most," he said.

In the other room, Uncle Marsh said he was going to

get his gun. The door opened then slammed.

I heard Susanna say, "You listen to me, Jim Kennison. You've got to make up your mind right now. You can't stop them, even with that old man. What kind of help could he be anyway?"

Daniel pushed himself out of the bunk and stood. The light from the barred window fell across his wound, which had reopened, the white gauze so deeply crimson it appeared almost black, but Daniel showed no sign of pain or discomfort. Blood spotted his fingertips.

"Jim!" I shouted. "Get in here! Quick!"

Jim came rushing through the door, his right hand gripping the butt of his .45, but when he saw Daniel, he pulled up short. Daniel swayed and grabbed the top bunk for support. "Go get Doc Gibbs," Jim said to me. "Hurry, Davy."

As Jim unlocked the cell, I dashed into the front office, passing Susanna as she entered the cell area. Before I reached the front door, Susanna screamed, a high piercing mixture of fear and pain, and something heavy hit the cell bars. A fraction of a second later, a shot rang out, the explosion thunderous in the confines of the jail. I halted, frightened into immobility.

Susanna continued to scream, and she stumbled into the doorway, her head arched back, her mouth agape, her hands clawing the air. A hand grasped her hair.

Daniel pushed her forward, the barrel of Jim's .45 jammed into her right temple, and I understood right then that when I found him picking at his bandage, Daniel was working at re-opening his wound and setting into motion his plan to draw Jim into unlocking the cell. I happened along at the right moment to aid Daniel.

"Open the door and get out of my way, Davy." Daniel's hand shook and the barrel of the single action .45 bobbed up and down. "Get out of my way or so help me—"

"You wouldn't shoot me," I said. "That wouldn't make any sense at all."

"Get out of my way—" His voice croaked like a dying frog. "—or I'll shoot this girl right here, right now."

Susanna had ceased her screams, replacing them with little chirping noises that sounded like a wounded bird. With her eyes, she pleaded for me to help her. I could do nothing but stand and watch. He pushed her toward me, I reached around and opened the door, and they lurched past. The rain fell in sheets now, blowing in at an oblique angle. Already the hard dirt had melted into sticky mud that, the moment they staggered into the street, stained the hem of Susanna's dress. The cold rain ran down Daniel's bare chest, soaking his bandage and turning his blood into colored water.

Despite the rain, the shot must have resonated throughout the town, and people were out of their shops. Old Mr. Wiggins and his son stood protected from the rain by their awning. Far down the street Mr. Misener watched from inside his livery. To my right, more than a dozen men, including Zeb Cain, piled out of Ernie's Bar. Lon Barron came from the bank and saw his daughter with the gun pressed to her head

"Susanna!" he shouted.

The men from Ernie's Bar charged as if to overwhelm Daniel with their numbers.

"I'll kill her!" Daniel screamed. "So help me God, I'll kill her!"

Lon leapt off the walk, stumbling, his large belly almost tipping him forward. He lurched in front of the mob, his arms raised, and brought them to a halt. Lon whirled to face Daniel and his daughter. "Let her go! Let my daughter go!"

Daniel twisted his fingers deeper into Susanna's hair, forcing her head back so that she looked up at the gray sky, her eyes fluttering as she tried to keep them open against the driving rain.

Cain stepped beside Lon. "You let her go, boy." He delivered his order in a guttural growl.

Lon placed a hand against Cain's chest and tried to push him back. Cain saw the desperation on Daniel's face, as we all saw it, but he didn't care. He wanted the girl out of the way so he and his boys could get at Daniel. Cain said louder, "You let her go, boy, if you know what's good for you."

Quite unexpectedly, Daniel smiled. "Come on, Mister Cain, come right over here and try to take her from me. I got a bullet for you and one for the mayor and maybe a couple more. If that's what you want, come right ahead. I'll be happy to oblige."

Cain paled. For some reason, he had never figured Daniel might use that weapon on him, and the thought shocked him into silence. Daniel's smile widened, and for one moment, one precious moment, I believe he reveled in his ability to shape events. All of his life, white people had pushed him around, and now, those same people, including Zeb Cain, feared him.

Lon Barron held out a hand as if offering a gift. "Let my daughter go. Please," he said.

"Daddy..." Susanna's plea was a whimper.

Men began to spread out, flanking Daniel. Mr. Misener and the Wiggins', father and son, had come up behind him. Daniel half whirled to face those on his right, then those on the left. He glanced over his shoulder and saw those to his rear.

Beside me, Jim staggered to the door, leaning against the frame, his left arm bleeding above the elbow, the sleeve dark with blood. He lifted a short-barreled .38, trying to sight it, but he couldn't keep his hand steady.

Surrounded, caught in a trap from which he saw no escape, Daniel must have given in right then to that bestial nature that resides in us all. He dropped his thumb over the hammer of the .45 and drew it back, and I knew, as every man there must have known, that he intended to kill Susanna and whomever else he could before they overwhelmed him. His finger tightened on the trigger.

I stood on the boardwalk, paralyzed, but I was not alone. Every man there was frozen, unable to act, too far away or too frightened by the horror about to unfold.

"Daniel!" The voice issued from across the street. "You don't want to do this, Son."

Uncle Marsh stood in front of our store, holding the Winchester he had gotten from Mr. Misener, the stock resting under his right arm. His expression was oddly sad, as if he already knew the outcome of these events.

"You promised me," Daniel said.

"I know," Uncle Marsh said.

Daniel swung the gun away from Susanna and snapped off a shot, the boom of the .45 as loud as a clap of Texas thunder, smoke issuing from the barrel in a white cloud. Cain spun away, a spout of blood erupting from his head. Susanna let out a scream so high and piercing that it could have broken crystal, and every man on that street ducked and dropped, trying to avoid the next shot, every man but Uncle Marsh, who tucked the Winchester into his shoulder. Daniel spun toward Uncle Marsh.

They both fired at the same moment, but Daniel never intended to hit Uncle Marsh. His shot went well over our store to punch a hole in the sky. Uncle Marsh found his mark. The bullet struck Daniel in the chest with a solid thud. He appeared to take a step back, then his knees gave way, and he went over backward, still gripping Susanna and taking her down with him.

Uncle Marsh lowered the rifle, and stepping off the boardwalk, crossed the fifteen feet that separated them. He knelt and disengaged Daniel's fingers from Susanna's hair, now a wet, tangled mess.

Lon Barron rushed to his daughter and lifted her in his arms, holding her while she sobbed into the crook of his shoulder.

Though the bullet had struck Cain, he remained on his feet holding the left side of his head, blood streaming through his fingers. He dropped his hand, and blood flowed down his neck onto his collar. Like a surgeon's scalpel, Daniel's shot had removed an earlobe.

Cain reached into his belt and drew out his fishing knife. Rain bounced off the serrated blade. He took half a dozen steps before Uncle Marsh said, "What the hell do you think you're doing?"

"I'm going to gut—" Cain began.

"I'm taking the boy home to his mother," Uncle Marsh said.

Cain touched his wounded ear. "Look what he did to me!"

Uncle Marsh worked the lever of the Winchester and lifted the barrel so that it lined up with Cain's belly. Every man there saw, but not a one, not Zeb Cain himself, possessed the courage to push Uncle Marsh any further. When I looked at my uncle's face, I understood why. His eyes held more than a bit of madness, almost as if he would welcome the chance to unload his weapon on Cain, or any other man who tried to stop him.

"Davy," he called to me.

"Yes, sir."

"Go with Mr. Misener and help him hitch up a team," he said. "Be quick now."

I hurried after him. As I passed Daniel, I cast a glance at the body. Up to that point, I'd had little time to feel anything, little time to react, but now I gazed into the open, dead eyes of my friend and saw the dark hole over his heart. By the time I reached the livery, I was sobbing.

It took less than ten minutes for Mr. Misener and me to hitch up the team and wagon. I drove up the middle of the street, the steady downpour soaking my clothes, my wet hair hanging in my eyes. Men and a few women stood under overhangs or inside stores, peering out. Except for the rain and the squeals of the wagon wheels, the town remained silent. I was still crying, but the rain blended with my tears. I kept my eyes straight to the front, trying not to show any emotion.

I halted the team beside Uncle Marsh and jumped down. Together we lifted Daniel onto the wagon bed. At that moment, I caught a glimpse of Jim Kennison through the open door of the jail seated at his desk with Dr. Gibbs stripping away the bloody sleeve of his shirt to get to the wound. Jim looked back at me with a quizzical expression that seemed to ask how this could have happened.

Aunt Esther came to stand on the boardwalk. "Davy, go put on some dry clothes. You'll catch your death otherwise."

"I want to go with Uncle Marsh."

"I'll keep watch until you're back," Uncle Marsh said.

It took me less than five minutes to dry myself and put on fresh clothes and boots. I donned my heavy jacket, and threw on a slicker and a rain hat. By the time I reached Uncle Marsh, I had gained control enough to stifle my tears. He thrust the rifle at me. "Don't let anyone mess with the wagon."

I spent an anxious three or four minutes peering into the rain, but no one made a move to interfere. Cain stood across the street, one hand holding a bloody kerchief to his ear. I kept my eye on him. If any trouble came, it would come from him. But I had no reason to worry. Uncle Marsh had cowed them all.

Uncle Marsh walked from our store carrying a blanket, which he spread over Daniel. We climbed up onto the seat, the wood groaning under our combined weight. "You take the reins, Davy."

He laid the Winchester across his lap and looked at Cain and the other men who stood with him, all soaked by the rain, their clothes sagging with the weight of the water. "Anybody follows, I'll take it they mean to do harm," Uncle Marsh said.

I flicked the reins. The horses, uneasy at standing so long in the downpour, lurched forward. We picked up the river road and headed west toward Boonesville. The Trinity swirled with fresh debris, evidence of hard rain upstream, and I wondered if we were in for one of those floods that happened every few years when the river overflowed its banks and inundated the bottoms. Already I noted a slight rise, less than a foot I judged, but a rise nonetheless. With a steady rain for a day or so, the river would jump the channel. Back in '03 before I came to live with Uncle Marsh and Aunt Esther, the water had come right into town, flowing down the middle of Main Street for a few hours before it receded. It didn't flood any of the stores, but in its wake, the water left behind piles of rubbish and waste, stinking up the town for more than a month until townsfolk managed to clean up the residue and dump it back into the river.

The downpour filled the ruts in the road, and the wagon wheels sank halfway to their hubs, but the team trudged onward. Several times I looked back at Daniel. One hand remained outside the blanket, its open palm collecting a little pool of rain. Except for the jostling of the wagon, the hand remained immobile, like the hand of a statue. The wet blanket formed an outline around his body, and I imagined him underneath the blanket, cold and growing colder. I had an urge to throw off my coat and wrap it around him to keep him warm.

Less than a hundred yards from the path that led to Boonesville, I made out a group of people standing in the rain. From that distance, I was unable to make out individual faces. Somehow, the word had already reached them. I reined in the team. Most had blankets thrown around their shoulders, and the rain pelted their bare heads and soaked them to the skin.

Without a word, Solomon stepped to the back of the wagon, Rachel at his side, and for a single moment, she looked up at me. I was numb inside—I had seen and experienced too much for a person my age—for a person any age—yet the sight of her still caused a tightness around my heart, a knotting in my belly.

Laying the rifle on the floorboard, Uncle Marsh

dropped to the ground and went to Sister Rose who stood surrounded by her people. He removed his hat, holding it across his chest, and spoke a few words I could not hear because of the rain. Even so, I saw the suffering buried so deeply in her eyes that I figured she would never lose it, not if she lived to be a hundred and fifty. But despite her pain, she reached out to grasp Uncle Marsh's hand, and without speaking, forgave him.

Solomon and two other men cradled Daniel like a baby, the blanket still covering him, one arm dangling free, and as they ascended the path, the hand bounced as if waving goodbye. The folks from Boonesville followed them, Sister Rose bringing up the rear.

Uncle Marsh climbed up beside me, and together we watched until the people disappeared among the brush and trees. As I pointed the team toward home, I glanced at Uncle Marsh and found his face as dark as the weather.

The rain beat against our faces, and the horses strained to keep the wagon from getting stuck in mud. Once we came to a place where the river swirled into a cut, eating away the earth in great chunks and undercutting an elm, which slanted far out over the water. Uncle Marsh waved a hand, urging me onward. I flicked the reins, and the wagon bounced over exposed roots.

We traveled a few yards further when we heard a thunderous crack and looked back to see the elm topple into the river, the entire upper part caught in the current, knotty roots holding to the muddy bank like arthritic fingers. With a groan, the tree surrendered to the water and left a gaping hole in the road that the river rushed in to fill.

By the time we reached the outskirts of Twin Forks, we caught up with the elm where it was wedged against the wooden supports of the old bridge. The current had soaked and blackened the bark, contrasting it with the white of the bridge. If left unattended, that elm, with the help of the current, would eat away the underpinnings until the bridge collapsed, sending it in pieces to the Gulf of Mexico, over two hundred miles downstream.

As we passed the first building on the edge of town, the Barron mansion, all cupolas and spires, I experienced the first chill that shook me like a man stricken with palsy. At first I thought it nothing more than a reaction to the cold water dripping on my neck and soaking my shirt collar. I told myself I was tired. Another chill struck, and then another, and I knew I could not blame my wet collar.

I drove the team under the hoist and into the livery, which smelled of fresh hay and horse droppings. A couple of horses in their stalls pawed the ground, acknowledging the arrival of their mates. I kicked the brake and wrapped the reins around the handle.

Mr. Misener stepped out of his office. "I wondered if you'd get back today. The river's on the rise."

"Road washed out behind us." Uncle Marsh climbed down, and I handed him the rifle.

I slipped down on the opposite side, trying to hide from Mr. Misener and Uncle Marsh, believing that they might think less of me if they spotted my shakes. Water ran off my hat and slicker, creating puddles on the dry floor. My hands felt like ice, and I couldn't stop them from shaking either, so I stuffed them inside the pockets of my slicker. Uncle Marsh stepped around the team, and I lowered my head, hiding my face under the brim of my hat. "Go home, Davy," he said, "Tell Esther I'll be along as soon as I help Mr. Misener with the team and wagon."

The town was shut down. Not one business had its doors open or its lights on. I trudged the hundred yards to our place and mounted the back stairs. The pain in my ribs was now paired with the shakes. Under the landing's overhang, I stripped off my rain gear. Without the extra protection, the cold cut right through my clothes. I stumbled into the kitchen, hoping I could make it to my room without Aunt Esther seeing me. I thought if I could just get underneath the covers and get warm, I'd be fine.

Aunt Esther caught me outside my door. "Uncle Marsh will be along in a bit," I said. I tried to control my voice, but it quivered and gave me away.

"You look frightful," she said.

I started to tell her that I was tired—tired and saddened—by all that had happened, figuring that would be explanation enough, but another chill struck me with the force of an earthquake.

Aunt Esther put me right to bed, covering me with so many blankets that I had difficulty shifting my weight. I stayed there for the next week, drifting in and out of consciousness, burning with fever or wracked by chills. On that first day, Dr. Gibbs came by, and after a cursory glance, declared I had influenza, perhaps the very strain that had taken so many lives during the great epidemic the year before.

Three days into my illness, when my fever rose to above a hundred and four, Aunt Esther took herself to Boonesville and returned with Sister Rose, who administered some of her medicinal herbs in sassafras tea. Within half an hour, my fever dropped. From that point, my sleep became less troubled, my mind more alert. I often awoke to find Sister Rose at my bedside.

I improved enough so that Sister Rose began reading to me for an hour or more each day, a few short stories by Mark Twain that made me laugh. Sister Rose smiled at the humor, but she couldn't bring herself to laugh, and I wanted to crawl into a dark corner and hide for enjoying myself.

A week after she brought me her potions, Sister Rose stopped coming, and I asked Aunt Esther about her. "She's opened her school. She's teaching little boys and girls to read and write. She said she'd drop by on Saturday to see how you're doing."

By then I had regained enough strength to sit up and read to myself, but I missed her. She remained my one link to Daniel. Even through the worse part of my illness, I couldn't take my mind off him. Not one person, man or boy, woman or girl in Twin Forks could I call friend, unless I included Rachel, but I feared she, too, was gone from my life.

No matter how hard I tried, I could not blot out the images associated with Daniel's death. Often I revisited those moments in my fevered dreams, so real I could feel the cold rain on my face and smell the acrid gunpowder. In the middle of such dreams, I would force myself to wake, too full of pain and sadness to stay in that world any longer.

I could have blamed Uncle Marsh—after all, he pulled the trigger—but he had only kept his promise to Daniel. I have no doubt that, if the town had gotten to my friend, they would have lynched him. He broke jail to avoid such a fate, and Uncle Marsh spared him that indignity.

Up until that point in my life, I doubt that I ever truly hated anything or anyone. But Zeb Cain and Lon Barron and the people like them had taught me well. I understood that they were products of a world that they had not made, yet I could not forgive them. They were evil men who had done evil deeds, and if I could, I would have wiped them from the face of the earth. One evening, as I sat in the living room reading James' *The American*, I looked up from my book. Uncle Marsh had his face buried in the newspaper, and Aunt Esther was repairing a sock.

"They're the ones who ought to be dead," I said. "Lon Barron and Zeb Cain. They're to blame for all that's happened."

"God will give them their rewards," Aunt Esther said.

"They deserve it right now, right here on earth," I said.

Uncle Marsh lowered his newspaper and looked at me with a mixture of pity and understanding. "People don't always get what they deserve. Sometimes the bad don't get punished, the good don't get rewarded."

The next morning Sister Rose came by, and I said the same thing to her. "You don't waste your life on hating," she told me. "You find other ways, better ways, to make your feelings work for you."

"Like your school," I said.

"It's a godsend."

Miss Pilgrim came by too, helping me to prepare for the exams I would take in May. She assigned readings and compositions, which she graded sentence by sentence, word by word. Sitting by her side, I agonized over every mark, every comment, but her criticisms forced me to work harder and longer until even I noticed an improvement in my writing.

One evening past nine, as we sat in the kitchen going over a composition I had written on Milton, she removed her thick spectacles to rub her eyes. Her face appeared more haggard than usual, the skin sagging around her jowls. I suggested that she might have taken on too much by tutoring me at night. "I'm afraid I'm going to have a lot of free time." When she saw that I didn't understand, she said, "I gave a few old textbooks to Sister Rose for her school. They were out of date and taking up space in the storeroom, but Mayor Barron found out. He's having me brought up before the school board. They mean to fire me." Reaching across the table, she patted my hand. "Don't worry, my boy. It's time I step down. The school needs new blood."

"I had teachers in Dallas before I came to live with Aunt Esther and Uncle Marsh," I said. "Not one was as good as you. Not one. You shouldn't have to go. No ma'am, you shouldn't."

She slipped the spectacles back over her nose, pushing them into place with a forefinger. "It's not as if I have a choice."

"Do you hate them, Miss Pilgrim?" I slammed an open palm on the table. "Do you hate them now?"

She stared across the table, her eyes made big by the thick glasses. "I hate what they stand for. Yes, I do hate that. As for hating them, at my age I have precious few years left to waste on hating any person. It takes too much energy."

30

Aunt Esther laid out a dinner of pot roast and mashed potatoes, and Uncle Marsh and I had seated ourselves when we heard the footsteps on the back porch. A knock sounded, and Uncle Marsh opened the door to discover old Mr. Wiggins, who was breathing a bit hard from the climb up the stairs. Uncle Marsh invited him inside, but the old man shook his head. "I was playing forty-two over at Ernie's, and I heard talk. Some of the boys are planning to pay a visit to that school tonight, the one run by your colored lady friend. Said they planned to get even for all the trouble her boy caused. Thought you'd want to know, considering everything that's happened."

He descended the stairs, his hand gripping the handrail to steady himself.

"Thank you, Mr. Wiggins," my uncle called after him.

Closing the door, he found Aunt Esther standing behind him, her hands caught up in her apron. "Don't suppose you have time for supper," she said.

"When I get back." He disappeared into their bedroom. Aunt Esther followed.

I figured if I asked to go, Aunt Esther would tell me

that I was still too weak, that any strain might put me right back in bed, but I couldn't let Uncle Marsh go alone, so I went to my room and slipped on my heavy coat.

I spotted the ax handle on the kitchen counter, the one on which Uncle Marsh had carved "truth" and "justice." I swept it up, gripping it in both hands like a baseball bat. The curve of the wood fit my hands as if it had been made for me, and a surge ran up my arms as if that handle possessed some supernatural power.

Aunt Esther stood on the landing and watched Uncle Marsh disappear into the night. I stepped past her and descended the stairs two at a time, expecting her to call me back, but she never uttered a word.

I caught up with Uncle Marsh halfway to Jim Kennison's office. From Ernie's Bar, loud, angry voices filtered through the closed doors. We saw no one, but with enough drinks in them, they would soon find the courage to march on Sister Rose's school.

We found Jim behind his desk, the lamps unlit, the room in deep shadows. Holding his left arm stiffly, he stood, keeping the desk between him and us. When Daniel had wrestled the gun from him, Jim had taken a bullet above his left elbow. The slug chipped bone. Uncle Marsh told me his arm might be stiff the rest of his life.

"Do you know what the boys over at Ernie's are planning?" my uncle asked.

"Yes sir, I know." Jim touched his wounded arm, as if to draw our attention to it. "You expect me to do something about it? But if I help you, Mayor Barron and Susanna will never speak to me again, not after what happened."

"What did happen, Jim?" Uncle Marsh asked. "You tell me. What happened when Daniel took that gun from you?"

"He jumped me when I went to help. He grabbed my gun and shot me."

"He shot you in the arm. He could've killed you, but he

didn't. He could've killed Susanna, but he didn't. I grant you, he tried to kill Zeb Cain, but hell—I almost did that."

"The boy took a shot at you, too," Jim said.

"He gave me an excuse to kill him—nothing more."

Jim grimaced as if he had a stomachache, and I could sense his insides churning. "I don't know what you expect of me," he said.

Uncle Marsh eyed him for a good ten seconds before he said, "You disappoint me, Jim."

"I'm bound to disappoint somebody, no matter what I do."

"There's only one person in this world you can't afford to disappoint." Uncle Marsh stepped to the door. "Come on, Davy."

I followed him outside. "But Jim—"

"Jim hasn't made up his mind whose side he's on," my uncle said.

"You could talk to him, persuade him—"

"A man has to have the courage to make up his own mind. Right now, there ain't nothing I can do or say that will make any difference." He pointed to the ax handle. "What do you plan to do with that?"

I pointed to the Winchester. "What do you plan to do with that?"

Smiling, he slapped me on the shoulder. "We better hustle. We don't want any of these boys from town beating us out there."

We crossed the bridge and caught the river road, the stars lighting our path. The earth had dried since the rain, and our boots kicked up dust that drifted behind us. Still weak from the influenza, I found the going hard, sucking in great gulps of air that burned my chest, but soon I fell into a rhythm, and the pain eased. Uncle Marsh never broke stride, though a couple of times he glanced at me to make sure I kept up.

At last we came to the path that led to Boonesville. I started to ask Uncle Marsh if we should go there to seek help, but I realized that that was a bad idea. If people from Boonesville joined us, the men of Twin Forks would single them out for retribution. It was best that we try to handle this ourselves and not put others in jeopardy.

Once we entered the woods, the trail narrowed, and Uncle Marsh took the lead. Deep shadows closed in like black ghosts. Except for our footfalls, the woods remained silent. Not even the call of a single bird broke the night's stillness. Only once did our approach send a possum or coon scurrying off into the brush, and I figured we must be the first to travel the road that night.

Less than a hundred yards later, I spotted a circle of lamplight illuminating the front of the schoolhouse. We broke into the clearing, and there Sister Rose, Solomon and Rachel waited within the light. On either side stood a half dozen men from Boonesville. One man carried a single shot .22, another man an axe, the rest pieces of wood picked from the ground. A bit wary, the men watched us approach, wondering, I suppose, if we were part of the group intent on burning down the school. Sister Rose knew better. So did Solomon and Rachel.

Sister Rose stepped forward, offering her hand. Uncle Marsh took it, and then he shook hands with Solomon.

All the time I kept my eyes on Rachel, but other than a one single glance, she focused on Uncle Marsh, almost as if she feared to look at me.

"Guess you know what's brewing," Uncle Marsh said.

"We not runnin'," Solomon said.

"Davy and me would be proud to stand with you."

"Things liable to get nasty," said Solomon.

"That they are." Uncle Marsh looked back the way we'd come. "Don't know how close they are behind us."

"We gots someone out there," Solomon said. "We knew you coming before you got here."

"I suspected you did," Uncle Marsh said, and I now realized that the rustling brush was no possum.

"Was LeeRoy that easy to spot?" Solomon asked.

"I don't think any of those boys from town will notice," Uncle Marsh said. "There will be too many of them, and most will be liquored up. We'll hear them coming long before we see them."

"If you and Davy want to stay—" He glanced at those around him as if asking for approval and said, "—we'd be glad to have you."

"If that's the case, can I make suggestion?"

"You have something in mind?" Sister Rose asked.

"Put half the men off in the trees to one side, half on the other. Solomon and me—we'll stay right here, meet 'em head on. Those boys will get quite a shock when they think they're surrounded. Surprise—that's a serious weapon."

"This is my school, Mr. Marsh," Sister Rose said. "I won't go off and hide. No, sir, I'm staying right here, with you."

"Yes ma'am, I suppose you will," Uncle Marsh said.

"I'll stay with you, too," I said. I wanted to impress Rachel, to show her that I had the courage to stand with her and her people, even though I was damned scared.

"No, Davy. That's not what I need from you," Uncle Marsh said.

I didn't bother to argue. It never did any good when Uncle Marsh believed he was right, and in this case, he was the only man among us with military experience. Everyone deferred to him. After a few more instructions, I followed three men off into the trees.

Then I noticed someone walking at my side and discovered that it was Rachel. My heart beat a little faster, and my face flushed.

The five of us crouched among the trees. I glanced at the men in whose company I found myself. Two were in their forties, gray hairs sprinkled among the black, but the third was no older than I, a kid who appeared underfed. He clutched a piece of oak with a large, wicked knot, which reminded me of a mace, those iron weapons used during the Middle Ages. Our eyes met, and I sensed a hostility that extended to me, as if he saw me as the enemy, too.

The trees and brush hid us well. The night remained black, except for the circle of light haloed around Solomon, Sister Rose and Uncle Marsh. As if he were no more than a shadow, LeeRoy, thin and wiry, slipped from the trees, but before he uttered a word, we heard them, as Uncle Marsh said we would, their voices full of liquored-up courage. Their torches lighted the woods and cast ghost-like shadows.

I looked into Rachel's dark eyes, the flames reflected in her pupils, and discovered with amazement that a calmness had settled over me. If by some chance I were to die this night, I would die in the company of people I respected and loved. Maybe when the end comes, a man can't ask for more than that.

Led by Lon Barron and Zeb Cain, his left ear bandaged, the mob stormed into the clearing, and in a way, they surprised me. I expected that they would come covered in white sheets, their faces hidden, but they must have felt so vindicated that they chose to do it in the open. I suppose that was why Tommy Barron—Tommikins—was there, his fingers hooked under his belt, marching right beside his father, the mayor.

I saw their faces in the torchlight, and I knew them all, every one a customer of our store, a few we even considered friends. Hank Sears, who looked like Abraham Lincoln without the beard, was there. So was Henry Wiggins, Old Mr. Wiggins' son. I looked for the preacher, but at least he had showed the decency to stay away.

Uncle Marsh worked the lever of the Winchester. That brought the mob to a halt, but the expressions on their faces said that they weren't afraid. After all, they faced one man with a rifle and two unarmed colored people, one a woman. What resistance could they offer against twenty men with shotguns and rifles?

"You can't stop us," Lon Barron said. "There's too many of us."

"You ready to die, Lon?" Uncle Marsh asked.

To give the mayor credit, he didn't show the least bit of fear. "You won't shoot me, Marsh. You may be a big war hero, but we know each other. Killing me will be a lot harder than killing some Kraut."

At that moment, we separated ourselves from the trees, but remained shrouded in shadows, far enough away for the mob to see us but not too clearly. We held our sticks and clubs as if they were rifles and shotguns, hoping the night would disguise the truth.

Mister Misener came along bringing up the rear, more a hanger-on than a participant, and he stood to one side near us. He carried no weapon, no torch, and his scrunched forehead showed more confusion than anger. When he spotted me standing with those from Boonesville, his confusion intensified.

"Davy?" he said.

I said nothing but stared straight ahead. Mr. Misener saw how few we numbered, and I feared he would give us away. I had always liked the man and believed him good and honest, but now I wondered if I'd misjudged him. After all, he accompanied Zeb Cain and Lon Barron. He was part of the mob. Yet, when I thought the worst of him, he said, "Tell Marsh I made a mistake, Davy. Tell him I ought not to listen to fools."

He swung around and headed back toward town.

Corpulent Pap Caldwell, who stood next to Cain, spotted us then, and he gave an inarticulate yell. Glancing from right to left and back again, they all saw us, but the shadows dancing from the torches must have made us appear larger than life and close to indistinguishable from the woods at our backs, as if the trees themselves formed part of our strength.

I kept my eye on Tommikins. His confident expression faded as he glanced at the shadows. We must have appeared a little like ghosts ready to swallow him up. "Daddy?" he said, a quiver to his voice.

Cain screwed up his courage and said, "You think a measly bunch of niggers can stop us? There can't be more'n...ten or fifteen of you." From the tone of his voice, I could tell he was guessing.

"I think if you boys start something, there are going to be a lot of dead bodies littering this place," Uncle Marsh said.

Lon Barron lifted a finger, pointing at Sister Rose. "That woman is dangerous. Look how her boy turned out. Now she's going to turn out a whole school like him. No sir, that ain't happening!"

"Get out of our way, Langston," Cain said. "This nigger school goin' burn."

Solomon stepped forward so that he faced Cain, moving in so close that their shadows merged from the torchlight. "All my life, your kind been denying mine and what's ours..."

Cain lifted his shotgun. I don't know if he intended to threaten Solomon or to shoot him, but Solomon knocked the weapon aside and grasped Cain by the neck, his thumbs disappearing in the soft flesh around Cain's windpipe.

Half a head taller and much broader, Cain looked as if he could throw off the old man like swatting a fly, but instead, his eyes rolled back in his head and he dropped to one knee. With both hands, Cain slapped Solomon on the arms and shoulders, but Solomon appeared insensitive to the blows. Cain's thick neck bent at an odd angle, and his arms slid away and fell slack at his sides.

A dozen men cocked their shotguns, and I feared right then that things were about to go terribly wrong. All it would take was one man, one hothead, to start something none of us could finish.

Uncle Marsh, too, must have thought all hell was about to break loose because he shifted his rifle so that it lined up on Lon Barron's big gut.

By now, Tommy Barron was truly frightened. "Daddy?" His high voice sounded like that of a small child.

It was a standoff—a Mexican standoff, I've heard it called—both sides at impasse. If one side takes action, the other does, and both sides lose. The faces of every person there reflected anguish and fear. People do stupid things when they're afraid. One man squeezes a trigger a little too much, a gun goes off, and everyone starts shooting. One thing kept that from happening. Those boys didn't know how many of us there were, but if we stood and did nothing, they would figure it out pretty soon.

"Look! Here's Jim Kennison!" a voice shouted.

Jim's long stride carried him so close to us that with one glance he, too, saw how few we numbered. In his right hand he clutched a sawed-off shotgun.

Another voice cried out, "We got the law with us now. Jim will set things right."

He strode up to Uncle Marsh, who never let his rifle waver from Lon Barron, and I believe that if trouble started, my uncle would have killed the banker. Lon might not have thought so, but I knew Uncle Marsh a lot better than he did. I think Tommikins, who stood looking directly into Uncle Marsh's eyes, thought so, too. His face had gone white.

Cain dangled in Solomon's grasp, his body jerking convulsively.

"Let him go," Jim said to Solomon. "Please."

Solomon wanted to squeeze the very life out of Cain—you could see it in the hard gaze of his eyes and in the set of his rigid jaw—but when Jim uttered the word 'Please,' some of the resolved went right out of him. Like discarding a bag of trash, he tossed Cain to the ground where the big man gasped for air.

Then, as I believed we had lost, as I am sure everyone there must have thought too, Jim stepped to Uncle Marsh's side and faced the mob. "You men got no business here. Go home," he said.

At first they were too stunned to react. They murmured and looked to one another as if to decipher the meaning of Jim's words. He hadn't taken the fight out of them, but he'd confused them. Lon Barron said, "What the hell do you think you're doing, Jim?"

"Here's the thing, Mayor," Jim said. "These people are in the right, and you're in the wrong. That's all there is to it."

"You saw what that boy was going to do to Susanna. She's still so scared she can't sleep nights. And he shot you."

"What that boy did has nothing to do with this," Jim said. "I know you're upset over what happened to Susanna—so am I—but burning down this school don't rectify that."

"Jim," Lon Barron said, "think about what you're doing here... And for what? A bunch of coloreds?"

Jim's mouth quivered, and the skin around his eyes wrinkled. A few seconds passed during which he teetered on the edge, ready to jump back to their side. All eyes were on him, and he must have felt the pressure.

He sighed as if surrendering, and hefted the shotgun, cradling it in the crook of his stiff arm, not aiming at anyone in particular, but the barrel, sawed-off to half its usual length, would spread shot in a wide arc. Jim said, "I'm sorry, Mayor, but you need to go home and let these people be." He laid a thumb over the right barrel and pulled back the hammer, then the left, each click a sharp crack in the cool night air.

Jim didn't want to use that shotgun, and perhaps in the end, his courage would have failed. But that's speculation. The mere threat of that weapon made the men around Lon ease away, trying to distance themselves just in case he cut loose. Only Tommikins remained close to his father's side, and for that small gesture, I admired him. Those in the back felt the pressure, and they retreated, too.

"My patience is wearing thin," Jim said with sudden force.

And so he vanquished them. First Pap Caldwell, fear written all over his fat face, broke rank and fled back to town. Another followed and another, then in pairs and then in small groups until Lon Barron and his son stood alone. Zeb Cain sat up and held his neck, as if trying to keep his head from rolling off his shoulders. Even in the firelight I could see the deep imprint of Solomon's fingers.

"You've thrown it all away, Jim," Lon said.

"I suppose I have." Firelight reflected off Jim's glasses, hiding his eyes, but his tone was one of resignation.

Uncle Marsh stepped forward, so that he faced Lon and diverted attention from Jim. "You were in the wrong, Lon. That's where you always seem to be."

"You bas—"

"Watch your mouth. My temper is on a short fuse, too." Uncle Marsh shot a thumb at Cain. "Better help him back to town. He needs somebody to lean on."

Lon tossed his torch in a bare patch of ground and moved to help Cain. But Lon had trouble getting a good hold, and Cain was too heavy. Solomon reached down, caught Cain under one arm, and jerked him to his feet.

"Tommy, get over here and help me," Lon Barron said.

Tommy Barron appeared frozen until that moment. He crossed the few feet that separated them, took Zeb Cain from the other side, and together father and son held the man between them. The expression of anguish on Tommy's face almost made me feel sorry for him.

Solomon said, "Mr. Mayor, I need you to hear what I gots to say. You best listen real close. If you or anybody from town come looking to hurt any of us—that includes Mr. Marsh here—you better know we gonna hold you responsible. You know me, and it might be you could come calling one night, and I'd find myself hanging from a tree. But there's others out there, too. You can't see their faces, but you know they're there. So if something happens to any of us, something's going to happen to you. You'll be jumping at every shadow you see, and one night, one of those shadows will jump back. You can call this a threat if you want, but it's a promise, too. Make no mistake. Anything happens to any of us, you may be walking around, but you is a dead man."

His words shocked Lon and shocked Tommy Barron. Shocked us all, I think, because no one thought Solomon capable of such violence. We all believed it now. We couldn't help ourselves because of the way he manhandled Cain and the tone in which he spoke to the mayor

"You understand what I is saying, Mayor?" Solomon asked. "You better say something, so I know you understand. Say it so we can hear."

Lon looked around, trying to see who lurked in the shadows. Fear pinched his face, fear of Solomon, fear of those he could not see. "I understand," he said.

"Now git, before we end it right now, right here," Solomon said,

Arm in arm, father and son stumbled off, bearing the weight of Zeb Cain between them. They walked through heavy grass, their boots leaving imprints that began to fade the moment they were made.

After that, we came to stand in the light with Uncle Marsh and Jim, Solomon and Sister Rose. We were all smiling, even the boy who first appeared so angry at me. We had won a battle. For that moment, we could savor and rejoice in the victory. I reached for Rachel's hand, holding it by my side. We stood together and awaited first light.

31

After that, I figured the town would turn against Uncle Marsh, and we would lose the store. But people are not always so predictable. Instead, the townspeople flocked to buy from us, as if they had come to admire Uncle Marsh even more for standing up to Lon Barron and Zeb Cain. That first Saturday after it happened, we waited on over two-dozen customers including Mr. Misener, Old man Wiggins, and even crotchety Dr. Gibbs. They all purchased something, even if only a handkerchief, as in Doc Gibb's case. Pastor Joyner came by, too, and bought a pair of socks, but not before he managed to get in a few words on God's Will.

Late Monday, as I was about to lock the front door, Jim stepped inside sporting a lopsided grin. "They fired me, Davy." I noticed the badge ordinarily pinned to his coat was missing. "The county sheriff himself drove all the way from Hollister to tell me."

Uncle Marsh and Aunt Esther came from behind the counter and stood next to me. "What reason did he give?" my uncle asked.

"Didn't give one...just said he needed my badge. Guess

we all know why.

"Lon Barron." Aunt Esther spoke through clenched teeth.

"He won't let me see Susanna."

Uncle Marsh wasn't a demonstrative man, not in the physical sense, but he laid a hand on Jim's shoulder. "You did the right thing. Don't let anybody take that away from you."

Jim looked at the floor.

"So what are you going to do now?" I asked.

"I got my stuff packed." He stepped aside to show us a large black suitcase he'd left on the boardwalk. "Sunshine Special comes through in a bit, heading for Dallas. Maybe I can find a job there. I hear Murray's Cotton Gin is hiring." He held out his hand. "It's been a real pleasure knowing you, Mr. Langsdon." He tipped his hat to Aunt Esther, too. To me he said, "Maybe you'd walk with me a bit, Davy." He reached down to pick up the suitcase. Grabbing my coat from behind the counter, I followed him. A bitter wind blew in from the north.

We passed the front of the Tower Theater where a single sheet glued to the wooden placard announced *Blue Blazes Rawden* starring William S. Hart who, decked out in his cowboy costume, both guns drawn, faced us as if ready to blast away. "Gee, that's a good moving picture," he said. "I saw it last night. That William S. Hart—now there's a real man for you."

We didn't speak again until we reached the train platform. Young Wiggins was there ahead of us pulling the lever that would flag down the train.

"I know this cost you a lot," I said.

"Do you?" he asked in a tone of surprise, as if he didn't quite believe me.

"It cost all of us something," I said. "Maybe we suffered one of those victories they call pyrrhic." A quizzical look came over his face, and I said, "It means we all lost—even the ones who won."

We heard the shrill whistle of the locomotive as it approached from the north. Down the tracks a black speck moved toward us.

"I'm real sorry you're going," I said.

He kept his eyes on the train until the Sunshine Special rattled to a stop, steam belching from the engine. He hefted his bag, faced me and thrust out his hand. I shook it. "Ain't no fun being a grownup, is it, Davy? Ain't no fun at all."

He boarded the train, and I watched it pull away. I caught one last glimpse of him at the window, his face blurred by the glass, and then he was gone.

I found Aunt Esther and Uncle Marsh behind the counter, the store empty of customers for the first time in almost a week. By then, I was feeling pretty low. "I thought I might go out to see Solomon and Rachel. I want to know how they're doing," I said.

Aunt Esther cast a worried glance at Uncle Marsh. "It's best you keep away for a while, son," he said. "Maybe a long while... You go out there and you might be seen as rubbing people's noses in it. They might take it out on Solomon and the girl. I don't think any of us wants that."

He was right, of course. So all through the summer I stayed away. I saw Solomon twice when he came to our store. The second time I waited on him. Accepting two dollars for a pair of bib overalls, I told him I wanted to come and visit, but Uncle Marsh had advised against it. "Your uncle is right about that, Mr. Davy."

"Please call me Davy." I handed him six bits change.

He took the three quarters, stuffing them deep inside his pants pocket. "Thank you kindly, Mr. Davy," he said, and with the overalls tucked underneath one arm, walked out.

A few days later LeeRoy shuffled through the front door and found Uncle Marsh in the rear unpacking a box of summer shirts. I was ringing up Mrs. Frankel's purchases, and I caught only snatches of the conversation, although I made out Rachel's name. After LeeRoy left, I did something I had never done before. I asked Uncle Marsh what they had talked about. He hesitated, and I thought I might have made him angry. That wasn't the case. His brow wrinkled before he said, "Solomon and Rachel have moved away, Davy."

My whole insides rolled into one big knot of hurt, and when I spoke, my voice cracked. "Where did they go? Where, Uncle Marsh? Where did they go?"

"Just away," he said. "That's all I know. That's all anybody seems to know."

"Why? Why would they do that?"

"Solomon thought it best. Who are we to say different?"

"But why?"

"You know why, don't you, son?"

"It's not fair," I said, and because I could think of nothing else to say, I said again, "It's not fair. None of it..."

"You're right, but that's the way things are. For now, we live the best we can and hope that someday things will get better."

I've got one last part of my story to tell, and I'm not very proud of it, although I'm not ashamed either. It concerns Zeb Cain.

Most Saturday mornings I walked the two miles to the schoolhouse. I'd add a coat of whitewash here and there or pull away the creepers and vines. Twice I flushed out a nest of possums from under the house, and once I interrupted a couple of raccoons frolicking over chairs and desks like raucous children.

I suspect most of the town knew what I was doing on those mornings. So one Saturday, as I was headed home, I encountered Zeb Cain as I rounded a bend on the old river road. The wagon was a quarter of a mile away, and the moment I spotted it, I knew it was Cain. His bulk filled the wagon box. As far as I knew, he had no business on that road. His farm lay in the opposite direction. I bent over and swept up a solid, water-smooth rock big as my fist.

The river flowed on my right—hog-back sand dunes sprinkling the surface of the dirty brown water—but the woods were on my left. At that point I could have easily slipped into the trees to avoid him. Why didn't I do it? I think the answer is simple enough: I blamed him for everything. If Cain and his buddy Blaylock hadn't come to the school that day, Daniel would still be alive and Rachel and her father would not have left. I hated him, and I wasn't about to give him the satisfaction of running away. So I kept walking and tried to keep my hands from shaking.

When we were less than ten yards apart, I stepped to one side to allow his wagon to pass, but of course that wasn't his intention. He kept coming until he was a few feet from me before he halted the team. Dropping the reins, he looked at me, his lips twisted into a smile. He glanced back up the road to see if anyone was in sight, and once he determined we were alone, he jumped down, his heavy boots raising a cloud of dust that swirled around him. "You still got time to skedaddle, boy."

Even from six feet away, I smelled his breath, heavy with liquor.

Reaching into his belt, he pulled out his long serrated blade that he used for gutting fish and rabbits. "Otherwise I'm going to split you from your belly to your chops. Afterward, I'll toss your body in the river, and no one will ever be the wiser."

Maybe he only meant to scare me. Maybe he actually intended to kill me. Either way he appeared unconcerned about the rock in my hand until I drew back and launched it with all my might. It caught him square between the eyes and sent him reeling back against the flank of one of the mares. His drawn knife pricked her flank, and she kicked out, catching Cain in his belly. He slammed into the ground at the same moment the team lunged forward. The right front wheel rolled over his neck, snapping it with a crack as loud as an ax chopping kindling.

Stunned, I stood there for the better part of five minutes staring at the still body with the head twisted at an oblique angle, the eyes open but sightless. I had often dreamed of wreaking vengeance on Zeb Cain, but now I found myself appalled by what I had done. My belly churned, and I felt sick to my stomach.

I regained my senses enough to see the trouble in which I had put myself. Snatching up the stone with which I'd belted Cain, I tossed it far into the river. I tore some brush loose and wiped away my tracks near the wagon. Afterward, I took off through the trees. I crossed the bridge into town without anyone seeing me.

Later that day, a farmer came along the river road and discovered Zeb Cain lying where I'd left him. Right away townspeople put his death down as an accident. He had spent the morning drinking at Ernie's Bar, and people speculated that he was so drunk that he'd taken the wrong road home. In his stupor, he had fallen off his wagon and his own team had run him over.

I never said a word to anyone, including Uncle Marsh and Aunt Esther. I've lived with my secret ever since. I suppose I should have felt far more guilt than I did, but I never felt much at all.

At the end of summer I took my scholarship and went off to school. Though Southern Methodist was less than twenty miles away, it proved to be a different world. For the next four years, my life was filled with books and studying. Whenever I came home, I asked Aunt Esther and Uncle Marsh if they'd heard from Rachel or her father, but if they had, they never told me.

One day, I ran into my former teacher, Miss Pilgrim, coming out of Wiggins General Store. She appeared frailer than ever as she hobbled about on a cane. "My boy, my boy," she said by way of greeting, "it's been so long. How are you?"

I told her of my trials and tribulations as a student. Then I said, "I've wondered if you know what happened to Rachel and her father."

"Oh, my dear boy, I received a letter from Rachel over a month ago. They live in El Paso." Her forehead wrinkled, and she said, "Solomon is getting old, and a bit feeble, as we all are. But he's fine. Rachel's fine, too. They all are."

After that I decided that someday when I got the money together, and the courage, I would board the Sunshine Special and ride it all the way El Paso. Someday...

One night less than a year after I left for Southern Methodist, Sister Rose's school burned to the ground. We never knew for sure the identity of the culprit or culprits, but we could guess. The loss, coupled with the loss of Daniel, devastated Sister Rose, and she packed what little she owned, and she, too, wandered off. We never heard from her again.

As for Lon Barron, he remained mayor for another term, then one morning on the way to the bank, his heart gave out. He was behind the wheel of his McLauglin Buick when he slumped forward. The car swerved off the road and slammed into the big elm in the front yard of the Frankel residence. Even before the car hit the tree, he was dead.

By that time Susanna was married to a bank vice president over in Hollister. I ran into her several times when I had business at the county seat. We said hello, but that was about it. Then one day as I walked the main street of Twin Forks, I heard the honk of a car, and a Dodge Touring convertible pulled up beside me. The top was down, and the wind had gathered her silk dress above her knees. She was beautiful still, her figure intact, her skin unfazed by the years. Perhaps she wore a little too much rouge, and where before she allowed her golden hair to drop below her shoulders, she wore it bobbed.

She was in town to see a couple of old maid aunts and wanted to know if I would have a cup of coffee with her. I noticed a patch of white skin where her wedding ring should have been. "Please, Davy. I need to talk."

I met her at the Eatmore, a one-room café next to the Tower Theater, the kind of place that uses linoleum to cover stained tabletops. For the first fifteen minutes or so we talked of the town and the people we knew. She asked what was happening in my life, but she wasn't interested in me.

"You said you needed to see me. What's so important, Susanna?" I asked

She placed her cup in the saucer and glanced around to make sure that no one could overhear. The only other occupant, Mr. Moody, the owner and cook, sat in the back reading a newspaper. "Except for my daddy, I never told anybody this. He said for me to keep it to myself, but...I don't see how it can hurt to tell it now."

I said nothing and waited for her.

"It's about that boy—the one who broke out of jail. I think about it all the time. I can't help myself. I saw him grab Jim's gun, I heard the gun go off, and I saw Jim fall. I don't think the boy intended to shoot Jim. The gun went off accidentally."

"Jim told me the same thing," I said.

"But then the boy grabbed me, and I was sure he was going to kill me. After all, I was Lon Barron's daughter. He must have hated me. Don't you think he hated me?"

I shrugged. "If it's any consolation, I never heard Daniel speak of you one way or the other."

Her eyes pinched as she recalled that day so long ago. "He apologized to me. He had a gun to my head, and he said he was sorry. Now why would he do that? Why would that boy say such a thing? Right then, when he had that gun to my head?"

"Daniel was a good person," I said, "but your daddy

and Zeb Cain were organizing a lynch mob. Daniel didn't want to hurt anybody, but he didn't want to be strung up either."

"But he apologized..."

I figured she would never understand. How could she? She didn't know Daniel. In reality, I doubted that she knew much about herself or the human heart that is so full of contradictions. I tossed a dime onto the table. "It was real nice seeing you again, Susanna."

So that's my story. I wish I could say it ended differently, that Rachel and I found each other, that we lived happily ever after, that Sister Rose rebuilt her school and it prospered, that good triumphed over evil. But if I said any of that, this would be a fairy tale.

When I was a small child, I believed in fairy tales. And monsters too, the kind that hid under your bed or in your closet, ready to pounce the moment you drifted off to sleep. As I grew older, I stopped believing in supernatural creatures that inhabit a child's nightmares. But that doesn't mean I stopped believing in monsters. On the contrary, I discovered that they do exist. They don't show their fangs or their horns or their pointy tails. Rather their deformities are on the inside and reshape their souls into something ugly and mean. Orvie Blaylock was such a monster. So was Zeb Cain. And although he wore the trappings of authority and order, so was Lon Barron. If I've learned anything, it's that we must be ready and willing to confront such monsters, for if we ignore them, we allow them to control our destiny.

"When a guy's got nothing to lose," Uncle Marsh once said to me, "he can face anything. But courage—real courage—comes only when a person is afraid of losing everything but still does what's right."

He was talking about Jim, about Sister Rose and Daniel, about Solomon and Rachel. But I knew one other to include on that list, and he stood behind the counter staring out the window of our store, his gaze focused on those who lived in our memories and in our hearts.